The Case of the Malverne Diamonds

An Inspector Anthony Slade Mystery

By Leonard Gribble

Originally published in 1936

The Case of the Malverne Diamonds

Published by Resurrected Press

This classic book was handcrafted by Resurrected Press. Resurrected Press is dedicated to bringing high quality classic books back to the readers who enjoy them. These are not scanned versions of the originals, but, rather, quality checked and edited books meant to be enjoyed!

Please visit ResurrectedPress.com to view our entire catalogue!

For updates on future releases, LIKE us on Facebook: http://www.Facebook.com/ResurrectedPress

ISBN 13: 978-1-943403-10-3

MORE MYSTERIES BY LEONARD GRIBBLE

Is this Revenge (1931) aka The Serpentine Murder
The Stolen Home Secretary (1932) aka The Stolen Statesman
The Yellow Bungalow (1933)
The Death Chime (1934)
The Riddle of the Ravens (1934)
Mystery at Tudor Arches (1935)
The Case of the Malverne Diamonds (1936)
Riley of the Special Branch (1936)
Who Killed Oliver Cromwell? (1937)
The Case Book of Anthony Slade (1937)
Tragedy in E Flat (1938)
The Arsenal Stadium Mystery (1939)
Atomic Murder (1947)
Hangman's Moon (1950)
They Kidnapped Stanley Matthews (1950)
The Frightened Chameleon (1950)
Mystery Manor (1951)
The Glass Alibi (1952)
The Velvet Mask (1952)
Murder Out of Season (1952)
She Died Laughing (1953)
Murder Mistaken (1953) with Janet Green
The Inverted Crime (1954)
Sally of Scotland Yard (1954) with Geraldine Laws
Death Pays the Piper (1956)
Superintendent Slade Investigates (1956)
Stand In for Murder (1957)
Don't Argue with Death (1959)
Wantons Die Hard (1961)

Resurrected Press Books in A. E. Fielding's *The Chief Inspector Pointer Mystery* Series

RESURRECTED PRESS CLASSIC MYSTERY CATALOGUE

Journeys into Mystery
Travel and Mystery in a More Elegant Time

The Edwardian Detectives
Literary Sleuths of the Edwardian Era

Gems of Mystery
Lost Jewels from a More Elegant Age

Anne Austin
One Drop of Blood
The Black Pigeon
Murder at Bridge

E. C. Bentley
Trent's Last Case: The Woman in Black

Ernest Bramah
Max Carrados Resurrected:
The Detective Stories of Max Carrados

Agatha Christie
The Secret Adversary
The Mysterious Affair at Styles

Octavus Roy Cohen
Midnight

Freeman Wills Croft
The Ponson Case
The Pit Prop Syndicate

The Uttermost Farthing: A Savant's Vendetta

Arthur Griffiths
The Passenger From Calais
The Rome Express

Fergus Hume
The Mystery of a Hansom Cab
The Green Mummy
The Silent House
The Secret Passage

Edgar Jepson
The Loudwater Mystery

A. E. W. Mason
At the Villa Rose

A. A. Milne
The Red House Mystery

Baroness Emma Orczy
The Old Man in the Corner

Edgar Allan Poe
The Detective Stories of Edgar Allan Poe

Arthur J. Rees
The Hampstead Mystery
The Shrieking Pit
The Hand In The Dark
The Moon Rock
The Mystery of the Downs

Mary Roberts Rinehart
Sight Unseen and The Confession

Dorothy L. Sayers

Anybody but Anne
The Bride of a Moment
Faulkner's Folly
The Diamond Pin
The Gold Bag
The Mystery of the Sycamore
The Come Back

Raoul Whitfield
Death in a Bowl

And much more!
Visit ResurrectedPress.com
for our complete catalogue

**For updates on future releases, LIKE us on
Facebook:
http://www.Facebook.com/ResurrectedPress**

FOREWORD

Leonard Reginald Gribble had a long and prolific career as a mystery writer, having penned over seventy-five novels spanning five decades. In addition to his mysteries he also wrote a number of non-fiction works as well as westerns, and during World War II he served in the Ministry of Information.

Gribble's career began during at the end of the 1920's when British detective fiction was undergoing a transformation. The whimsical, eccentric private detective as epitomized by Hercule Poirot or Lord Peter Wimsey was starting to give way to a different type of detective, one that worked within the official police force, either Scotland Yard or one of the county police. Partly, this was a response to the new wave of "hard-boiled" detective stories coming out of America, which were both more realistic and more action packed. This new style of detective story, dubbed by some the "Hum-drum" school, relied more on hard-work and forensic evidence than on the inspiration of the "little grey cells." There was less emphasis on the puzzle factor and more concern for the psychological aspects of the crime. And, while there was more action, there tended to be less of the humor and wit that marked the novels of authors such as Anthony Berkeley.

The detective in this new style wass university educated, often of middle class origins, though there were exceptions, and with few of the personality quirks of the detectives of earlier eras. They usually held the rank of Inspector or Chief Inspector and were often assisted by a trusted Detective Sergeant. Examples of this new style detective can be found in Nagio Marsh's Inspector Roderick Alleyn, A. E. Fielding's Chief Inspector Pointer—or Gribble's Inspector Anthony Slade. The typical plot involves an initially baffling crime, the patient investigation and following up of clues, and the final burst of action as the criminal is apprehended. That this new style found favor with the reading public is witnessed by the fact that it continued to be popular with subsequent generations of readers and writers, as seen by the popularity of writers such as Colin Dexter and P. D. James.

The Case of the Malverne Diamonds is a typical example of the style. It begins with the theft of The Malverne Diamonds, also known as The Tears of Death. The most important aspect of the theft is that the safebreaker is discovered unconscious before the empty safe while the diamonds themself are missing. Clearly, this is something other than a simple crime, and Inspector Slade spends the rest of the novel sorting through red herrings and false clues as he works his way through to the surprising solution.

Despite his long and successful career, the works of Leonard Gribble have not been readily available today. It is therefore with pleasure that Resurrected Press offers this new edition of *The Case of the Malverne Diamonds*.

About the Author

Leonard R. Gribble (1908-1985) was a British writer of mysteries, criminology books and even westerns. He was born in Devon, England. During World War II he served in the Press and Censorship Division of the Ministry of Information. In addition to those mysteries under his own name, he was published under at least a half-dozen pseudonyms. Many of the mysteries published under his own name feature the character Inspector Anthony Slade.

Greg Fowlkes
Editor-In-Chief
Resurrected Press
www.ResurrectedPress.com
www.Facebook.com/ResurrectedPress

I.

"I don't like it, Bill. I don't like it one little bit." Shadows veiled the brightness of the girl's dark eyes; a worried note crept into her pleasantly husky voice. "Think, Bill, it might mean your . . . going back *there*."

The young man's face went stiff, his lips compressed in a colourless line.

"Never, Tessa. They won't do that to me, not again."

The smouldering cigarette between his lean fingers broke, and he tossed the crushed remnants into the grate. "There's a big debt owing me for last time. I was framed—"

"You were . . . unlucky, Bill."

"Framed, Tessa!" he all but shouted. His breathing was heavy and laboured, as that of a man struggling with some deep-born emotion. "Framed." He repeated the word slowly, slurring the vowel. "But not this time." He paused, took a fresh cigarette from the open packet on the table, and touched it with flame from a lighter. "This time things will be different." He laughed. "The very name fascinates me. The Tears of Death. If what the newspapers say is true plenty of men have died for that string of diamonds—plenty. They've changed hands a hundred times. Men have cheated and stolen and killed for them, but that has only increased their value. A hundred and fifty thousand pounds. Think of it, Tessa. A hundred and fifty thousand pounds. . . ."

His eyes were dreamy. A pulse throbbed wildly in the slim curve of his throat.

The girl shivered.

"I'm afraid, Bill," she murmured.

He didn't appear to hear.

"That means a certain thirty thousand for us. Thirty thousand pounds . . . perhaps fifty thousand. Some of those stones are big. They could be cut and cut again, and still fetch a big price. Think what we could do with thirty thousand pounds, Tessa; think what it would mean for us, for you. . . . And perhaps fifty thousand."

"Would we be happier, Bill?"

"Would we?" He sounded incredulous at her lack of faith. "Listen, Tessa, nobody can be happy without money. We know that. Think how your own mother had to screw and scrape. And mine . . . the fight killed her. Do you think I can ever forget that dirty little slum, the leaky roof and damp walls? It bred misery, Tessa. Romance! It sounds all right in books, on paper. But see how it works out on a few quid a week, and those never very sure. Romance and the opportunity to enjoy life comes with money. We've proved that—"

"We've been happy, Bill."

The protest was wrung from her. He was almost brutal in the way he flung that protest aside.

"We've tried to be, Tessa. My God, we've tried! And I got framed for a job I never did. Then you had to take that offer of old Reisenberg's, to keep things afloat. The old swine! I'd like to—"

"It's all right now, Bill. He hasn't been pawing me again. Don't dig that up. I had to do something, and the money was good."

"It was filthy. I'd sooner steal—d'you hear?—than go about life knowing my wife's got to—"

"Bill, shut up!"

She was white and trembling. The young man went towards her with a clumsy gesture invoking forgiveness.

"I'm sorry, Tessa. I know there's no muck sticking to you. But it's the whole set-up of things that gets under my skin and makes me mad. I boil up so that I want to rush out and smash things with my two hands. Don't you know that feeling?"

After a pause she said, "I did when you went . . . inside, Bill."

The word roused him. He strode back to the table, and

his clenched fist pounded the threadbare cloth.
"With thirty—maybe fifty—thousand pounds we can get out of the country, make a fresh start. Don't you see? We can be ourselves—"
"With fear of the police always with us?"
"You're a woman. You let your feelings get the better of you."
"Bill, for the last time, will you give it up—the whole idea? You've got the offer of a job. Bill . . . for my sake!"
The black hair brushed across the crown of her head was level with his mouth; her face was tilted upwards, red lips slightly parted.
"A job. Forty-six bob a week. And you ask me, for your sake, Tessa." Wondering surprise mingled with disbelief in his quiet tone. "No!" The word trembled vibrantly. "For your sake, Tessa—for mine—for both our sakes I'm going through with it. Those diamonds . . . those Tears of Death shall bring us happiness, Tessa. I swear it. I won't bungle the job. I've been studying—"
"Studying?"
"Sure. I didn't want you to know. Look." He brought a book from beneath a pile of magazines. "*Historic Sussex*. That's the title. Get the idea?" He flicked over several pages. "Pictures of old castles and manor-houses, with maps and descriptions. There's a beauty of Steyning Towers. I've been studying it. I could go through the place blind-folded."
He left the book in her hands, and she felt cold fingers caressing her throat. The book was a weight in her hands, and the diagrammatic sketch of Steyning Towers on the page before her eyes blurred and took grotesque shape.
"So you've made up your mind . . ."
"That's more like my Tessa," he said, with assumed heartiness. "Sit down. I want to talk. I've got it all doped out."
She sat in a chair at the table, while he paced the small room, cigarette smoke following the jerky movements of his head. She wanted to shout and scream,

do anything to stop him from this mad venture, but she sat mouse-like, silent, listening.

"I can climb the North Tower, Tessa. There's a turret window that will be easy to open—"

"The place will be wired," she said softly.

He laughed.

"I'm not easily caught that way, old girl. . . . Then a flight of stairs to the main building. A balcony runs round a big hall, with east and west doors. That way I can get to the living-rooms, and through the South Tower to the sleeping apartments."

"How will you know where the Tears are?"

He smiled down upon her.

"Where would any woman conceal jewels in a place like that, Tessa?"

"In a safe, I suppose?"

"Of course."

"But the safe—you don't know where that is, Bill."

"Don't I?"

He winked, and again those cold fingers circled her throat with icy touch. He saw realization dawn in her dark bright eyes.

"Then you—"

"Now you've twigged it, Tessa. Those four days last week I wasn't in Northampton; I was down in Sussex, getting my bearings, as you might say."

"You were careful, Bill?"

"As a cat. And now listen to this. I've got everything set—"

"I gathered that."

"Smart girl. But you don't know the half. Set for tonight."

"To-night!"

He nodded.

"I've hired a car, changed the number-plate, and I've worked out a complete time-table. See? This is a big thing for us, no sense in not taking every precaution. But in case there's a hitch, I want you to come back . . . alone."

"No, Bill! No!"

She half rose. He caught the hands she upraised, and gently pushed her down again.

"Alone, Tessa," he repeated, his voice thin. "You're not being dragged into anything. I've promised myself that. I had to promise myself that . . . and it wasn't easy. You see, it meant admitting that there is a risk—small, but a risk. Well"—his chin jutted at a determined angle—"it's my risk, all mine, something I won't share with even you, Tessa."

She rose and crept into his arms. They were strong about her, and their pressure gave her false confidence.

"You're a damned, pig-headed, blind fool, Bill, but . . . oh, God, I love you!"

Minutes later they sat at the table together, and studied the time-table Bill had worked out. Fear stole back into Tessa's heart, brooded in her eyes. Bill's limbs and wits were nimble, his hands strong, his eyesight good, and he was clever at opening safes. There had been jobs in the past, small jobs, about which he had laughed. Then he had been jugged for a crib-cracking he had not committed. That had made him savage. He wanted to strike back. But not blindly. He was taking every care, as he had said. His timing and preparation were thorough.

She glowed with strange, bewildering pride, and pride fought fear for possession of her mind.

"See?" Bill was saying, his voice thick. "That's where you wait in the car. Give me thirty-five minutes, Tessa. No more, no less. If I'm not back with you then drive on. You understand?"

She nodded. She knew she had capitulated; her last reserve was gone.

They began their meal in silence, and finished it in a state of forced hilarity. In the tiny scullery Bill stood at her side, wiping the hot dishes as they came from the suds in the sink, and she thought she would never forget that strange smell of soapy dishes, fried fish, and cigarette smoke.

In the little living-room the radio was on low, as Bill liked it. A dance-band unwound a mechanical tune and she found herself thinking to its broken tempo. She wanted to cry and she wanted to laugh. She wanted to fling her wet arms round Bill's neck and she wanted to throw the thick Woolworth jug with the damned silly flowers all over it at him. She wanted . . . She was near to breaking down, and realized it. Her nerves were on edge.

"Might finish them for me, Bill. I want to slip upstairs a minute. I don't feel so good."

"'Course I will, old girl. *Tum-rum-rum-tiddlee-um*," he sang, to the music of the radio, and playfully smacked her rump as she slipped past.

"No more cotton dresses, Tessa," he called after her, "when we get that thirty thousand ... or maybe fifty. Silk, satin, what the hell you like!" He was happy, and each minute the heady wine of his reflection was becoming more intoxicating. "*Tum-rum-rum-tiddlee-um-pum.*"

Nearly an hour later they were in the car Bill had hired. Bill sat before the wheel, Tessa at his side. Again silence lay between them, an invisible barrier neither probed nor scaled. They left London, and the southern suburbs flashed by in a steely twilight.

"Not a bad little bus, is she?" said Bill.

"Not at all bad," agreed Tessa.

That ended the effort to make conversation. Beyond the built-up area Bill opened her up. The little car bounced and rattled, but she was speedy. Tessa sat rigid, sucking deep gulps of the cold night air flung in her face. Bill stared straight ahead, gaze fixed on the unwinding ribbon of road revealed in his headlights.

An hour and a half after leaving London Bill drew the car into a country lane.

"Remember the map, Tessa?" A sense of urgency and caution caused him to drop his voice to a whisper. "Good. This is the spot I marked with that letter A. I want you to wait here. Thirty-five minutes, mind. No more, no less. How's your watch?"

They compared watches, and Bill stood up. He was dressed in dark clothes, a black muffler was round his throat, ready to be drawn over his face, and black woollen gloves covered his already rubber-covered hands. The tools in his pockets did not jingle.

"Good luck . . . Bill!"

Their kiss was long. In the darkness something cold and moist touched one of Bill's cheeks, and Tessa blinked rapidly.

"Remember, Tess, thirty-five minutes . . . that's all."

His tall figure merged with the darkness, for the car was parked under some trees, its lights off, and only the sound of the wind came to her.

"Thirty-five minutes," she repeated, staring at the radio-lite dial of her cheap wrist-watch.

An hour and thirty-five minutes passed, and still Bill did not return.

II.

When one recalled that Sir Julius Malverne had met his death in a 'plane crash only a brief six months before, one may be forgiven surprise upon encountering the radiant happiness in Lady Malverne's eyes. Certainly she was the most charming widow Detective-Inspector Anthony Slade had ever met. There was something vital, full of joy-of-living about her. To the discerning detective it appeared that the woman had been released from a cage. She was spreading her wings in her new-found freedom. Her manner confirmed this impression.

"I am not worried about the necklace, Inspector," she confided. The two were sitting in the library. Slade and his chief assistant, Sergeant Clinton, had arrived at Steyning Towers, the Malverne Sussex home, an hour before. "My husband had it insured for its full value— actual value, I mean, not intrinsic. But I'm afraid such a jewel does not impress me greatly. That is why I have asked Mr. Reisenberg down here. For myself, I frankly would not have troubled Scotland Yard. But Mr. Reisenberg is a gentleman who takes precautions."

She made a pretty *moue*. She was fair-skinned and blue-eyed, and her dove-grey frock suited her good looks. She could not be termed a beautiful woman by any save an insincere flatterer, but there was humour in the expression of her mobile lips and at times subtle provocation in her eyes. She was an interesting woman, with considerable charm of manner and of self.

"Mr. Reisenberg has a reputation for taking precautions, Lady Malverne," said Slade. "He is a successful business man. I presume he advised you not to have the necklace brought to Sussex."

"He did, Inspector. But I thought that childish. I see

no real danger in having the necklace here, especially as two Scotland Yard officers will be on hand to guard it, and the insurance company have sent one of their own detectives. A kind of double-locking of the gate, and unnecessary."

"A necklace worth a hundred and fifty thousand pounds, Lady Malverne, is a great temptation, and there are still a lot of crooks in the world."

She laughed.

"You sound like a school-teacher reading me a lesson."

"I'm sorry. I meant only to—"

"I know, I know," she interrupted quickly. "It's just that I don't see the *need* for all this fuss. I don't mind it a scrap . . . especially as I haven't to stay in London over the week-end."

Slade knew to what she referred. One of the few guests at Steyning Towers was Kurt Swensen, the laughing Swedish-American who had astonished the athletes of the nations at the recent Olympic Games. Gossip-writers in the Press had weeks before linked the names of Lady Malverne and the tall Swede. Swensen had not returned to the United States, and Slade had found him at Steyning Towers.

"Will Mr. Reisenberg take the necklace with him, Lady Malverne, in the event of his purchasing it from you?"

"That remains for Mr. Reisenberg to decide, Inspector. I don't want to bore you, but I don't care. You perhaps will not be able to understand that. Women are supposed to covet jewels and bright gauds. I may be different; anyway, I don't. My husband"—her voice hardened—"as you doubtless know, collected jewels. He bought the Tears of Death necklace when the Countess of Beaune offered it for sale. But it has always remained in a strong-room in London, with the other gems of his collection. Now he is dead, I personally see no reason why the strong-room should continue to hold them. I don't want them. I've sold most of the other jewels of the collection, and now I'm anxious to get rid of the Tears. I've got a feeling that they are not a lucky possession. Silly of me, because I've always pooh-poohed the suggestion that jewels have any potency for good or evil. Yet you know their history, Inspector. At times I'm quite frightened by my possession of that necklace."

Slade nodded gravely.

Most newspapers in the British Isles had printed the history of the celebrated Tears of Death once it had become known that Lady Malverne intended to disperse her husband's celebrated collection. The Tears comprised a necklace of matchless diamonds, four of which had histories as dark and horrible as that of the Koh-i-Noor. Like the famous diamond in the collection of British Crown Jewels, the four Tears had commenced their wanderings after the sack of Delhi by the hordes of Genghis Khan. With the Koh-i-Noor, they had been stripped by ravishing Mogul hands from the Peacock Throne, and they had travelled in different directions to the ends of the earth, finally to be collected and brought together by the grandfather of the late Earl of Beaune. The Eye of Allah, the Star of the South, and the Rose of Persia had remained, for the most part, in the East until exploring Europeans had heard the legends that had arisen about them. The fourth Tear, known widely as the Catherine diamond, had been presented to the Russian Empress by a Mongolian prince who had visited her Court.

"I understand the necklace is in a safe in the South Tower, Lady Malverne," said the detective.

His words, spoken quietly, roused her from dreamy contemplation of a tinted finger-nail.

"That is so, Inspector." She laughed. "Don't tell me you are expecting a burglar."

Slade interpreted the words literally, and chose another tack.

"If you don't mind, Lady Malverne, I'd like to go over the Towers before it is dark. I'm rather lost at the moment."

She rose, smiling.

"Like Mr. Reisenberg, Inspector, you take many precautions for a short week-end."

"Probably like Mr. Reisenberg, Lady Malverne, I have learned the value of those precautions."

Did she sweep him a swift, appraisive glance? The Yard man could not be sure, but he fancied that her hand trembled as she moved towards the door. Or was it fancy?

"Brooks will give you every assistance, Inspector," she said, and the dove-grey figure passed on to where her guests waited in the lounge.

Slade strolled back to the morning-room, where Clinton awaited him.

"Looks like we've got a quiet week-end for a change, Clinton," he announced. "A small house-party, a house like a fort, lost in the heart of the country, and a necklace that would give a millionaire heartburn. Pity we didn't bring our rackets."

Clinton glanced at his chief.

"What's wrong?" he asked. He knew from Slade's manner that the chief of the Yard's Department X2 was puzzled by something.

"If I could tell you, Clinton, I'd feel considerably happier than I do." Slade returned his sergeant's inquiring stare. "It isn't the place, though one has to get used to it. It isn't the people. I've only glimpsed one or two, and Lady Malverne is about what I expected . . . only, perhaps, a trifle more so."

Clinton grinned.

"That puts her in the plus class," he opined.

"I should say it does." Slade sat down and crossed his legs. "It's not the place nor the people, then what is it? Logic replies atmosphere. But have you felt the atmosphere of the place, Clinton?"

"No," said the sergeant, looking round the room, "but then I'm not an archaeologist. This place is pretty old; old enough to be a ruin, I should say. But even a ruin wouldn't affect me much atmospherically. I'm pretty cold-blooded."

"Bunkum," Slade grinned. "Lady Malverne said Brooks will escort us on a tour of the place. I think we'd better get the idea of all the twists and turns."

"There aren't any lifts in those towers?" queried Clinton, with a very straight face.

"Not this week-end," Slade replied gravely.

Brooks, the butler at Steyning Towers, a saturnine, lean-faced individual, who walked like a cat and had a trick of raising his brows very slightly when receiving a request—a trick which proved disconcerting to many—took them on an excursion of the large, rambling house. The Lord Steyning who had visioned it and spent a fortune upon its erection had died at Naseby. Since then the memorial he had built for his family name had passed from rich family to rich family. Only a rich family could afford to maintain Steyning Towers as a country residence; and in these days of super-tax and land tax only a very rich man could enjoy the beauty and old-world privacy of the Steyning estate.

Sir Julius Malverne had made a tremendous fortune during the War. Tinned foods, boots, leather equipment, khaki cloth, he had owned factories that had worked night and day on Government orders. When the high-tide of War profits receded he sold out, at a handsome sum, his shares in the various companies he had formed and directed. Reinvestment in the staple industries later proved his commercial wisdom. He bought Steyning Towers after the Verrock family had bled itself white to try to keep it, married, and settled down to collect precious stones.

Why Lucie Birchall ever agreed to become Lady Malverne was a perpetual mystery to her friends. Some attempted an explanation with the suggestion of foolish reaction to a broken romance. Certainly everybody agreed that red-haired Tommy Witchart had been a purblind idiot to get drunk at the Hunt Ball, and it served him right when Lucie returned his ring. But Tommy shouldn't have shied and left the field, and anyway he should have known that there were snakes in Kenya. Or was it Tanganyika? Lucie had been terribly upset, of course; but the fact remained that Tommy *had* left the field . . . open to Julius Malverne, with his chinking coin and agate-hard eyes, his baronetcy—paid for in hard cash—and his passion for gems. When Lucie became Lady Malverne she virtually retired from the world. Julius had a queer streak in him; he had the outworn notion that a wife was a chattel, and he was not the kind of man to treat a chattel kindly. Rumour had it that Julius's 'plane crash had been more than fortunate for Lucie . . . and Kurt Swensen.

However, no foul play had been proved, and Lady Malverne had not been a hypocrite and gone into mourning.

Something of all this was passing through Slade's mind as he and Clinton followed the butler from room to room, along corridor and staircase. Brooks had made himself acquainted with the history of the old house. He had a fund of anecdote and story to tell, and in his quiet voice, empty of emotional inflexion, he told them of sword-fights and midnight trysts that momentarily transported them to another age. He was standing in the doorway of a large room, raftered, hung with drab-coloured tapestries, through which a keen draught blew cuttingly, and he was saying, "Sir Malcolm drew his sword as he ran . . ." when the dressing-bell rang.

The two Yard men, who were ostensibly 'guests' for the length of their stay, retired to change. Upon going downstairs they were met by a rotund, bouncing individual with bright eyes and a round, almost bald head. Gems glittered upon Max Reisenberg's pudgy fingers. Coruscating opals burned in his shirt-front.

"Glad to see you, Inspector. You too, Sergeant." The beady black eyes danced, travelled, and returned to Slade's face. "I'm not sure I shouldn't prefer to be in my own office than stuck out here, miles from anywhere." A surprisingly white finger rubbed his blue-black jaw reflectively. "I can't get used to this place. It doesn't seem real. More like a movie set. I feel I'm acting all the time. Understand what I mean?"

"Vaguely, Mr. Reisenberg."

"Perhaps I'd better—Ah!" he broke off as a woman in blue approached. It was that shade of hard blue that, in electric light, hurts the eye. "Madge, meet Mr. Slade and Mr. Clinton, from Scotland Yard. Gentlemen, my wife."

The woman's attitude was as hard as her blue frock. She gave each Yard man a limp hand and said, "Pleased to meet you" with transparent insincerity. The paint on her face was skilfully applied, but distress signals lit her narrowed eyes. She was a woman set against her wrong background, and she knew it. Her eyes and her accent proclaimed that she was out of place.

They chatted generalities until another man drifted towards them.

"You've met Mr. Butterick, Inspector?" Reisenberg inquired.

Slade murmured his regret, and found himself shaking the hand of the insurance company's representative. Butterick was a negative type of man, thirty-fiveish, with sandy hair and a clipped sandy moustache. He looked like a seedy Army man whose health had broken down and forced an early retirement. His upper lip was very full, and when he spoke his words were chewed and mangled. His voice had a dreary intonation that quickly grated on the ear.

He was plainly nervous, a man whose sense of the fitness of things was swamped by the impressiveness of the surroundings in which he found himself. He slipped out of the conversation without anyone being aware of it.

Lady Malverne and a young giant with corn-coloured hair approached.

"Swensen," Reisenberg murmured. "A lad who knows a good thing—when it falls into his hands."

Crude but expressive, Slade thought. Typical of Max Reisenberg, whose acumen as a business man was not unknown at the Yard. Merchants in Hatton Garden who have regular agents travelling to and fro between London and Amsterdam must expect the police to survey their activities with something more than a disinterested glance. Max Reisenberg had always had the mental courage, in the past, to take the police bull by the horns.

Swensen bowed to Madge Reisenberg, and for an instant longer than was necessary held his yellow head over her wrinkled hand.

"Charmed, Mrs. Reisenberg," he said, a slight accent broadening his American vowels.

As he raised his head he stared straight at Slade.

"From Scotland Yard, Inspector?" It wasn't a question save for the lilt of his voice. He held out a frank hand. "I have read so much about the English police in fiction," he said as his grip challenged that of the detective, "that I am a trifle disappointed."

Lady Malverne laughed. Reisenberg's roving eyes came suddenly to rest, and he opened his fleshy mouth to emit what he thought would pass for a chuckle.

"What did you expect, Mr. Swensen?" Slade smiled.

"Oh ... an eagle face, hawk eyes ... in fact, Inspector, a *rara avis*."

"And instead?"

Swensen laughed easily.

"Instead I find a man with whom I might sit down and have a chat about athletics. I said I was disappointed. I must enlarge—pleasantly disappointed."

There was a high polish to the Swede's manner. He spoke without embarrassment and his English was not a stumbling-block. He was a graceful giant, and damned good-looking, as Slade admitted to himself.

Other people drifted into the lounge. A Mrs. Clammer, elderly, but seemingly sweetly futile. Slade gathered that she was a friend who was now a companion-of-sorts to Lady Malverne. There was a Captain Furniss, a distant cousin of the late Sir Julius. He apparently had one topic of conversation: how Julius's death could have been avoided if he had allowed some one to overhaul his 'plane. In the Captain's manner was more than a suggestion of open defiance towards Lucie Malverne, and this defiance was also directed towards the Swede. Slade noted that Swensen spoke little or nothing to Furniss, while Lady Malverne treated him to a series of brief smiles in which she cleverly mingled toleration and boredom.

At sound of the gong a general drift towards the dining-room was apparent. The meal was excellently served, and Slade for one enjoyed the cooking and selective care that had gone to the preparation of the various courses. Afterwards the company divided itself into groups, Slade and Clinton taking the opportunity to capture Brooks's attention and mention the advisability of completing their survey of Steyning Towers before the guests retired for the night.

"Very well, sir. I shall be ready in quarter of an hour," said Brooks.

In that fifteen minutes the two Yard men finished their excellent cigars. The late Sir Julius had had a rare taste for Havana leaf. Ten minutes had passed when Butterick approached.

His sandy moustache bristling, his sandy hair somewhat ruffled, and the same subdued expression on his face, he paused before Slade, and said, "I wonder if you could help me on a point, Inspector?"

"I will if I can," Slade assured him amiably.

"Just when is the necklace to be—ahem!—actually offered to Mr. Reisenberg for his inspection?"

"I don't know, Mr. Butterick. Perhaps to-night. But Lady Malverne may intend waiting till the morning. Why? Have you something on your mind?"

Butterick blinked.

"I'll be candid, Inspector. I'm uneasy. This place, it's so large. A thief could conceal himself—"

"It's wired," Clinton said bluntly.

"It's not only that." Butterick threw away the stub of a cigarette. "But I feel my position rather keenly. I'm not exactly"—he smiled, revealing poor teeth—"accustomed to this environment, and when I have a job to do—as I have here—I can't settle down. I'm a man with a one-track mind. I can't at the moment get off the single-line track that those diamonds are a risky, very risky thing to have lying about in an isolated place like this."

"I think the Tears of Death will be safe," said Slade quietly. "There are three of us here to protect them, you know."

Butterick shrugged.

"Of course, if you feel all right, Inspector—about the necklace, I mean—there's no need for me to get hot under the collar, I suppose." He paused, shot a look from Clinton to Slade, then asked, "Reisenberg, presumably, has a client behind him? Doubt if he could raise all that coin himself. Got any idea who's after the diamonds?"

Slade shook his head as the telephone shrilled insistently. Brooks unhooked the receiver, placed it to his ear, said quietly, "Just a moment, please. I will tell her," and went in search of his mistress.

"What on earth can Barry be 'phoning about from Paris?" asked Lady Malverne's voice some moments later.

"You will soon know," murmured the deep tones of the tall Swede. "Perhaps he intends to warn you about me . . . again."

He added the last word after an appreciable pause. Clinton glanced at Slade and nodded.

"Silly Kurt!" said Lady Malverne's voice, gently remonstrative. "Barry is just a young man with ideas, and young men shouldn't have ideas . . . some ideas . . . should they, Kurt?"

The question was a subtle challenge. Swensen's laugh rang melodiously.

Slade rose softly.

"Let's get out of this, Clinton." He turned to speak to Butterick, but the insurance company's detective had disappeared.

"Who's this Barry fellow?" Clinton asked.

"Her half-brother, Barry Birchall. Lives in Paris most of the year. So far as I can gather, he violently disliked his half-sister's late husband."

"Why isn't he over here now?"

"There is a thorn called Furniss, Clinton. I take it that Lady Malverne had no desire to have the Birchall-Malverne wrangle continued . . . until after the Swensen episode has decided itself. Then Captain Furniss won't count a row of brass hooks."

Brooks appeared.

"Now gentlemen, if you are ready."

He led them along rock-walled corridors, lit with electric light and hung with tapestries, to the South Tower. He explained the general plan of the rambling house, picked up the survey of Sussex history where he had left it before dinner, and half an hour passed before they reached a room before which Brooks hesitated, his sardonic face lit with a secret enthusiasm.

"In this room, gentlemen, is the safe holding the famous necklace, brought by Lady Malverne from the late master's London bank."

A massive oak door frowned at the three men. The hinges were strips of heavily nailed wrought-iron. It looked more like the door to a dungeon than to one of the private chambers of the master of the house.

"Have you a key, Brooks?" Slade inquired.

"No, sir. There is only one key. Lady Malverne has that."

"The door is always kept locked?"

"Always, sir."

Brooks moved to continue, and Slade took a couple of paces after him. Neither saw Clinton reach out a hand to the octagonal iron handle of the door. The Sergeant turned the handle, and pushed.

The door opened without a sound.

"Wait a minute," said Clinton, calling after the others.

"I thought you said, Brooks, this door was always kept locked. Look at it."

Brooks's mouth gaped.

"Why, I don't understand," he frowned. "I've always understood there has been only the one key, and I know Lady Malverne had it after Sir Julius was killed."

"Perhaps Lady Malverne has been showing the necklace to Mr. Reisenberg," said Slade, remembering the insurance company detective's question.

Brooks, however, shook his head.

"I don't think so, sir. Lady Malverne told me she would take the necklace from the safe to-morrow."

"Well, we'll look inside." Slade stepped into the darkness of the room and fumbled for a light switch. He found it and flooded the room with yellow light. "Good Lord!" he exclaimed, swinging about and staring at a corner of the far side of the room.

The door of an iron safe was open, and on the floor in front of the safe was sprawled the body of a young man. A doctor's stethoscope and an oilskin case of tools lay on the floor beside the body.

Slade motioned to Clinton to close the door of the room. He turned and examined the safe. Not finding the necklace, he ran his hands over the still figure.

"The necklace is gone," he announced slowly.

"Gone . . . stolen!" muttered Brooks in an awed voice. "It's enough to make Sir Julius turn in his grave. He worshipped that necklace."

Clinton stared at Slade and pointed to the sprawled body.

"How does that fit in?" he asked.

"When he comes round we shall soon know."

"He isn't dead?"

"No. Some one gave him a hard crack over the head and . . ."

The Yard man shrugged. The rest was open to anyone's guess. Clinton voiced his.

"—and made off with the diamonds."

"It looks like it," said Slade. "The open door, the open safe."

Clinton pointed again to the body.

"He had to get in some way—and somewhere."

"If he's who I think he is that didn't present him with much of a problem," said Slade.

"Who is he?" Clinton asked.

"A clever safe-opener named Bill Pegwell. Hasn't long been out." Slade frowned. "There's something I'm trying to remember. It'll come to me in a moment . . . something about Pegwell's wife, a girl who got a job somewhere . . . now, where was . . ." The Yard man straightened. "I remember. Mrs. Pegwell is employed by Reisenberg."

Clinton's eyes widened.

"My Lord!" he exclaimed. "What a set-up!"

III.

"Brooks!" Slade turned to the wide-eyed butler. "I don't want news of this discovery circulated. You understand? Not until I am ready."

"Yes, sir." The sallow promontory in the centre of the butler's scrawny throat wobbled uncertainly. "But Lady Malverne, sir ... I don't like the responsibility of not telling her—"

"I'll take the responsibility, Brooks," said the Yard man. "I believe the staff are all accounted for. No newcomers?"

"No, sir. We're all, as you might say, old retainers. Been here since Sir Julius bought the Towers."

"Very well, Brooks. Go downstairs and carry on normally. If anyone inquires for me, I am still inspecting the South Tower."

"Very good, sir."

After another backward glance Brooks opened the door and moved silently outside. As the massive door closed the young man on the floor groaned. His eyes opened, and he tried to sit up, only to fall back with a muttered "Ouch!" as pain stormed his head.

Clinton brought forward a chair, and the two Yard men helped the other man into it.

Through a lattice of fingers the young man stared at the open door of the safe. Black straight frown-lines were incised in his forehead. His hair, matted with blood, stuck out at crazy angles from his head.

"What hellish luck!" he muttered.

"Depends how you consider it," said Slade.

"Eh!" The young man reared himself, winced with pain, and slumped wearily back in the chair. "What d'you mean, depends?"

"You came after the Tears of Death necklace."

In time the young man caught himself.

"Tell me more," he invited.

Slade studied the drooping shoulders, the defiant poise of the bloodied head. He felt that this young man might prove more than ordinarily difficult.

"Your name's Bill Pegwell. Only recently out after a job."

The droop of the shoulders became more pronounced.

"All right," said the young man, "you've labelled me. No use saying you haven't. It wouldn't have taken you long, anyway."

"No, not long. Well, Bill, where's the necklace?"

The thoughtful eyes lifted from gazing at the open safe.

"In the pocket of whoever slugged me."

The Yard men saw the young man's body straighten, and a cold, calculating look changed the expression of his face.

"You've thought of something," said Slade. "Better let's have it. You're going to need help."

"The hell I am!" flared Bill. "Did I get it last time? No, I was framed. I tell you—"

"Tell me what I want to know, and it'll be easier."

Bill's under lip pouted.

"I can't."

"You mean you won't."

"Take it how you like. I say I can't."

"Because of some one else?"

"Hell, leave me alone. My head's spinning like a top."

"Bill"—Slade eased a persuasive note into his voice—"you've got a wife, haven't you? I remember she took it badly when you went inside last time."

Bill's hands trembled. The fingers locked tightly, so that the flesh was pinched over the knuckles, under his gloves.

"Leave her out of this. Leave her out, I say. You've got nothing on her." Desperately Bill told himself he must regain control, but he made the effort too late. Both Slade and Clinton, watching every muscular move in the young man's face, saw his eyes turn swiftly to the window, then drop hurriedly. "You've got nothing on me."

"Sure, Bill? Isn't that your kit of tools?" Slade pointed to the safe-breaking tools beside the open door of the safe. "That dark muffler round your neck looks like a mask, and you're wearing rubber gloves. You don't think we've got *nothing* on you, do you?"

Bill threw a wild glance at the detective's set face. There was quiet humour in the Yard man's grey eyes, and something else, something that sent a cold feeling down Bill's spine.

"All right, it's a pinch, but I was outed before I got the stuff."

"That's better, Bill. You're talking more like a reasonable person. Go on."

"There's nothing else. That's all. I came here, got in, opened the door, and that's all I know. I came to with you shaking me."

"What about the person who knocked you out? Any idea who it could be?"

"No, my back was turned. And whoever it was had a tread like a cat. I wouldn't have taken such a wallop if I'd heard a step. I'm pretty speedy on my pins, and I reckon I've got good ears."

Slade thought for a moment.

"How did you get here, Bill?"

The other's suspicions returned. He shot a narrow, scrutinizing glance from Slade to Clinton, and what he found in the face of each man did not reassure him. He pushed the point of his tongue over suddenly dried lips. One thought was in his mind. They mustn't know about Tessa. She must be kept out of this. She must!

"That's my business," he muttered. "I came alone, if that's what you're getting at."

"In a roundabout way it was, Bill. But there's no call to lie about it."

Slade spoke lightly, but the words flayed the young man. He sprang to his feet, his face twitching from the spasm of pain that shot down his neck at the sudden movement.

"I'm not lying!" he shouted, brandishing a gloved fist, and swaying uncertainly on his feet. "I came alone. Think I'd let anyone in on a job like this?"

His sneer was not very successful.

"You'd have been a fool to try a job like this without arranging a quick get-away, Bill. Come by car?"

"No, train."

"How did you get from the station, four miles away, to Steyning Towers?"

Bill sat down. This was a puzzler. He realized that he had spoken too quickly, had jumped without thinking where he was landing. . . .

"Don't spend long thinking up another lie, Bill. You came in a car, and you didn't come alone, did you? You've got that car parked somewhere near, Bill, and there's some one waiting at the steering-wheel. You planned it as a smash-and-grab raid."

Bill's head rolled, and for a moment his eyes closed with pain and a hand went to his head. The fingers, when he took them away, were smeared with blood. He gazed dully at the stain, but his thoughts were elsewhere. Tessa must get away. He must play for time . . . for time.

He wiped the blood from his fingers slowly, rubbing his hand against his coat. "What are you charging me with?" he demanded.

Slade's mouth relaxed. He nodded towards the safe.

"Being concerned in the disappearance of Lady Malverne's diamonds. For disappearance I may substitute a stronger word later."

Would Tessa realize something had happened? Would she go, keep the promise she had made? Bill was torn with anxiety. She had been right. The cards had been stacked against him. It was a trick. Suspicion flared in his mind and lit his eyes.

"Was it you who—?"

His clenched hand tapped his head.

"You're not being bright, Bill." Slade grinned wryly. "If I had had any say in the matter I should have preferred to take you with the diamonds."

Bill's hand dropped down again. He was defeated. He knew that now, and the truth seared. Yes, he had walked like a fool into a trap. His hand had been on the necklace. In the ray from his torch the brilliance of the diamonds had been like whirling dagger-shafts of light. No, it hadn't been a police-trap. Some one else had been after the diamonds. That some one had coshed him and got clear.

Resentment, fierce as a flame, strong as a sudden-turned tide, welled in him.

"By God, I'll get even!" he growled.

Slade caught Clinton's eye.

"We're wasting our time," said the Sergeant.

Slade turned to the seated man.

"Bill, I don't know what to do with you," he said frankly. "I come in here and find you knocked out. I should treat you as a victim of assault, I suppose. Yet it's plain you came to crack a crib. Plainer than that: you did crack it. But you got cracked in turn. No, I don't know what to do with you."

"What d'you mean?"

Doubt, mistrust, were in the one of his voice.

"If I show you I show my hand." Slade folded his arms as he stood contemplating the other. "On the other hand, if I let you go, say nothing, somebody's suspicions will be lulled. But I've got no more right to let you go than I have to give you the necklace when I find it."

Bill's cockney humour appreciated the point.

"Let me go, and we'll forget the necklace. Call it a deal. You may never find it."

"That would be so much worse for you, my friend," Slade reminded him.

Clinton put in a word.

"Think it may be a plant?" he asked his chief.

Slade looked at the blood-matted hair crowning Bill's blunt face and shook his head.

"Friends don't hit as hard as that, Clinton. Not even to put up a good bluff. This lad's lucky to be alive." The words gave Slade a thought. "Did you tell any pals you were coming here, Bill?"

"Say, what do you think I am?"

"A young man who's sorry he didn't keep his hands out of mischief."

Bill's only rejoinder was a lugubrious scowl. His only comfort in those slowly passing minutes was the reflection that it couldn't be long now before Tessa drove off ... if she kept her promise. But would she? She was the sort of girl that sometimes takes things into her own hands, with startling results. That job at Reisenberg's. She had kept the rent paid on the rooms, and if he knew anything about Tessa had kept the Jew in his place. But supposing she didn't drive away. . . .

"Still got that something on his mind," Slade said, speaking to Clinton.

"Yes, he's just giving his head another ache trying to forget it. Probably the missus has been stepping out."

This was an old game with Clinton and Slade, baiting a man. However, on this occasion Clinton never knew how close his last shot sped towards the mark.

Bill slewed round in his chair.

"Give over, can't you?" he grumbled. "I've had enough of sitting here like a damned fool. You've got me, but you haven't got the sparklers. All right, the game's still open, and I'm in the pot. Let's get on with it."

He rose, again staggered uncertainly forward for a few steps. He stopped when Slade's firm grasp closed on his shoulder.

"Don't get riled, Bill. Those diamonds are more important than you just at present. But you're not going to help yourself by being a fool and keeping your mouth shut."

"Tell me what to say," Bill jeered.

Clinton took a step forward, a hard look on his face. He lifted a hand, but it fell to his side. Some one outside had touched the handle of the door. In a flash Slade was across the room and it was plunged into darkness. As though by unspoken consent, the three men in the room held their breath, and the door opened slowly. In the widening rectangle of light grew a bulky figure. It moved so that the light slanted across the fleshy face.

There was a short gasp, and a shape bounded forward.

"Stop him, Clinton!" cried Slade.

But Clinton moved too late. Bill was past him and upon the man in the doorway.

"Reisenberg—you swine!" Bill grunted, as his fists drove like pistons against the Jew's face.

A thin bleat spilled from Reisenberg's burst lips, and he toppled backwards, the lithe, piston arms of the young burglar still smacking into soft flesh. Reisenberg collapsed, and his feet tripped the man clinging to him. Bill swayed and swirled sideways.

A blow on the side of the head, delivered by an enraged Slade, settled the issue.

"Get 'em inside quick, Clinton."

The two men were hauled inside the room where the broken safe still gaped open. Slade closed the door, and switched on the light. Bill dragged himself upright, his young body bending like a bamboo, and a storm raged in his eyes.

"Reisenberg, that's who crashed me! He'd do anything to get me out of the way. Tessa must've asked too many questions, and he caught on. So he got rid of me—or tried to. Laid for me, and afterwards came back to make sure I was dead—"

Bill paused for breath.

Reisenberg dabbed his mouth with a handkerchief. His battered lip was bleeding freely, and there was a growing discoloration under his right eye.

"Pegwell. . . ." The Jew's sound eye discovered the open safe, and his lips pressed tightly together. "So, you're here on a job, you dirty crook."

"Crook!" Bill sucked breath sharply, struggled futilely in Clinton's restraining grip. "You dirty double-twister, you took the necklace. I get it. Pretend you're going to buy it. You've got some rich client. Yes, you wanted to make a lot of dough in a hurry—"

Reisenberg's little eyes snapped.

"Apparently I wasn't the only one."

Bill's spate of words rushed on. "And you wanted Tessa!" He struggled again, and Clinton pushed him down in a chair.

Slade spoke. "Interesting to know you're not strangers. Just why did you come up to this room?" he asked Reisenberg.

The Jew scowled.

"I don't like your tone, Inspector."

"You don't have to, but I should appreciate an answer to my question."

Each man had bared a blade and the ring of steel was in the room.

"I saw the butler come down, and I was . . . curious. Does that satisfy you?"

"It's a reason," said Slade non-committally.

"What do you mean by that?"

"I mean you've made me . . . curious, Mr. Reisenberg. The Malverne diamonds have disappeared."

"Surely you don't suspect me? There's the obvious answer."

A finger pointed to Bill, who writhed under Clinton's hands.

"Take it easy," soothed the sergeant, and gave some practical aid towards that end with a push downwards.

"He hasn't swallowed a hundred and fifty thousand pounds' worth of diamonds," Slade observed laconically, "and I did come in here and find him stretched out on the floor. Some one in this house has those diamonds."

"You can search me—"

Reisenberg was a little taken back at the promptness with which Slade adopted the suggestion. But the diamonds were not on him.

"You don't think I got police down here to catch me in a fool's trick like that, do you?" he grunted, wiping another smear of blood from his cheek.

"What I don't think doesn't matter, Mr. Reisenberg. What I do think is that some one has been very clever, very far-sighted. I shall want to question you later."

"Go ahead. I'm not putting up any objection, am I?"

Slade turned to his assistant.

"Take Bill downstairs and lock him up in some room that isn't used. And watch him."

"Right." Clinton nodded and gave the young cracksman a prod. "Come on, young fellow, we've got to be moving."

"What about me?" Reisenberg sounded anxious.

"You may go and repair the damage you've sustained, Mr. Reisenberg. I shall find you when I want you I've no doubt."

With that Slade left them. He went downstairs and made his way to where Lady Malverne and the Swede were amusing themselves in the drawing-room. They were alone, and the piano at which they sat was strewn with copies of jazz songs. As Slade entered he was greeted with a crashing discord in the treble clef and a peal of hilarious laughter.

IV.

The laughter died.

"What is wrong, Inspector?" Lady Malverne rose from the piano-stool, dropped a cigarette into a tray, and the soft light of the room touched with fire the jewels on her hands and round her throat. "You have news?"

Swensen stood back, a puzzled, half-expectant look on his fair face. His corn-coloured hair was slightly ruffled, so that a forelock all but swept into an eye.

"Unpleasant news, Lady Malverne. I should like to see you alone."

She glanced from Swensen, who bowed with rather mocking grace, to Slade, who stood erect, his attitude a subtle challenge. For a moment it appeared that she deliberated. To the watchful Yard man it seemed that she was about to object to Swensen's absence, when some other reflection changed her mind.

"You will excuse me, Kurt?"

"Why, of course, my dear."

His eyes possessed her with a frankness that sent mounting colour into her cheeks. With a brief nod to Slade, the Swede walked out of the room.

"Will you sit down, Inspector? Now"—they were seated facing each other—"this unpleasant news. Something has happened."

"It has. The diamonds are gone."

She sat very still, gazing straight before her.

"Gone!"

The word was a hollow echo of the last word uttered by the detective.

"A burglar with a record was found by the opened safe, Lady Malverne. He had been brutally beaten over the head, and was unconscious—"

"He won't . . .?"

"No, he won't die. But he hasn't the diamonds. He says he had opened the safe, got his hands on the necklace, and that's all he remembers before he found me bending over him. You realize the implication?"

"Naturally." Her voice had lost its timbre. Some of the colour, the vividness faded. Her glance was suddenly bleak. "The thief is here."

"With the diamonds."

"Yes, with the diamonds." She said it tonelessly. "What do you propose?"

"I am afraid I shall have to make a search."

She started. "Will that be . . . necessary?" Something was on her mind.

"I don't see how I can avoid it, Lady Malverne. There is a thief here. I believe a clever thief."

She reached for her cigarette-case. Slade was ready with a light. She inhaled deeply. That something was on her mind still. Slade wondered if she suspected Swensen. Did she sense that she was about to face an abrupt and brutal disillusion.

She was mentally alert. She glanced up and read the thought in his mind, and cleverly tried to prepare herself.

"Have you any suspicion, Inspector?"

"I will be frank, Lady Malverne. No. This young safe-breaker we've caught has a grudge against Mr. Reisenberg. He accuses Mr. Reisenberg of stealing the necklace."

"Would that be possible?"

"Until I have checked Mr. Reisenberg's movements since dinner—yes. But then the same conditions apply to anyone here. Mrs. Reisenberg, Captain Furniss, Mrs. Clammer . . . Mr. Swensen."

The tip of her cigarette glowed, but her fingers were steady as she removed it from her mouth, and her voice was calm as she said, "That is so, of course."

But she did not allow her gaze to meet Slade's. The Yard man, desirous of knowing just how strong were her defences, added, "Even yourself, Lady Malverne."

"Indeed. Doesn't that require an explanation?"

There was reserve in her manner now. She had succeeded in detaching herself from the emotion that had all but betrayed her.

"I am sorry if I am blunt, Lady Malverne."

"One doesn't apologize for bluntness these days, Inspector." She had trust in herself; she looked up, cold, aloof, wary. "I have generally found that the blunt person eventually proves to be the sharpest, in another sense."

Slade realized that he was matched against a worthy opponent. Yet was she an . . . opponent? He hesitated so to classify her. How much was caution, how much feminine doubt?

He said, "The explanation is simple. You are insured, Lady Malverne, against theft."

He left it at that, knowing that she would see to what he was pointing. He was not mistaken. She nodded slowly.

"Yes, I suppose, Inspector, an ingenuous mind must seem somewhat incredulous to you, but I hadn't realized the implication until you pointed it out. A hundred and fifty thousand pounds and the necklace would be—what do you say?—a nice haul."

Bitterness coated the words, made utterance difficult. She threw away the cigarette, plucked a crease from her gown.

"Well, you are probably thinking a foolish woman brought it on her own head. You may be right. I can only say, Inspector, that you must consider yourself free to undertake such investigation as you see fit. The staff will help in any way you—"

"I'm afraid I cannot expect much from the servants, Lady Malverne. Suspicion in this case must extend below-stairs as well as above."

Her shapely shoulders lifted.

"That is for you to decide. Now, if you will excuse me, I should like to be alone for a little while."

"Of course."

Slade rose, but he had not reached the door before it was opened and Reisenberg entered. He looked round the room with the air of a conspirator in a third-rate melodrama, closed the door with excessive care, and came forward. He had repaired the damage done to his features by Bill, but his eye was almost closed.

"This is a pretty kettle of fish," he began, talking at the woman rather than to her. "Down here, miles from anywhere, and a necklace worth a hundred and fifty thousand lifted under our noses. Something smells— smells badly."

His mood was black, and it was plain that he was not willing to be pleasant. He took a cigar from a case, bit off the end, and lit it. His white fat hands fluttered in front of his face as he resumed.

"I want to get out of this place quick. So the quicker the police are through with their job, the better it'll suit me. I don't want to remain here a minute longer than I've got to, not a minute."

Lady Malverne regarded him contemptuously.

"So far as I am concerned, Mr. Reisenberg, you are free to leave now. I might remind you that I am the owner of the necklace," she added caustically.

"You're insured. If I'd paid over it would have been a dead loss for me."

"You imply, Mr. Reisenberg, that you don't think it will be recovered?"

"I don't care a bean whether it is or whether it isn't. My interest in the deal is finished. I'm getting out from under. See? I should have had more sense than let myself be brought down here on such a deal. It wasn't asking for trouble. It was broadcasting."

He mopped his face with his bloodstained handkerchief. His cheeks had a greyish tinge, and the opals in his shirt-front seemed to have lost some of their fire. He swung round on the Yard man.

"What are you going to do?"

"Search every one's rooms."

"Think that'll recover the diamonds?"

"No," said Slade bluntly. "This job's been planned."

"That swine Pegwell's in on it."

"Think so?"

"A blind man could see how the case ties up. Pegwell lays down with a crack over the head. That kept you here running round in circles. Meantime the stuff's cleared out of the place."

"How did Pegwell know I should find him just when I did, Mr. Reisenberg?"

The Jew frowned.

"It's your job to answer that. Don't think I know, do you?"

"He says you took the necklace. He seems to have some reason for not liking you."

Reisenberg winced.

"That's nothing to do with it. I did that little crook a good turn when I gave his wife a job after he'd been sent to stir. This is how I'm repaid for my generosity."

Lady Malverne said: "If you two gentlemen will forgive me, this is all a trifle over my head. I hardly consider my presence necessary at the debate."

"No," said Reisenberg, his voice rising, "but it's necessary to hear what I've got to say." He moistened his lips, spat a piece of cigar-leaf from his teeth, and moved forward several paces. "My wife's a jealous woman, and a jealous woman's unreasonable. When I say she's very jealous you'll know how unreasonable she can be." He paused, considering his next words carefully. "I don't want her to see that fellow Pegwell."

"I'm afraid I shan't have anything to say in the matter," said Lady Malverne.

"Maybe not. But I don't want Mrs. Reisenberg even to *know* he's here. Get me? Pegwell's wife works in my office. She's a good worker; that's why I keep her. But I've told you, my wife's a jealous woman."

Slade saw that Lady Malverne was more amused than

anything else at this request.

"If it eases your mind, Mr. Reisenberg, I've forgotten Inspector Slade has a . . . prisoner."

"Thanks," said the Jew, heaving a sigh of relief. His gaze swivelled. "You, Inspector?"

"My job's to find the necklace, not to nose out divorce court evidence."

Reisenberg scowled.

"That wasn't what I meant at all," he grunted, turned about, and left them.

"Rather effective, Inspector," smiled the woman, "and cleverly blunt."

Slade left her. He found Clinton. The sergeant had locked Bill Pegwell in a room from which escape was impossible.

"Seen Butterick?" asked Slade.

"No."

"Then he doesn't know?"

"I haven't told him. What about Reisenberg?"

"Come on. I want to break the news first, Clinton."

They found the insurance company's detective reading a magazine in the smoking-room and carrying on a silent participation in a one-sided conversation. Captain Furniss was explaining with considerable volubility why within five years India would cease to have a British Emperor. "Spend millions to educate 'em to stand on their own feet," he was saying as the Yard men came in, "and what do you get for it? A kick in the backside when you're not prepared for it. That's India. That's the Indians. We've been too dashed lenient, sir. Pampering 'em and—"

Butterick was rescued from the remainder of the peppery Captain's tirade. Slade explained briefly what had happened. The sandy-haired man asked a stream of questions, all prefaced with why, and when, and how. The only answers Slade could supply were unsatisfactory and disheartening.

"Well, thank heavens you two Yard men are here!" he exclaimed. "The company will expect action."

"The company will get action," promised Slade. "I'm going to run a rule over the whole place, and I'm starting now. I want you to keep an eye down here, if you will."

"Of course, anything I can—"

"That'll be all, I think."

Away from Butterick, Clinton said to Slade, "You don't think he's much of a detective, do you?"

"I'm not concerned with what sort of a detective he is, Clinton," Slade replied. "All I want is first look. I don't want to have to blame some one else for a slip-up, that's all."

By midnight the two Yard men had completed their search. The news that the necklace had disappeared was known to every one in Steyning Towers by then. But when Slade and Clinton had finished their search they had not found the diamonds or any clue to their whereabouts.

"Where can they be?" asked Clinton, tired and puzzled.

"Cached somewhere. We'll give somebody time to move them. That'll be our chance. Things look more hopeful by daylight."

Reisenberg approached.

"When can I get away?"

"To-morrow, if you're lucky," said Slade.

"You can't hold me here—" the Jew blustered.

"I'm not holding you here," Slade pointed out sharply. "But if you leave suddenly I shall put you under arrest. That's all."

Reisenberg glowered, and went away without another word.

"I'd like to know what's on his mind," Clinton muttered.

"You'd sleep easier if you didn't," was Slade's reply. "Hallo, Butterick." The insurance detective had passed the retreating Reisenberg. "Anything to tell me?"

"No. That Swensen's worn my nerves out, that's about all."

"How?"

"Walking about. He's like a cat on hot bricks. Can't seem to settle down. Lady Malverne's shut herself up in her room, and he's at a loose end. You found something?"

"Yes, but not what we were looking for. I'm going to have a look outside as soon as it's daylight. You'd better get some sleep."

"I can't sleep. No good trying. My job depends on this."

"Well, let's get a drink. I feel in need of something myself."

"But do you think the diamonds are still here—inside, I mean?"

"I don't know. If they aren't, inside is still the best place to find out where they are. I'm certain of that."

"I don't follow."

"Never mind. Let's get that drink."

V.

Tessa stretched out a hand, switched on the dashboard light, and glanced at the face of her wrist-watch. Her dark eyes were troubled. Bill had been gone nearly an hour and thirty-five minutes.

She switched off the light and pushed her spine hard back against the seat. Breathing hurt, and there was a troublesome lump in her throat. She tried telling herself that she was not afraid, that Bill could look after himself, and would be all right. But her efforts were not convincing. She knew she was trying to lull a growing conviction.

Something *had* happened?

A breeze disturbed the trees under which the little car lay in the country lane. Between the melancholy soughing she heard the sharp, broken screech of an owl. The sound played on her nerves. The more she tried not to hear it, the louder it seemed to fill her ears, mockingly. She had wanted to smoke, but had told herself no. Smoking would be a risk. A small risk, perhaps, in that isolated spot, but sufficient if there was some one behind the hedgerow or walking along the lane. And Bill must not be exposed to any risk from her.

She had had plenty of time for thinking, for taking herself to task for ever agreeing to this madcap scheme. Yet out of her recrimination arose a strange pride of Bill. Not many men would have attempted this thing. Not many would have had the pluck, the cold nerve to go through with it. And he was going through with it for her.

A warm wave of satisfaction that this should be so swept over her, and she sat enjoying the sensation it imparted. Cold doubt followed on the heels of her satisfaction. Something *had* gone wrong! She knew it. Ice lay next to her heart, which beat heavily, like a leaden thing. Tessa knew herself to be hard-moulded. The world had not been kind to her until she met Bill. She had fought and fended for herself, and in her own assessment of personal values managed to keep herself unsullied. She was glad of that when she met Bill. She and Bill had their own code by which they lived, and that code demanded a shining honesty in any matter where the other was concerned.

But how could she be honest now? She had promised Bill she would go after thirty-five minutes. That promise was broken. She was still there, waiting. Hope had succeeded hope, but Bill had not come. In the background of her mind was another thought, one that hurt and seared. Bill would not come now. Something had gone wrong.

Wrong.

Dread italicized the word in her mind. With futile despair she tried to figure out what it implied. Was Bill a prisoner? Was he hurt? Had he been shot?

Impatience seized her mind. She had to strive hard for control. Desperately she wanted to leap from the car, to run to that house of dark shadows in its expanse of starlit parkland, to shout Bill's name, and demand that he be given back to her.

Again reaction set in.

The hard-moulded young woman told herself she was becoming hysterical, and that would be no way to help Bill. Something cold and tingly touched the side of her nose, and she realized with amazement that tears were trickling down her face. In the darkness she repaired the damage to her make-up. Bill didn't like a shiny nose.

It was after putting her compact away that she turned on the dashboard light and glanced at her watch. It was almost ten o'clock.

Pressing her back against the seat, she tried to understand what this implied. Bill had made his plan with care. He had left her at five-and-twenty minutes past eight, calculating that he would be at the house in seven minutes. Another four to locate the room with the safe. That was cutting it fine, but Bill had said four was enough, and he should know. A quarter of an hour for the actual job. Bill had said that would allow him time to sleep on it. Nine minutes to get away.

He should have been back by nine o'clock.

It was ten . . . must be gone ten by now.

In an agony of doubt and mental torment she reached forward and whirred the self-starter, throttled down the cooled engine, and without switching on her headlights drove slowly out of the lane. She was retreating, leaving Bill to his fate, and there was nothing she could do about it. Her last despairing survey of the situation had revealed clearly to her the danger her presence was to Bill. If he was caught search might be made for an accomplice. Her capture would only serve to make things worse for Bill. That was why he had insisted upon her leaving after thirty-five minutes . . . but no, she corrected herself, that wasn't the reason; not because it would make things worse for him. He had been thinking of her, not of himself.

Thought rotated in a vortex, until she could not think clearly. She was miserable and defeated, and the drive back alone, without Bill, would be a journey without hope.

Swiftly she swung the steering-wheel, to avoid crashing into a projecting tree, then braked as she came to the main road, running past the grounds of Steyning Towers. She changed gears silently, and was about to switch on her head-lights when her glance, travelling up the road instinctively, to note any oncoming traffic, saw a figure detach itself from the shadow of the tall hedge bounding the Steyning Towers estate.

Bill!

Her lips parted eagerly to cry his name, but in that moment before the word could be uttered she knew with instinctive certainty that the person in the road was not

Bill. She glanced round. Trees drooped their foliage over the entrance to the narrow lane, and the car was probably hidden from the figure she was watching. The low note of the engine would not be heard above the deeper moaning of the wind.

Luck was with her. Here might be a chance to help Bill. This might be some one sent to reconnoitre, discover if an accomplice was awaiting Bill's return.

Her mouth set grimly. Now was her chance to chalk up something on the credit side for Bill. If anything had happened to him . . .

She saw the figure begin to run, and thought stopped dead.

The person in the road was a woman!

Tessa hesitated, listening to the idle ticking over of the engine, undecided what to do. Could this woman know anything about Bill's failure to return? Logic, cold and hope-dispelling, said no. The woman might not be anyone who had even heard of Steyning Towers. She might be a chance traveller who had lost her way.

But chance travellers did not appear out of boundary hedges past ten o'clock at night and suddenly break into a sharp run ... without reason.

Tessa decided to give the woman a fair start, and then to follow, if necessary drive slowly past her, with her headlights glaring full on her, and to wait again farther on. She could not, she realized, play that sort of hide-and-seek for long, but she might discover something, and, anyway, it was a chance; and Bill . . .

It was the recurrence of Bill in her thoughts that decided her, and set her upon the strangest adventure in which she had ever engaged.

She drove slowly along the lane, the twin beams from her headlamps cleaving the darkness like sabre blades. Ahead the running woman dodged from one side of the road to the other. Only when the car had almost come up with her did she turn her head, and Tessa caught her breath. In a pale porcelain face two flashing dark eyes glared round apprehensively. The woman was running with her hands clutched in front of her, holding her coat. In that moment as she stared into the pretty face of the stranger a wild idea flashed into Tessa's mind. She braked, and put out her head. "Can I give you a lift?" she inquired.

Breathing hard, the woman came close. "Would you be so kind? I'm afraid I missed the last bus, and I've a train to catch."

It was glib, but the words sent a strange, tingling sensation through Tessa's body. She thought she recognized in them some half-confirmation of what she had supposed. And, besides, this woman was not English. She spoke English well, and had no trouble with the words, but she spoke with a faint, yet unmistakable accent.

"No trouble at all. Glad to give a fellow-sufferer a help." Tessa opened the door so that the other could get into the seat beside her. "This isn't exactly a Rolls, but it gets there all the same."

"It's most kind of you. I am really very grateful."

The woman smiled, but pointedly ignored the seat beside Tessa and climbed into the back. Tessa thought with regret that she wouldn't be able to inspect the stranger in the light from the dashboard, but on the drive to the station she watched the woman in the driving-mirror. She lay back in the rear seat, eyes closed, face very pale. Under a small, tight-fitting black hat reddish hair peeked. The lips were a bright stain in the whiteness of the face. But the clutched hands did not relax their fast hold on the woman's coat. That clutching grip intrigued Tessa. Was the woman in pain, or was she clutching something to her?

The station, a small, box-like affair with dim lights, was perched on a small hill. Tessa swung round in the tiny yard, and stopped. She got out. The stranger followed her.

"You won't know how kind you have been," she

smiled, and her smile revealed teeth that made Tessa envious.

"Oh, forget it," said Tessa heartily, every bit of which was assumed. "How are you off for money? I haven't much, but if you've only a small distance to go . . ."

Something happened to the woman's eyes, which were darker than Tessa's own. It was as though she pulled a veil over their brightness.

"I have a return ticket to Brighton," she said. "Thank you again, and good night."

As she watched the woman walk into the station Tessa knew that she had lied. Instinctively the woman had realized that Tessa was probing, and she had tried to cover up. She had said she was going in the opposite direction, hoping to fool Tessa.

But why?

Tessa knew that the woman was bound for London, but why lie about it?

Why had she come so suddenly from the Steyning Towers hedgerow?

Where had she been?

... Bill .. .

She did not know how, but in some way, she was convinced, this woman was concerned with Bill's failure to return to her, and the thought hardened her heart and steeled her resolve. This woman, this foreigner, should not escape her. If Bill had got himself in a mess perhaps this woman would be able to help. Perhaps she could be forced to help. She might have evidence that—

Tessa got into the car and drove it a quarter of a mile into the nearest village. She had no trouble in stabling it in an all-night garage. Stuffing the receipt into her handbag, she turned back towards the station. Once out of sight from the village street, she ran. She had taken a chance. London-bound trains that would stop at the small wayside station at that time of night would be few, and would be steamers, not electric. If she was to follow the woman to London and find out where she went aground, she had to leave the car. She could not afford to dump it by the wayside. It would be found, the registration and engine numbers checked, and traced to the place where Bill had hired it, despite Bill's precaution in changing the number-plate. That would look bad for Bill.

Tessa's wits were nimble. She had placed the car safely out of the way of the police. Now remained the woman.

She approached the gas-lit station warily. The uninviting waiting-room was filled with gaunt shadows. She walked in, went to the booking office, and inquired about the next London train. It was due in twenty-three minutes, she was told, and it was a very slow train, stopping at nearly every station, as it picked up and dropped quite a lot of local produce.

Tessa bought a third-class ticket and hid herself among the shadows on the platform. The other woman had disappeared.

Those twenty-three minutes dragged by. To Tessa they seemed longer, even, than the minutes spent waiting in the car parked in the narrow country lane, with the wind and an owl disturbing the night silence. A few other people came on to the platform. A farmer with his wife. The latter was very voluble on the subject of dog powders, and when her husband tried to change the conversation to dry-feed for cattle she would have none of it. None of the powders she had tried had done Sparkles any good. With lack of marital tact the husband inquired if she had tried gunpowder.

"That should put the spark back into him, by gum!" he guffawed.

The effect on his spouse was certainly explosive.

Tiring of listening to this sort of rural humour, Tessa wandered some feet away, where a country courting couple were giggling and all but choking. Three minutes in their proximity nearly drove the restive girl frantic.

At last the train wandered in, roaring and belching flame and smoke, but doing little exciting in the way of making progress. Tessa got in a non-smoker in the rear, and watched the others get into forward compartments. The guard wandered up to have a word with a station attendant, they laughed hoarsely at some joke or other, and then the whistle blew. The train was moving when Tessa saw the strange woman run from a door marked "Ladies' Waiting-room" and climb into a first-class carriage. She heard the slam of the door as she sank back against the upholstery, and for several moments kept her eyes closed.

The chug-chug of the engine was lulling, and she would have dropped off to sleep had she not pulled herself together with the mental reminder that she must keep watch at every halt the train made. There was at least a chance that the other woman might elude her by getting out at some intermediate station. She must not drop off to sleep. She glanced at the sign on the window—"Non-smoking." Habitually when travelling by train she chose a non-smoking compartment, because men usually travelled in smokers. She had followed her habit in this case. But it was a habit that could be broken in part, and she proceeded to break it. In glaring defiance of the notices on the windows and over the seats she took a cigarette from her handbag and lit it.

Then began a long vigil.

However, the foreign woman did not alight at any of the country stations. She remained on the train until it pulled into East Croydon. Tessa saw her walking briskly along the platform towards the farther exist. As the woman reached the long incline Tessa got off the train and started in pursuit. She quickened her step until she had diminished the other's lead to some twenty yards. They followed each other out of the station to a bus stop. It was late, gone midnight, but a few 'last' buses were arriving and collecting the late-comers. Tessa, waiting in a shop doorway, saw the other woman climb aboard one, and she ran across the pavement and managed to get on before it had gathered considerable speed. A side-glance revealed the other woman inside, her back to Tessa. Tessa climbed to the top deck, and resumed her watch on the other woman's movements. When at last the stranger got off the bus Tessa was already moving out of her seat. She dropped to the pavement in time to see her quarry walking into the courtyard of a large block of modern flats. An electric flare illumined the name Dunbar Court. Shrubs and trees spangled the fore-court, and a runway for cars sloped down to a long line of garages.

Tessa saw the woman she was following push open swing glass doors and step forward to a flight of stairs. Tessa passed through the swing-doors as the other woman rounded a wide bend in the stairs. Apparently, as it was after midnight, the lifts were not working.

Moving silently, listening to the steps of the woman half a flight of stairs ahead, Tessa mounted to the third floor, and paused. The steps had stopped. Cautiously she crept upward to the next flight, and, flattening her slim figure against a wall, pushed her head round a corner, to see the other woman disappearing through a green door on which the brass numerals 73 shone brightly.

Tessa straightened, and breathed a sigh of relief. She had run her quarry to earth. This was where the woman lived. However, that list of questions formulated in her mind in the darkness as she ran along a Sussex road remained to be answered, and, after proceeding this far, Tessa was in no hurry to leave her self-appointed task uncompleted. She debated the wisdom of boldly calling on the woman and surprising her into an admission. But recollection of the suave manner in which the woman had got into the rear of the car and avoided a close scrutiny by the woman offering her a lift, caused Tessa to reflect that perhaps she was up against some one who would prove to be no mean opponent. A woman, perhaps, accustomed to finding herself in awkward situations, and to bluffing her way out.

Tessa's indecision was terminated by her observance of a door with a bolt-locking device. Instantly her mind was made up; here was an exit to suit her purpose. The door must lead on to a balcony or elevated garden of sorts. Anyway, it would most likely provide her with a means of reaching a window of the other woman's flat.

She opened the door silently. The bolt-locking device was well oiled, and slipped back with scarcely more sound than a quiet click. She stepped out on to a balcony running the length of that side of the block of flats, protected by a concrete wall topped with an ornate railing. All this she saw in the light shining from an uncurtained window. A tremor of excitement ran through her body, for she realized, as she turned to face the stream of light pouring from the window, that it must be in the flat of the woman she had trailed from the roar near Steyning Towers.

Her excitement, for some wholly inexplicable reason, continued to mount. She walked to the balcony wall, looked over at the street-lamps below, and moved back to the wall of the flat. She now saw that curtains had been hastily pulled to, but that one had dragged against a window-seat, leaving a gap near the sill. It was through this gap that the light streamed out across the balcony, touching a bed of chrysanthemums.

Tessa crouched under the window, and cautiously raised her head. She saw the other woman, her coat and hat flung across a settee, seated at a table speaking into a telephone. All at once the woman pushed down the receiver and took a packet of cigarettes from a pocket of her overcoat. She lit one, inhaled deeply, and as she threw back her head Tessa saw the light from a blue-shaded lamp shimmer along the red waves of her hair.

There was a look on the woman's face that defeated Tessa's mental analysis. Was it apprehension, greed, or relief? It might have been any one, Tessa decided. She waited, watching the woman smoke cigarette after cigarette. And to Tessa's mind came an explanation. She was putting through a long-distance call and was waiting to be called back.

Nearly half an hour went by, and Tessa was painfully aware that one of her legs had gone to sleep and there was a severe crick in her neck. But grimly she stuck it out, waited for a 'phone call that she was sure would come through.

It did, nearly forty minutes after it had been asked for. But Tessa was not to know that that particular call had necessitated the clearance of a submarine cable.

The woman grabbed the receiver eagerly. Tessa saw her lips pouring words into the instrument. And once the woman laughed, tossed back her head in an arrogant gesture, and her white teeth gleamed against the red slit of her mouth. Tessa heard the sound of that laugh through the window, but, although she listened closely, trying to catch the words the woman spoke she was not successful. She tried to read the formation of the words on the woman's lips, but the movements were far too quick for her to follow. With a feeling of being baulked, she desisted, wondering what would be the next move for her to make.

Tiredness was assailing her limbs, and she was cold. Even thought of Bill had now less of its original poignancy, although regret and misery still lay deep and cold in her heart. But she had ceased to think of what the years would mean while he was again serving time in prison. The dark grey months were one with the night that surrounded her.

Her lassitude was dispersed momentarily by the rocking sound of another loud laugh from the woman at the telephone. She seemed to be shouting at the person at the other end of the wire. Tessa saw her frown, her left hand make an airy gesture, and then plunge into an inner pocket of the coat flung across the settee.

Tessa's eyes, tired and hot, and aching for the want of sleep, brightened, and she took a deep breath. She blinked and stared again, unbelievingly. But unbelief changed to amazed wonder.

"Bill—oh, Bill!" she murmured.

The numbness departed from her leg, the crick from her neck. She forgot her discomfort as she remained crouched there, fingers grasping the window-sill for support. The woman in the flat was again speaking rapidly into the 'phone, which was held close to her mouth, and as she spoke her gaze was lowered to a cascade of light pouring from the extended fingers of her left hand.

Tessa knew that she was looking at the Malverne diamonds, that fateful necklace known as the Tears of Death.

VI.

True to his word, Anthony Slade was in the grounds of Steyning Towers at daybreak. In the east the sun poked flushed fingers over a high ridge of trees. There had been some rain about two o'clock. Slade had stood at the window of his room watching it. Now the air was cleaned and fresh, and the first songs of the birds rose clear and piping. Slade had finished his examination of the ground near the house, and was strolling along one of the paths towards a distant summer-house, partly hidden by trees, when he became aware of a figure running along a converging path.

He paused, thinking for the moment that the other person must have observed him. But the running steps continued, and then, between some bushes, he saw the bathrobed figure of Lady Malverne springing towards the summer-house. A floating laugh met the detective's ear. He glanced back. Another bathrobed figure was chasing the first. In the early morning sunshine Kurt Swensen's yellow hair gleamed like burnished brass.

Neither of the runners seemed perturbed by loss of the jewels or the disturbance of the previous night. Slade recalled Lady Malverne's first acceptance of the news, her reaction to the doubt and suspicion that had immediately assailed her mind, and realized that he was seeing another facet of a remarkable woman. She might be suspicious of Swensen—furthermore, there might be cause for her suspicion; cause of which Slade knew nothing—but to Swensen she would reveal no change.

Or was she herself a clever, scheming woman?

Slade walked down the path to the summer-house, and saw beyond it a small shelving beach and a clear lake of water. White arms were thrashing the silver surface of the lake and laughter rose in ripples. Slade stood in the shelter of a rustic arch and watched. He saw the swimmers racing neck and neck, and then gradually one pulled ahead. It was the Swede. The detective saw him reach the farther bank, turn, and laughingly await the arrival of the woman. Together they rose, turned back, and headed once more across the stretch of water, to the accompaniment of joyous splashing and laughter.

Slade was minded of a couple of children on holiday. The scene was fair, the sweet air of morning was a tonic for the blood; it was a setting where carefree laughter should echo and light hearts be unfettered. He watched the bobbing heads. The woman turned on her side, the bright green of her rubber cap a splash of bold colour, and called to the man swimming a few yards to her right. Slade could not catch the words, but they brought a resounding laugh from the Swede, who suddenly disappeared under the water, and some seconds later reappeared a considerable distance ahead.

The woman made haste to follow, and they were keenly racing again for the opposite shore. Swensen's athletic figure pulled itself from the water, and stood waiting for Lady Malverne. Slade could not but help admire the technique of the Swede as a swimmer. He was fast and powerful. Equally the Yard man admired the Swede's physical grace. A maroon swimming-suit encased his trunk, from which his limbs projected, brown and tapering and muscular. Above the laughing face the yellow hair gleamed wetly in the thin sunshine.

Across the intervening space Slade heard the woman's call as she came out of the water.

"What about a dive, Kurt?"

"I'll race you round to the spring-board, Lucie."

Another race was on. To Slade it was a frolicsome gambol by two youngsters bent on getting the most out of life. Imbued with the same spirit of fun and love of motion, they were playing in a little world apart, and the thought made the Yard man feel an interloper. He felt that he had no right to witness the playing of these two people so obviously attracted by each other by something stronger than mere mutual liking.

Yet the watching detective made no move to go. He was aware of another feeling, one of caution, a feeling that told him to remain, to watch. Caution whispered that there might be a development. Perhaps, after all, Lady Malverne was not happy in her mind about the loss of the necklace . . . and Swensen.

From what he remembered of the newspaper articles on Swensen at the time of the Olympic Games, Slade had conceived an impression that he was not particularly well endowed with this world's goods and chattels. What if Lady Malverne had decided she could not marry him? What if thought of losing a rich wife had turned his thoughts in other directions . . . jewels, the necklace of diamonds that was worth a considerable fortune in itself?

There were a number of possibilities in the combination of individuals and circumstances that intrigued Slade. These possibilities, not completely framed or thought out, lay in the back of his mind, ready to be drawn to the fore if occasion turned his thoughts in that direction. But the fact that they were there, dormant, probably accounted for that feeling of caution which caused him to remain, watching.

Some minutes later he was thankful that he had remained. He was able to arrive at the spring-board without Swensen leaving his sight. And Lady Malverne disappeared for a matter of only seconds while she made the dive that resulted in a tragic discovery.

Standing in the same position Slade saw the man and woman arrive at the diving-platform, saw the woman run out on to the spring diving-board, raise her hands above her bright green cap, and saw her lift herself gracefully as a bird in flight. Her arching body cleaved the water with scarcely a splash, and involuntarily Swensen applauded. The Swede ran lightly on to the spring-board, and began a trip dance, slapping his hands loudly against his thighs, bending slightly, as though peering to see where the woman swam under the water.

The next thing of which Slade was aware was a figure breaking water quickly, a flurry of white arms, and a shrill cry.

He could not hear the words, but there was no mistaking the portent of that cry. Something was wrong. Fear and a demand for help were blended in that shrill sound.

Swensen, about to spring into the lake, was stayed by Slade's shout as the detective ran swiftly round the margin of the lake. The Swede waited, alternately shifting his gaze from the approaching detective to the swiftly swimming figure of Lady Malverne.

Lady Malverne was the first to reach the diving-platform, but Slade was within earshot as she gasped out her first words after landing.

"There's a car in the lake, Kurt! I nearly crashed into it. And there's a dead man inside!"

Swensen put a protecting arm round the trembling figure of the woman. It was obvious that she was badly shaken by her discovery. Her eyes were wide and round, and her lips twitched grotesquely.

"There, Lucie, steady yourself. Here's Inspector Slade."

The woman stared at Slade as the detective slowed his fast pace.

"Good morning, Lady Malverne. Good morning, Mr. Swensen. I was at the other end of the lake, and heard Lady Malverne's cry. It was obvious that something was wrong."

They had nodded when he said good morning, and when he finished Swensen said with a brief grin, "Out hunting early, Inspector."

"The best time of day to find an undisturbed spoor," Slade returned lightly.

"Well, you've got one now. A dead man in a car," said Swensen. "Looks like an accident."

The woman shuddered.

"It's horrible. And, Kurt, I'm cold. Would you be an angel and get my robe?"

"Sure. Wait there. I'll be right back."

Slade watched the Swedish-American athlete's clean-limbed figure sprinting round the lake. He ran with effortless ease and grace. Small wonder, thought Slade, he had broken so many records at the Olympiad. He turned to the woman.

"Did you recognize the car, or the man in it, Lady Malverne?"

"No. It was all so sudden. I found myself gliding down beside it, and I was startled. It was a queer sensation, being startled like that while under water. I had a feeling of faintness, as though I suddenly wanted air. . . . And then I saw the white face staring at me through one of the windows." She shuddered again. "It was horrible! . . . The eyes . . ."

Slade waited until Swensen returned with the bathrobes. The Swede wrapped one round the woman and slung the other across his own shoulders.

"Well, Inspector, what do you do now?"

Slade looked at him meditatively.

"You suggested an accident, Mr. Swensen?"

His tone added the mark of interrogation.

"Naturally. There's a path across there." Swensen pointed. "Beyond is the thick hedge running by the road. Perhaps the car skidded on the road, lost control, broke through the hedge—and, that path being an incline, what could the driver do?"

Slade felt that the last words were a sudden amendment of something the other had left unsaid. Mentally he gave the Swede full marks for an alert brain. It was true, there was a path where the other had pointed.

"We'll see," he said.

"But—but the man!" said Lady Malverne.

"I'm afraid a little delay will not make any

difference— now, Lady Malverne," the detective said gently.

Her face dropped into her hands.

"Do you mind if I go in, Inspector? I don't feel I want to be here any longer."

"Certainly. But before you go, perhaps you would show me whereabouts the car lies?"

She pointed to a spot some yards beyond the edge of the diving-board, then turned and without another word ran back round the lake towards the summer-house.

Slade became aware that the other was looking at him closely. .

"You think, Inspector, this has something to do with . . ." The Swede paused. There was no need to say in full what was in his mind.

"It's possible, Mr. Swensen." Slade's tone was noncommittal. "Let's look at the path. There may be tyre-tracks."

There were, tracks that very obviously showed that a car had run down the path from the hedge. The hedge itself told a story too. It was broken, and snapped branches and fallen leaves lay on the ground. Further, the tyre-marks were sufficiently clear to prove beyond doubt that the car had left the road beyond the hedge, burst through, and travelled to the lake as Swensen had suggested. Only on the concrete margin of the lake, which was about twelve or fifteen feet wide, were there no signs of the car's passage to its fatal resting-place.

"Apparently you were right, Mr. Swensen," said the detective.

Swensen smiled. It was a boyish smile, and there was a suspicion of a twinkle in the blue eyes.

"I hope you won't hold it against me, Inspector."

Slade remained non-committal. He could not make up his mind about Swensen.

"Why should I?"

"Oh, I don't know. It might have occurred to you that I had previous knowledge. Actually I didn't know a thing.

But I remembered the path as I had noticed it when running round the lake, and a possible solution came into my mind at once. I am not usually very deductive."

Swensen's manner was open and friendly. It was not, Slade had to admit, too friendly. The Swede was normal, and was behaving naturally.

Of course, the thing might have been an accident, but Slade doubted it. To his mind it looked as though the car had been deliberately driven through the hedge. Besides, the path curved, so that the hedge was hidden from view of anyone standing by the lake. Had the car lost control the chances were a hundred to one against its following the course of the path into the lake. More likely, it would have crashed into a tree as it swept aside from the path at the bend. And if driving of the car into the lake was deliberate, the possible connexion with the stealing of the diamonds was too apparent to need stressing.

Slade followed the gravelly surface of the path back to the bend. There the tyre-tracks slewed round, and were more deeply incised.

He pointed to them.

"You drive a car, Mr. Swensen?"

"Yes. I haven't driven in England, to be exact. But I've got an old roadster at home in the States. Why?"

Swensen's blue eyes had clouded.

"Don't those deeper ruts suggest anything to you?"

"No, I can't say they do. How do you mean exactly?"

"Wouldn't you say the car was steadied at this point, the brakes applied, so that the locked wheels dug deeper into the surface of the path?"

The Swede's face lengthened.

"Sure, that's right, Inspector. But if the brakes were on, as you say, then—"

He hesitated, looking at Slade. The detective nodded.

"Then it wasn't an accident," Slade finished for him.

"We'll soon see. I want a swimming-suit, and then we'll take a look together ... if you've no objection."

"No objection at all. In fact, I'm desperately

interested, if you can understand that. I'll run and fetch you a swimming-suit and towel right now. You can change in the summer-house. A spare suit of my own should fit you."

Slade had not been in the summer-house four minutes when the other returned.

"Here you are, Inspector. For that service you can give me a cigarette, if you've got one. I was in too much of a hurry to remember mine."

Slade gave the Swede a cigarette, and he smoked while the Yard man got out of his clothes and into the swimming costume.

"Ready?" asked the detective.

"Sure."

Swensen threw away the cigarette and they trotted round the lake together. Side by side they flung themselves into the water. Legs paddling, they sank, one on each side of the submerged car. The wheels were embedded in the soil of the bottom.

They rose and broke surface together.

"You saw?" said Slade, shaking water from his ears.

"I did," nodded Swensen. "He's in the back. That settles it ... it wasn't an accident. What do we do, get him out?"

"Yes. You'd better come round this side. You grip the door and hold it back. It'll need a hefty tug against the pressure of the water. I'll get him out. That suit you?"

"Suits me fine. When you've got him out hold his shoulders, Inspector. I'll grab his feet, in case he slips. We shan't have a lot of time to waste."

Without waiting for an answer the other swam round to where Slade was treading water.

"Okay, I'm ready."

They dived. Slade saw one of the Swede's arms stretch out and his hand grasp the handle of the door. The other hand joined it. What seemed like minutes passed before the door moved open. With legs kicking furiously Swensen dragged it wide enough for Slade to manoeuvre in the opening and grasp the dead man's shoulders. His back muscles felt as though they were tearing apart under the strain. He pulled, wriggled this way and that, and at last, when he thought he would have to desist and rise for air, he felt the weight of the dead man slacken.

He was through the opening, climbing through a greenish haze, his lungs singing for air.

Suddenly his mouth parted, and he gulped great gasps of air as the sunshine made him blink.

"Gee, Inspector, that was an effort!"

He saw that he and Swensen were clinging to something extending between them, the body of a man that lay face downwards in the water. They paddled to the shore, and dragged the body after them and rolled it over. The face of an unknown man stared back at Slade.

"Know him, Mr. Swensen?"

The Swede shook his head.

"Never seen him in my life before. At least," he amended carefully, "not to my knowledge."

Slade felt in the man's pockets, for the corpse was fully clad in a lounge suit, socks, collar and tie, and shoes, but found nothing. Even a tailor's tab had been cut from the inside pocket of the jacket. There were laundry marks on the linen, but, as Slade realized, it would take some time for those clues to prove of any value; and by the time they had established the man's identity—if they did—it would most likely be too late to make use of the information.

"Somebody did a thorough job, didn't they?" Swensen observed.

"A very thorough job," Slade agreed, pointing to a clean-lipped hole in the side of the man's head. "And whoever it was meant that there should be no mistake."

"Say, what about the car? Didn't think to look at its registration number. Not that it would mean anything to me, of course."

"I noted its number first time we went down. The car was registered in London, but that might not be much help. Feel like helping me with him to the summer-house, Mr. Swensen?"

"Yes. I'll take his legs."

They carried the dead man round the lake to the summer-house and deposited the body on a rustic seat.

"I'd like you to wait here while I get into my clothes, Mr. Swensen."

"Carry on, Inspector."

Five minutes later Slade was dressed. He placed the costume and wet towel over the back of the rustic seat on which the corpse lay.

"Now I'd like you to fetch Sergeant Clinton, if you would, Mr. Swensen, and I must ask you not to mention this business to anyone in the house. This is murder, and alters the complexion of things."

"I understand. Could I trouble you for another cigarette? I've been out here some time now."

With his bathrobe wrapped round him, and smoking a cigarette, Kurt Swensen ran back to the house. A few minutes later, by which time Slade had completed a further examination of the corpse, Clinton arrived.

"Lord, this alters things!" were the sergeant's first words.

"Considerably, Clinton. We've got to take new bearings, and quickly, or we'll find ourselves at sea without chart or compass."

VII.

Max Reisenberg turned a sour face to Captain Furniss. There was something not altogether wholesome in the look on the big Jew's face.

"Did you recognize him?"

The Captain wrinkled a bony nose, puffed out his chest, and cleared his throat noisily.

"Egad no! Utter stranger. Never seen the fellow before in my life. It's—it's a damned mystery, begging the ladies' pardon."

The ladies at the moment consisted of Mrs. Clammer, tearful, dressed in grey, with a grey look on her face, and Madge Reisenberg, fiercely silent, watchful, blowsy, and masking her thoughts behind a smile that was in effect a savage grimace.

"Murder's not a nice thing," Reisenberg opined.

"Nice!"

"I said not nice." Max's temper, like himself, was on edge. His face, where Bill Pegwell had manhandled it, was still puffed up and discoloured, and, what was worse, he was afraid that his somewhat naive explanation— namely, that he had collided with a bathroom door—had not gone down smoothly with his wife. "And I meant—not nice," he added truculently.

Captain Furniss's nose continued to wrinkle. He didn't like Jews when he was in a good humour, and this morning his humour was definitely bad.

"We're all suspect," he said, with a faint touch of malice.

He grinned when he saw Reisenberg's start. "When that lorry arrives and the car's pulled out of the lake, and the doctor gets the bullet, that Scotland Yard man will know more. Well, I've knocked about the world, but I never thought till this morning that a clear conscience was an asset. I don't know how you feel," he added, staring at the Jew.

"I feel this isn't any place for me," said Reisenberg, wantonly refusing to rise to the bait.

Mrs. Clammer broke in, her voice scared.

"Has nobody identified him, gentlemen?"

"Nobody, ma'am," said the Captain.

"Not even the servants?"

Furniss shook his head.

"It's a mystery, a complete mystery," he reaffirmed sententiously.

"What I want to know," said Mrs. Reisenberg, too clever to meet her husband's roving eye, "is who's the prisoner in the North Tower?"

Mrs. Clammer perked up. "Prisoner?"

The Captain's chest again assumed military proportions. "Prisoner, ma'am?"

"I saw breakfast being taken there on a tray. The servants aren't housed there, and the guest chambers are in the South Tower. Besides, that Yard plain-clothes sergeant has been snooping round the North Tower all night. I couldn't sleep," Mrs. Reisenberg explained in answer to several inquiring glances. "I had a headache, and I had to go to the bathroom for water to swallow some aspirin. I saw him."

Reisenberg, who in thirty years hadn't learned what a clever psychologist his wife was, fell into the trap she had set and ridiculed the suggestion she had made, thereby confirming her suspicions that her spouse was keeping something to himself. And when Max kept something to himself it was because—as she had found out from long experience —he had urgent reasons for not wanting her to know.

He said, "Nonsense, Madge! A prisoner. It's absurd. You've been reading some trashy novel and got hold of a damned silly notion."

But Mrs. Clammer and the Captain were quite obviously willing to consider the possibility.

Said the Captain, "There's something going on here that we haven't been told about. That insurance detective's face shows it. I don't like that man, don't like his looks."

"I don't envy him his job of going back to his company," put in Mrs. Clammer, "and reporting that the necklace has been taken from under his nose, as it were."

The Captain turned to Reisenberg.

"Would the thief get the full hundred and fifty thousand pounds for it, Mr. Reisenberg?"

A disturbing thought came into the Jew's mind as he watched the Captain, but he put it on one side, as being impossible. Furniss, he considered, was mentally and physically incapable of pulling the job that had been pulled, although there were strange ducks abroad, getting their fingers on to things.

He frowned, as though considering the question deeply.

"Whether it is worth actually a hundred and fifty thousand pounds, Captain Furniss, is a question that can be answered only by the purchaser." Reisenberg shrugged. "Intrinsic value, you know. Historical association, and all that. There are people—many people—prepared to pay for what I call a curio value. If the thief knows his trade—or, rather, my trade"— Reisenberg smiled thinly—"he might be able to get six figures for the necklace, even though it is known to be a stolen article. If the thief is just a thief"—his tone made the distinction very clear—"he'll be lucky to get . . . whatever he does get."

Captain Furniss thought the Jew was annoyingly vague, and purposely so, after his last pause.

"I see," he said.

Reisenberg picked up a newspaper, and conversation drooped like a plant denied nourishment. No one in that room heard the soft fall of departing footsteps in the corridor outside. Sergeant Clinton trod on the balls of his feet. He met Slade outside the room where the corpse of the stranger taken from the lake was lying under a sheet while a local police surgeon probed the wound for the bullet.

"How are they taking it, Clinton? Hear anything?" asked the chief of the Yard's Department X2.

"They're upset and curious. The Clammer woman's a bit frightened, I think, and the Captain fidgets as though he's received orders to lead a front-line attack. Reisenberg's anxious to get out, and his wife's on to something. She's dropping feelers about the prisoner we've got hidden away in the North Tower."

Slade smiled unpleasantly.

"That woman's a cross between a terrier and a tom-cat, and a bad cross. There's one comfort. If Reisenberg was a murderer she wouldn't be here."

"It wouldn't be easy to catch a cross between a terrier and a tom-cat," Clinton grinned. "Reisenberg may be just out of luck."

"He will be if his wife sees Pegwell. I want you to bring him down, Clinton. He may know who the dead man is, and be able to give us a lead."

"I get it. You mean this dead man may be the fellow who was waiting to spring Pegwell after he'd lifted the stuff?"

"Yes." Slade nodded thoughtfully. "Pegwell didn't try this lay without having a means of getting away in a hurry. That's ten to one on a car. Well, we've found a car in the lake, a car with a London registration number. And in the car a man shot through the head. A deliberate stroke of business, Clinton."

The sergeant rubbed his jaws.

"When will the car be out of the lake?"

"In about an hour."

"Well, don't you think it might be an idea to tell Pegwell we've found his car? Say there was an accident, the car ran through the hedge, crashed into the lake. That bit of bait ought to set his teeth snapping for a good bite."

"Clinton, that's more than an idea. It's pure inspiration. I think I can improve on it, however. A bit ghoulish, but the devil's driving us hard, so our needs must be the excuse. I'll have him down and tell him in there, with the corpse covered up. But we won't say who the corpse is. If I'm not wrong he'll want to find out quick enough for himself. Either he'll be surprised or he won't."

Slade eyed his Sergeant.

Clinton's grin returned.

"I feel like a chef with a nice fat goose I'm about to put in the oven."

"He'll go in the oven—when we've plucked him," promised Slade.

Bill had spent a restless night, and had eaten little breakfast. Most of the meal taken to him remained on the tray by his chair. He looked up morosely when Clinton unlocked the door and entered.

"What d'you want now?" he asked gruffly.

Bill had lost his spick-and-span appearance. Dark bristles shaded his cheeks, and his hair had not been combed. He had loosened his collar and tie and had not fixed them again.

"We've got something to tell you," said Clinton, "and show you. Come on."

Bill shuffled to his feet, shooting the plain-clothes sergeant an uneasy glance.

"I don't want to see anything, and you can tell me here."

"Not this I can't," Clinton smiled. "And you'll want to see it all right. How's the head feeling?"

"Like the dome of St. Paul's. But get this straight. You're not fooling me with any smart tricks. I was framed last time I did a stretch."

"That's what they all say."

"Well, you're listening to a fellow that means it, for a change."

"Were you framed last night?"

Clinton's tone was sceptical.

"I was unlucky. I reckon I was owed something for that frame-up."

"As much as a hundred and fifty thousand in sparklers, Bill? That's a pretty big round figure. You must think you're worth something to somebody."

"Cut out the sarcasm," growled Bill. "I've still got a debt to settle for that crack on the bean, so you'd better keep Reisenberg out of my reach or you may have a murder on your hands."

Clinton gave the other a straight look.

"Come on," he said briskly, "and stop bleating."

The local police-surgeon and the inspector of the Sussex County Constabulary who had accompanied him to Steyning Towers in answer to Slade's 'phone call, took a stroll in the grounds while the chief of Department X2 waited alone in the room with the sheeted corpse for Bill's arrival.

The bullet had been recovered from the bone of the dead man's skull, in which it had become embedded. It was badly flattened, but Slade was certain it was fired from a thirty-eight automatic. It might be a thirty-two, it was difficult to say, but Slade thought not.

The door opened and Clinton came in with Pegwell. The cracksman saw the outline of a human form under the white sheet, and nodded.

"What's the idea? Playing bogey-man with me?"

There was a broad streak of contempt in his tone. Slade watched him closely. He saw that Bill was worried about something, but that he was desperately ready to hide his worry under a cloak of assumed ease.

"Bill," said Slade, "we've got your car."

The other's eyes dilated. Faint dark lines appeared at the sides of his mouth, which was suddenly pulled down at the corners, as though by hidden wires. Slade could see that the news had hit him hard, but he was wary, not ready to be rushed into a tricked admission.

"Who told you it was mine, the chauffeur, I suppose?"

The same desperate lightness was in his voice, but it

was near to cracking. The eyes wandered to the figure of the corpse, then sped to another part of the room. Slowly white spots gleamed along the ridges of the straining knuckles of the young man's hands. The hands relaxed and the white spots faded.

"Unfortunately no, Bill. There was an accident. The chauffeur is dead."

This time Bill was not proof against the shock of the detective's words. Immediately into his mind flooded pictures of Tessa's young body broken in a car smash, her brave eyes glazed in death, and something rose within him and tore at the muscles of his throat, so that he could not speak. Sweat dewed his forehead, started from the pores over his shoulders, and he felt it trickling against his spine. His mouth worked, but no words came. He could think of nothing to say, and black seconds of time swept over him. He felt numbed.

Inside him a voice whispered, "No, it isn't true. It can't be. Tessa's alive." He did not know that voice was his own mental reaction to a terrible, nerve-shattering interpretation of the detective's cunning words. But it gave him hope. Something stirred and fought in his mind. "Not Tessa, no, not Tessa."

"An accident."

He barely recognized his own voice, and when he knew what he had said he could have laughed. After that wild emotional storm all he had said was, "An accident." Nothing about Tessa, nothing about . . .

"The car crashed through the hedge, Bill, swept on to a path in the park, and I suppose in the darkness the driver failed to regain control."

It sounded as though it might be true. That dark fear returned to his mind, hung like a black curtain over his thoughts, veiling what he wanted to think.

"And . . . what happened?"

His voice was pitched higher. He knew now. He told himself he must keep his voice lower. He mustn't give himself away—Tessa away.

"The car plunged into the lake, Bill. The water was pretty deep at that end, about twenty feet, I think. There was no escape."

The words droned and echoed in his brain. No escape. Tessa, the cold water gurgling through the window spaces, stealing her life, rising over her pale face, with its satin-smooth skin. . . .

The picture was horribly clear.

He had brought Tessa to this. He had asked her, and she had given her life. That was Tessa. They had found her. Tessa under the white sheet, her beauty chilled to cold clay, and these men would stand around and stare at her, not knowing what a lovely thing she had been.

His Tessa. . . . She hadn't wanted the diamonds. Tears of Death . . . *death.*

He did not know he was moving forward, like a man in a trance, hands outstretched to tear that sheet from her face.

His Tessa. . . .

The eyes of the Yard detectives met behind the slowly moving man. Clinton's mouth pursed at one side expressively. Slade nodded.

The Yard man took a couple of paces and placed his hand on Bill's shoulder.

"Don't be hasty," he said. "You'll get a shock, Bill."

Bill shook his head, more to clear the fog in his brain, than in denial.

"Not now," he whispered.

"Don't you think you'd better tell us the truth before you lift that sheet?"

"The truth? What is there to tell you? You know . . . now."

Slade was puzzled. The words suggested that his problem had been reduced to a fundamental simplicity. What did he know . . . *now?*

As Bill's hand was hovering over the edge of the sheet Slade said, "I warn you, Bill, he's not a particularly nice sight."

Something clicked in Bill's mind, clicked and whirred like a motor starting up. His hand drew back slowly. He did not touch the sheet. He looked round, met Slade's puzzled gaze, and suddenly his eyes narrowed.

He knew now. It was a trick.

The fools!

But he must be careful. They had almost got him. He must be careful. Everything depended on his keeping his nerve. They'd got nothing on him. Not a thing. Unlawful entry with intent. . . . That didn't mean a damn' thing. No, he could still hold his own.

The fools!

Slade frowned. The sudden change in Bill was perplexing. He had been disturbed, worried, and he had been about to pull aside the sheet when Slade spoke. The words stopped him. He hadn't flinched at the thought of not seeing a nice sight. It wasn't that. Slade, whose gaze had not left Bill's face, had seen the dawn of fresh intelligence in the narrowing eyes. His words had had a definite meaning for the other, and that meaning was a mystery to the Yard man. He felt annoyed that at the last minute his subterfuge had failed.

Or would it still work?

"Well, don't be shy," he said, pulling aside the sheet, revealing the face and chest of the dead man. "Recognize him, Bill? That's your partner, isn't it? That's the man who drove you down here?"

For moments there was silence. Bill seemed to the others to sway uncertainly on his feet, as though his strength was leaving him.

Suddenly the room trembled in the gale of a gushing roar of laughter. The sound had burst from Bill's lips. His head was thrown back, and he was pouring laughter into the room, recklessly, swamping feelings and drowning thought.

"Hey!"

Clinton sprang forward and grabbed the young man's arm. He shook him. The effect was to send the sound trilling in a wild arpeggio.

"Stop it! D'you hear? You're crazy!"

The sound stopped.

After its frantic release the silence was almost painful. Slade winced. He had been witness to something he could not understand, could not fathom, although in his mind was revolving an idea. There had been a cause for that laughter. A cause sufficiently strong to send Bill Pegwell off at half-cock.

And the only clue he had was the words he had spoken: "I warn you, Bill, he's not a particularly nice sight." . . . Not a particularly nice sight. In those words lay the cause of the laughter. Bill had expected to recognize the figure under the sheet, but those words had prevented recognition.

Clinton was saying, "Well, do you know him? Speak, man. He's been murdered, shot through the head. Understand that. Murdered. If he's your partner you'll want to do something about it, won't you?"

Clinton was impatient, and there was deep-seated annoyance in his tone.

Bill's eyes dropped to the sergeant's face. He did not look again at the corpse.

"I've never seen him before in my life," he said soberly, "and you didn't find a gun on me."

VIII.

Two hours later three men sat in the summer-house in the grounds of Steyning Towers, and the face of each wore a frown of perplexity. Inspector Frenton, of the local force, felt that Fate had dealt harshly with him that Sunday morning. He had planned to take his wife and two children to see his sister at Eastbourne, and had looked forward to the trip for days. Now he was listening to a Yard man telling him he would have to be responsible for the custody of an arrested burglar. The trip to Eastbourne had been rudely wiped off the slate, and that wouldn't improve his wife's temper. She had bought a new dress, because she thought the occasion warranted it, and, anyway, she always felt that her sister-in-law expected to see her in a new dress whenever they met. The kids would be gloomy too. Young Harry had made up his mind to go to Beachy Head.

Unhappily Inspector Frenton pulled his thoughts back to the present and the problem before them. He accepted a pouchful of tobacco from Slade, and felt for his matches.

"To be perfectly candid, Slade," he said, tamping the ash in the bowl of his pipe, "I don't see where my holding Pegwell is going to get us. This is your pigeon, and Doctor Lumsden's evidence doesn't make it any less so."

"Lumsden said, so far as he could decide at the first examination, the unknown was shot about five o'clock yesterday afternoon. Before I got here, Frenton. Clinton and I arrived about half-past. The time puts it in your province; it's a local case."

"It's a damned nuisance." Frenton cast round wildly and plucked at a distant bloom of hope. "We don't know where he was shot. That's a London car. He might have been shot in London."

"Sorry, Frenton, you're not giving me the slip that easy," Slade grinned. "London registration plates. It might have changed hands in Sussex last week. It isn't a new car. But the point is this, I want to isolate the case, not get it tangled up with a lot of insurance issues in London. See what I'm driving at?"

"Vaguely. I've got a better idea of a lot of routine stuff you're pushing on to my shoulders. I'm not grumbling about that. Don't mistake me. But if I can shift that headache on to some one else I'm going to. Nobody's going to get any thanks for this business. The necklace in the blue, a man murdered, and God knows what it all means and where the solution lies—if there is one."

"You don't like the way the case is shaping?"

"I don't like anything about it. I'm a country policeman, Slade, and it's years since I thought of catching murderers redhanded. That was all knocked out of me by the time I got my sergeant's stripes. I've grown up. I concern myself with trespassing gipsies, motorists who like to knock it back, neighbours with complaints, and suchlike. That's my job. I'm not a London detective. Big jewel robberies and slick shootings are not my meat. I don't know how to carve those joints. See what I mean? I'm not happy holding the dirty end of the sort of stick you've picked up down here."

Slade nodded. He liked the local inspector for his forthright views and lack of personal vanity. The man knew himself to be a uniformed policeman and not a trained detective, and wanted to keep to his own work. That showed his wisdom.

"Look, Frenton," said Slade. "Tell you what I'll do. Cooperate, and I'll see you're not expected to do a lot of red-tape stuff for the local records."

Frenton glanced up, somewhat mollified.

"You will?"

"Certainly. I want help. I'm willing to give some in return, and I prefer to work with a friend any day than a man who won't pull his weight."

Slade could be equally frank. It was this frankness that usually won others to his viewpoint and ensured the smooth working of his cases when they took him into the sphere of a local force.

"Good enough," Frenton nodded. "That's plain English of the sort I speak myself. Now let's have what's on your mind. You're the detective, mind, and yours is the responsibility."

Slade turned to Clinton.

"Give me those notes," he requested.

The Sergeant produced a black notebook and Slade flipped over a few leaves.

"I want Pegwell locked up locally, and I want the local men to get me plates of the fingerprints of the dead man, photographs, etc., and I want that car held. That all right?"

"Perfectly. You don't mind explaining, do you? I like to know why I do a thing."

"That's fair. Pegwell gave me an idea. He thought there was some one under that sheet whom he knew."

"He didn't act like it," grunted Clinton.

Slade turned. "He did, Clinton, until I spoke those last words. Remember? There was a clue in those words, and I've thought it over and decided there's only one word that gives a real clue—the word 'he.'"

Clinton sucked his teeth, while the local man screwed his face into an expression suggesting laborious mental work.

"Don't get it," he said at last, shaking his head.

"He," repeated Slade. "He expected me to say 'she.' I had the sex wrong. That was Pegwell's surprise. Get it? He had an accomplice, but she was a woman. There's no two answers to the riddle. A woman, and I've an idea who she is."

Clinton nodded.

"His wife."

"Right, Clinton. Bill Pegwell flared up when he saw Reisenberg. His wife works in the Jew's office. Well, I think we can assume that Reisenberg has tried to make himself a nuisance."

"He wouldn't have to try hard, from what I've seen of him," grunted Frenton.

"Pegwell can't get it out of his mind. He's got a bee in his bonnet about being framed the last time he was sent in for a stretch, so it looks as though he'd set himself this time to pull something big and steer clear of the rocks for a while."

"He'd got his plans set nicely," Clinton affirmed. "How he got in that room the way he did, and had the safe open, beats me."

"You forget, Clinton, Steyning Towers is a show-place of sorts. In any book on the county you'll find mention of it and a full description."

"That's right," said Frenton. "Some of the books on these parts have maps of the Towers. It's asking for trouble."

"This time there's been an answer, and I think you can depend on it that Pegwell got his information about the architecture of the place from some topographical work or other. However, that's neither here nor there. What is more interesting is Bill's knowledge of the necklace."

"It's been spread in the papers pretty freely," the sergeant pointed out.

"True, and a round figure suggested as its market value. What I'm driving at is this. Bill Pegwell knew the right time to try his grab. He was at the safe when the house was full, but no one was near the room with the safe. He might have guessed the time they would be at dinner, but that would have been chancey, very chancey. I think Bill knew. He had inside knowledge of the guests arriving and roughly the times. He knew how and when to work. The fact that he was interrupted doesn't alter this other fact."

"I don't see where this is getting us," demurred Frenton, his blunt face puckered.

"Briefly, Frenton, here. Bill got information from his wife, employed in Reisenberg's office. That means one of two things: either she's sufficiently familiar with Reisenberg to be sure of getting the information, or she came by it secretly in some way."

"I follow you that far," the local man nodded, stirring the ash in his pipe-bowl with a match.

"All right, then," resumed Slade. "Now, Reisenberg's a fly individual. He's nobody's fool, and I should say he's about as trusting of other people as a tiger-shark. He's got where he has by not allowing other people to make mistakes that would affect him in any way. We at the Yard have got nothing on him. Frankly, we'd like to have, for Reisenberg's a shark that preys in deep waters. There have been rumours about stuff he has handled, but rumours unsupported by concrete evidence soon lose their potency. Reisenberg knows that, and that's why he's like a cat on hot bricks every time he sees me in the same room with him. He's afraid of two things: my getting something on him, and his wife discovering from Bill Pegwell something that I have no doubt Mrs. Pegwell has told her husband."

Frenton's broad face showed signs of the local man's mental struggle to keep track of just where Slade was leading him.

"So we can discount Mrs. Pegwell getting anything from Reisenberg—information about this trip to Sussex, I mean —because he trusts her. That's right out. It leaves us with the other alternative. She came by that information without Reisenberg knowing."

"Does this really help us?" queried Frenton. "It's getting a bit beyond me, I'll admit."

Slade smiled.

"I've got to take you on a roundabout trip to make things perfectly clear. You said you wanted them explained."

"That's right, I do. But this sort of thing's giving me a headache. It's worse than one of the missus's Sunday puzzles in the paper."

"No," Clinton disagreed, with a broad grin, "not as bad as that. They're terrible. My wife's afflicted with the same complaint, and I'm expected to do the work. Not that we've won anything yet."

"Like us, still trying," said Frenton, and, turning to Slade, he added, "Righto, let's see where this leads us. Though I'm not promising I'll remember it."

"You needn't," grinned the Yard man. "Fact is, I'm not sorry for the chance to get it all untangled myself. As I was saying, it's pretty clear that Pegwell's wife got her information about the party here without Reisenberg knowing—or thought she did."

"Eh?"

Frenton frowned.

"Or thought she did," Slade repeated. "That's the point I've been leading up to. She might have got the information, but probably she gave herself away in doing so, and Reisenberg, being clever and never one to jump at the obvious, thought it over and arrived where the Pegwells were intending to start from. If he didn't know Bill was out of prison, he could have found out easily enough. That would have verified his suspicion that something was afoot. Perhaps afterwards Bill's wife tried to verify things by pumping Reisenberg because he suddenly proved willing to talk about things down here. And Reisenberg that way discovered enough to assure himself he was right. In short, it's possible that Reisenberg, with knowledge of a deliberate attempt to steal the necklace, laid counter-plans. Remember, some one did cosh Bill Pegwell badly, and the necklace is missing. That some one's been mighty spry. The spryness suggests Max Reisenberg."

Frenton pursed his mouth.

"Now I get it—yes, of course, if he knew he could have been the one to bash Pegwell over the head and grab the diamonds."

"Always remembering," put in Clinton, in his staid

voice, "that Reisenberg did turn up after we'd found Bill Pegwell."

"Yes, but wouldn't that count the other way?" asked Frenton. "Couldn't expect a man to walk back into the lion's den, could you?"

"With the lion laid out cold—why not?" said Slade. "It was a bold move—or would have been, in the circumstances we're debating—and calculated to be reckoned as you've reckoned it, Frenton. Another case of the double-bluff. Oh, no, Max Reisenberg is more than clever enough to think out a telling move like that. But all this brings us to Max Reisenberg in one pan of the scales, and the rest in the other pan. Furniss, Mrs. Clammer, and Lady Malverne; I think we can rule them out meantime. When I questioned them they gave each other a rough sort of alibi for the time Bill was laid cold. Butterick says he was watching Swensen; he evidently doesn't trust foreigners of any kind. Mrs. Reisenberg, I think, we can place as an appendage of her husband, for the purpose of this particular tally. So we've got to take our pick of the bunch, and Reisenberg stands out by a mile."

Clinton had something to offer for consideration.

"What about if Reisenberg and Bill Pegwell are in this together?"

Slade flashed his sergeant a keen glance.

"Mean the knocking out was a put-up job?"

"Something like that, to put us wide off the real track." Slade thought it over. The theory had been considered before.

"It might be," muttered Frenton.

"No, I don't think so," said Slade. "Far too risky. Suppose we hadn't turned up when we did. That was luck, remember. Our going into that room was not part of the preconceived plan. We *happened* on Bill lying on the floor by the open safe. There's no other way of looking at that. There was no purpose to serve in arranging a complicated set-up like that unless they were sure Bill would be found. Besides, it would have been safer if he had got away with the necklace. But would Reisenberg have trusted him? Not Maxie—oh, no! Again, Bill's accusing Reisenberg of beating him over the head and stealing the necklace was spontaneous. It wasn't thought out. No, Clinton, I don't think we need puzzle about that possibility for long."

"Put that way, I agree," said Clinton. "But as some one's in this thing up to the neck there must be some real clue. What about 'phone calls? There was that one from Paris, wasn't there?"

"That doesn't help us. That was Lady Malverne's half-brother, having another row about her selling the diamonds. He couldn't do much from Paris."

"Unless he spoke to some one else," said Frenton.

"He didn't." Slade killed the idea with cruel sharpness. "He spoke to Brooks, who brought his mistress, and she hung up when the brotherly advice was finished. We can't suspect her. She is rich, has plenty of jewels. That wouldn't make sense. On the other hand, there is Swensen. He may be genuinely in love with her. My own feeling, from what I've seen, is that he is, and doesn't care a broken button for her money. But there is the possibility that he might have come with designs on snatching a fortune."

"But you say Butterick was watching him when the diamonds were taken." Frenton gave proof that he was following what Slade said. "That doesn't square."

"Butterick's hazy about the actual time. They were all on the move, you know. It was after dinner, and they hadn't properly settled down. I'll be candid. At the moment Reisenberg's standing out away in front of the others as suspect number one. Second, I can't help placing Swensen. There's Furniss and the Clammer woman, but they are members of the family. Anyway, I can't see the Captain knocking anyone out without having some one standing by to take the weapon when he'd done the job. He's that sort, pretty futile. Mrs.

Clammer I suspect, is a good deal more shrewd than people probably give her credit for being. But she couldn't tackle a strong young animal like Bill Pegwell, nerved up for a ticklish job."

Slade paused, and relit his pipe.

"Where do you proceed from there?" asked Frenton. The local man's interest was captured. Slade smiled as he added, "Working it out this way, it gets sort of fascinating. You know, a bit different from taking down names and addresses and looking after dog-licences."

"There's a lot of routine work in this game, Frenton."

"So the mystery-story writers tell us. But you can't compare the two routines—the ordinary uniformed man's and the plain-clothes man's. Look at this case, for instance."

"Yes, you were asking where we proceed now. I think, Frenton, now you've agreed to hold things down locally, I'll try something with Mrs. Pegwell. She's the link between her husband and Reisenberg."

"Always supposing she was his accomplice on this job," put in Clinton.

Slade glanced knowingly at his sergeant, but Clinton did not flinch, although he knew what was in his chief's mind. Slade occasionally referred to Clinton as his mental brake.

The sergeant was a stickler for facts, and Slade knew that when a theory of his passed Clinton's factual scrutiny it was basically sound.

"True, Clinton; but the implications in this case would justify her being gathered into the fold of witnesses even if she hadn't been here. She is, what I said, a link. I'm hoping she'll prove the weakest in the chain. If she weakens and breaks there's hope."

"Of course, she might not have anything to tell you," said Frenton, without realizing just how damping his words really were.

"True enough. If she can tell us nothing we've got to start afresh. But if she can I think she'll lead us back to

Reisenberg. One thing I'm pretty certain of, the diamonds aren't here, unless they're hidden for a considerable time, to be gathered up later."

"You don't think she—Pegwell's wife's got them?"

Clinton offered the suggestion with the air of a man throwing an idle pebble into a pool.

"No. Pegwell would have taken them out of the house himself—yes, I'm pretty certain about that. But, anyway, I'll have a much stronger pull with Mrs. Pegwell when her husband's in a cell down here, Frenton. I may have to bring her down to see him. I should say she's the kind to drive a bargain, and she'll probably lie to cover up her husband's tracks."

"It'll be all right with me, whatever you arrange," said Frenton handsomely, all thought of the trip to Eastbourne gone from his mind.

"Fine," nodded Slade. "Well, I won't hold up things any longer here. And if I'm going to save you a lot of red-tape performance, Frenton, I'll have to get on to the Yard at once. Before I let the others depart I want a word with Mrs. Clammer, just to be sure she hasn't been pulling any wool over my eyes, and I think another word with Maxie is very obviously on the slate."

The three men returned thoughtfully to the house.

IX.

While the local men were taking finger-prints and photographing the dead man, and while Max Reisenberg superintended the packing of their things, Slade sought Mrs. Clammer. The Yard man had conceived an appreciative regard for the little woman's intellect from the few times he had spoken with her. He adjudged, furthermore, that she was one of those rare women, one who could keep a secret.

He found her on the veranda of the library, a roll of grey knitting on her lap, her needles clicking, her eyes, as grey as the ball of wool at her feet, watching him as he approached.

"You haven't come to tell me you've found the diamonds, Inspector," she greeted him.

"No, I haven't. Would you mind if I sit down, Mrs. Clammer? I'd like to ask you one or two things—general things."

"I see." The grey eyes still watched him. The needles kept up their steady work, fast but unhurried. "Yes, pull up another deck-chair." A pause as the chair was opened and Slade sat down. "Smoke if you want to. All men are the same. They can get to the point more quickly if they're smoking. That is, if they're the sort that don't run out of matches," she added archly.

Slade smiled. As he filled his pipe he wondered what sort of man Mr. Clammer had been. Interesting, or his wife would not have married him. At least, that's how he visualized the marriage.

"And you're not interested in knitting, of course," she went on, realizing that his mind was occupied with thought of herself.

"Well, I'm more interested in the Malverne diamonds, Mrs. Clammer, that strange necklace known as the Tears of Death."

"You think I can help you?"

"In what way do you mean help, Mrs. Clammer?"

She put down her knitting. "Inspector," she said, "we shall get along much faster if we don't fence. You know very well I meant help you to find the diamonds—that is, provided they have to be found."

"Now you are fencing, Mrs. Clammer. You think that perhaps I shan't be *expected* to find them?"

"Does what I think matter so much?"

"It matters, Mrs. Clammer, because you know the Malverne *menage* so much better than I do. And before I leave here I'd like to feel that I'd covered all the ground for survey."

"So you wish to waste your time on barren soil, Inspector?" There was an archness to the words that captured Slade's attention. She resumed her knitting. Deftly the stitches were knotted and run along one needle. "Or are you merely taking compassion on a lonely woman?"

Was there bitterness underlying that last, slightly impulsive question? Slade saw that she regretted having uttered it by the way she caught her under lip between her teeth.

"Mrs. Clammer," he said, "diamonds worth a hundred and fifty thousand pounds are a temptation to anyone in this house except Lady Malverne."

The grey eyes twinkled.

"Isn't your philosophy somewhat earth-bound, Inspector?"

"If you mean I must always keep my feet on the ground —then yes, it is."

"I didn't mean that, but your answer is apt. Well, Inspector, I'll make things easier for you by being very blunt."

"Thank you, Mrs. Clammer. I was hoping you would understand."

"Captain Furniss is an old fuss-pot. He foams at the

mouth and makes terrible noises in his bath. But he isn't a thief, and for all his tall tales about what he did and didn't do in India the sight of blood almost sends him into hysterics. A fuss-pot, did I say? He's an old woman—in a purely masculine sense, of course."

"You are delightfully explicit, Mrs. Clammer."

"I am nothing of the sort, Inspector. I am a scandal-monger, and that's what you were betting on when you came to sound me."

The grey eyes were twinkling again.

"Really, Mrs. Clammer—"

"Oh, don't bother to protest. It would spoil the effect—for me. But to get back to Furniss. He was one of Julius's poor cousins, and he's one of the many—there are quite a lot, believe it or not—who harbour the notion that Julius's end wasn't entirely accidental. You remember the story of his 'plane crash?"

"Yes, distinctly. The inquiry proved nothing."

"How could it, when everything was burned to a cinder? That's the one really troublesome bee in Jim Furniss's bonnet. Julius's crash. He was expecting something from Julius. He never had reason to expect it, but that's Jim Furniss. There's quite a bit of Micawber in him. When the will was read he got nothing, as he might have expected. That made the bee develop a sting. Lucie more or less took compassion on him, but compassion's wasted on Jim. That Indian sun, besides drying up what few wits he had, warped his body and his soul. Anyway, so much for him, Inspector. He hasn't got the diamonds."

She paused.

"Nor have I," she added, keeping her eyes lowered. "Heaven knows I could do with a hundred and fifty thousand pounds, nobody more so! A husband who thought he was a Monte Carlo bank-breaker left me just beyond the hightide mark. The only bank my lovable idiot of an Arthur broke was mine. Actually, I'm no real relation to Lucie Malverne. Her father married twice, as you know, Inspector. She has a half-brother, Barry. I am

Barry's mother's eldest sister, though I'm not taking the blame for that. However we must keep to the diamonds. As I told you I haven't got them, but I'll continue to be frank with you; had I had a chance to put my hands on them and no one been any the wiser I'm not sure I shouldn't have taken it. Lucie's disgustingly rich. She's a sweet child, but when I think of all the loot her husband rooked from his fellow-countrymen it makes me feel positively socialistic. Not that I should be a socialist long if I had a hundred and fifty thousand pounds. Don't get a wrong idea of my political stability, Inspector. I'm like most other people."

For a space the only sound was the clicking of her needles.

"How do brother and sister hit it off, Mrs. Clammer?"

"Half-brother and half-sister," she amended. "It makes a big difference. Barry has a grudge against Lucie. He thought that when she married Julius she ought to have seen that something was done for him. Instead, Lucie dried up emotionally. The marriage was a mistake of course—at least, until Julius's 'plane fell down in flames." Her gaze met Slack's squarely, and did not flinch. "Lucie wouldn't ask any favours of him, least of all for her own relatives—or near-relatives, as I know. And now Barry has a bee in *his* bonnet."

Slade waited. If Mrs. Clammer expected him to put a question she was disappointed.

"He dislikes Kurt Swensen, intensely. There's been a quarrel about that good-looking Swede already. Or should I call him an American? He's naturalized, I understand. Anyway, I suppose an American by any other name will recognize himself."

"And what is the reason for Lady Malverne's half-brother's dislike of Mr. Swensen?"

"Baldly—Barry's jealous. He gets that from his mother. She was a cat who, unfortunately for a lot of people, purred like a kitten. And I was her sister. Barry's jealous of Lucie."

"But he's her half-brother," Slade pointed out. "The same blood—"

"Oh, I don't mean in that way. It's her wealth he's jealous of. He was peeved about it before Julius's accident; now he's crazy. Perhaps crazy isn't the right word, after all. Certainly, though, he is intensely jealous of Lucie's wealth, and he hates and loathes her determination to sell Julius's jewel collections."

"There is a reason for that, you think?"

"There is, although what I think may not be the right reason."

"It will be interesting, I am sure of that."

"Perhaps. My feeling is that Barry's jealousy is based upon his dislike—amounting almost to hatred—of Swensen. He's got the impression that Swensen, by sweeping Lucie off her feet, has cheated him out of participation in what Julius left. Though why the young fool should imagine he had any right to participate is more than I can say. Except that my sister Jane was his mother."

Slade pondered this. Mrs. Clammer's forthright words had cleared in his mind the somewhat hazy picture he had received of the Malverne family as it was now constituted.

"When was Lady Malverne's half-brother last in this country, Mrs. Clammer?"

"Last week. He went back to Paris on Tuesday, I think it was."

"He lives in Paris quite a lot."

"Practically all the time when he's in funds, though if you knew much about him you'd find that statement somewhat contradictory. He lives there because he says it fosters his creative instinct, though what he means by that I'm not sure."

"Is he an artist or a writer?"

"He's nothing but a lazy good-for-nothing. He's got a brain, which was a gift from his father, who was killed at the explosion that occurred at his mine in Mexico, but

Barry'll never use it. There's too much of his mother in him. You may think I'm hard and scathing regarding my own sister. Perhaps I am. I have more than reason to be."

Slade saw the woman's face square rigidly. The fine lines at the side of her nose disappeared as the skin of her face stretched taut, mask-like.

"Was the quarrel between your nephew and Lady Malverne serious?"

"She showed him out of the Town flat."

"As bad as that?"

"Worse. She told Kurt Swensen to throw him out, which he did. Barry's nursing a pride that must be stinging like the devil."

"Then isn't it surprising that he rang up his half-sister yesterday?"

"Surprising, yes. But Barry is always surprising. That's what makes him Barry."

"Do you think he rang up solely to ask her not to sell the necklace?"

This time Slade received no immediate reply to his question. The woman looked up inquiringly.

"Just where are you leading me, Inspector?" she demanded. "Up which garden path? Are you trying to get me to draw a question-mark after Barry's name?"

"I was wondering, that is all."

"Won't do you any good. Barry rang up all right, and he gave his sister a terrific shouting on the 'phone. Must have made the Channel cable blister. But every word was utterly in character. Anyway, how could Barry, in Paris when that call came through, be here to lift that necklace? I know that's what you're turning over in the back of your mind, Inspector. But even you can't take a man from a Paris address and put him in the middle of Sussex in just over half an hour."

She was right, of course, and Slade put the fantastic idea that had crossed his mind outside his consideration.

"Perfectly true, I can't. You have his Paris address, of course."

"Naturally. 34 *bis* Rue de Savarin."

Slade rose.

"Thank you, Mrs. Clammer, you've been most helpful."

Again that arched expression changed the look in her eyes.

"I haven't been anything of the sort, Inspector. I've told you a lot of tittle-tattle, and I've given you the impression that I'm a sour old grouch who had no reason to love her sister Jane. But"—the grey eyes smiled—"I'm thankful that you wasted your time. It isn't every one who'll give me long of their company."

There were tears, bright as early morning dew, in the grey eyes. Slade turned away before they fell, aware that Mrs. Clammer had a problem of her own to solve, perhaps, of its kind, more difficult than his.

He rang up the exchange, and got them to check the call that had come from Paris on the previous evening. The records showed that the Paris call was entered as incoming from the Paris number Abelard 7810. He noted the number and hung up. As he passed into the lounge he ran into Max Reisenberg.

"Excuse me Mr. Reisenberg, I wanted to see you before you left."

"Yes, Inspector, what is it?"

"You'll be at your office to-morrow?"

"Yes."

"Good. I rather think I shall drop in to see you. What times does Mrs. Pegwell go to lunch?"

"Between one o'clock and two."

"All right, then. Expect me about five past two."

The Jew's eyes glinted like specks of polished obsidian as he moved away.

X.

Lucie Malverne looked up from polishing her finger nails at sound of a tap on her door. She rose as Kurt Swensen entered.

"What is it, Kurt?"

She could see the brooding trouble in his face.

He shrugged his wide shoulders and spread his arms in a Continental gesture he sometimes adopted. But the cloud did not lift from his face.

"They have gone, all except the two men from Scotland Yard, Lucie."

"Well, I'm glad of that, anyway. This has been a weekend of surprises. I lose a diamond necklace, and find a corpse in my lake." She did not shudder this time at mention of her discovery. It was as though she had steeled herself inside, hardened her emotions; her words rang with a metallic sound, causing the man to lift his glance. "What about that little man Butterick, has he gone, Kurt?"

"Yes, moaning about his lost job. He said he would get in touch with you to-morrow, and then the company's solicitor will write you. Furniss has gone too. Didn't take much to send him packing."

"Judith?"

"No, I think the Old Guard remains, and of course myself—"

"Kurt, what is wrong?"

"Wrong, what should be wrong, my dear?"

"That's what I want to know. Nothing, of course, should be wrong, but it's obvious something is. You're changed. You're . . . brooding."

He dug a cigarette-case from his pocket and lit one.

"Possibly."

"About what?"

They were both aware that the other was rigid, mentally alert, like fencers about to exchange the first parry and thrust.

"A necklace of diamonds."

"Kurt!"

The cry was wrung from her.

"Oh, it's no use, Lucie, don't you see my position now? I've been thinking about it all morning, all last night too. What will people say now? Furniss will chatter. I'm a fortune-hunter, and you've held me off, so I improved the shining hour by lifting the equivalent of three-quarters of a million dollars from you."

"Kurt, you mustn't! Stop!"

"No." He shook loose from her groping hands, stood apart, smoking quickly. "Now is the time to do anything but stop. There've been enough of these ugly rumours, Lucie. Your husband's 'plane crash'—"

"Jim Furniss's silly ideas."

"And a lot of other people's, don't forget that."

"But what do I care what they think?"

"You will, my dear, after what happened yesterday. It's impossible to expect the idle tongues to stop from wagging until—"

"Until what, Kurt?"

"Until those diamonds are restored to you."

"Very well, we'll wait."

"How long?"

"Does that matter?"

"Every minute of it matters, darling. Don't you see, it's one of Fate's brutal contrivings? Together, with this net of suspicion around us, how long do you think our love could last?"

She smiled bravely.

"Are you doubting me?"

"No, nor myself. Individually we know our love is strong, strong to withstand any test of time. But together it is another matter, Lucie. One cannot live the days and weeks and months without rubbing shoulders with the crowd. I know what I am talking about. My parents, when they left Sweden, were very poor. I've seen both sides of life."

"So have I, Kurt."

She said it very softly, and his expression changed. He took her hands.

"I know. That very experience in common helps to make us . . . us, Lucie. But we don't want to spoil it, we don't— we shouldn't—want to run the risk of spoiling it."

Apprehension darkened her eyes.

"Tell me, Kurt, what do you mean? What is on your mind?"

"You've held back hitherto, Lucie, because of Barry. You wouldn't marry me because of his threats. You wanted to wait. Well, it suited me, because I had no wish to be taken deliberately as a fortune-hunter. Not that that would trouble me. What other people think never worries me at all; and all men at heart are fortune-hunters. It depends what one considers one's fortune. You without a cent would have been my fortune, Lucie—"

"I love you, Kurt."

"But although," he went on quickly, "I didn't care a damn what people thought about me, I did trouble about what was said concerning you. You can see, then, Lucie, we both held off, thinking of the other. I'm being very truthful, because now we must face the truth."

"But, Kurt, I'm ready to marry you now, this minute."

"Of course, because you see further danger for me."

"Don't, Kurt!"

"I must, darling. The police are suspicious of me. Every one will think as they do. I *could have* done it. Then there is the mystery of the car and the body in it. I didn't help things with my idea of how the car got into the lake. That Inspector Slade is no fool, but he won't overlook what to him must have seemed my 'glibness.'"

"Kurt, you mustn't think like this."

"I must, for both our sakes, Lucie. Probably the only

person in this house, apart from yourself, who doesn't think I did it is Judith Clammer, but she wouldn't say so, you know that. But I didn't. I know nothing about the robbery or the murder—"

"Of course you don't. That's obvious to the police. No weapon has been found."

"They will argue that I could have concealed it. As they will argue I could have concealed the diamonds. You see? No, darling, I can't remain and let the eyes of the world be focused on you because I am standing with you, suspected."

"Kurt, this is nonsense, I won't allow it. If you're thinking of leaving—"

"I have gone a stage beyond thinking, Lucie darling. I have packed."

"You have . . . packed!"

The news bewildered her, like a glancing blow that had numbed her nerve centres.

"Yes, and I am leaving Steyning Towers to-day. I shall stop in London. I'm not turning tail altogether. If the police want me they can get me." His tone was grim, the hard light had returned to his eyes. "But, for the last time, Lucie, I love you too much to remain. You must see my argument. It's the only one possible, in the circumstances. We've been together, in each other's company, a long while now, some months—more than long enough to antagonize your half-brother and to set Furniss against me—"

"They don't count."

"They do—very much."

"Of course, if you prefer . . ."

She stopped as he smiled.

"Don't go into a pouting act for my benefit, Lucie, it's not in your line. You know what I prefer, and I know what you prefer, but because we're living in this twentieth-century civilization we can't enjoy our preferences. We've got to remember there is such a thing as public opinion, which is always the opinion of a very

few shouted loud enough for every one to hear. I don't
wish to be rude about your family, darling, but Barry and
Furniss are excellent shouters of the kind I'm talking
about."

She sat down, limp, realizing that he was adopting
the only possible way out. But whither did their diverging
paths lead? She shuddered as she tried to glimpse the
darkness ahead of them.

"I'm afraid, Kurt."

He put his arms round her shoulders, lifted her face,
and gently kissed her red lips.

"My little Lucie mustn't be afraid," he whispered.
"Time, they say in story-books, is a great healer. Well, we
won't give it anything to heal. We'll pay no fat fees to Dr.
Time, because we don't like his bedside manner, eh? We'll
keep our love and our hearts whole, my darling, and
when"—he straightened, and his voice changed—"those
diamonds have been recovered and the newspapers have
finished plastering the story across the country—then,
oh, my sweet—"

She stayed further words with her eager lips.

At last, "You think I should stay here, Kurt?"

"You will be out of the centre of the storm," he said.
"This business is not going to be a nine days' wonder.
Murder and a big jewel robbery, a car in a lake, found by
the mistress of Steyning Towers when swimming with
the blonde Olympic whirlwind, as they have been kind
enough to dub me, and the fact that Lady Malverne
would transact the business in Sussex, and not in
London—all that, my dear, will tie up very neatly with
the not-yet-dead rumours of your husband's death. You
see? It won't be pretty, will it? You won't want it dinning
in your ears, morning, noon, and night? You don't wish to
be driven frantic, to hate the sight of me, the thought that
I—"

His voice had been rising; now it trembled.

"Kurt!"

She had twisted round, sprung up, and flung her arms

round him. His breath was hot against her neck, and as she stroked his fair hair she thought how silky it was.

"I'm sorry, Lucie. I guess it's wearing me down. You see, I've thought and thought about it until my brain aches, and my ideas tread upon each other. I can't—"

"Then don't try, Kurt, my dear."

Her voice soothed as the gentle touch of her fingers soothed.

"I don't want to make things more difficult for you, my darling," she murmured, "but sometimes I wonder if you know—if you even *could* know—how very much I love you. You've given hope of a real life, my darling, you've brought colour and brightness into a life that was drab and oh, so very dull. You've—"

There she paused as a heavy hand struck the door.

Her body grew taut, as though she held her breath and dare not release it. The man held by her arms stirred. She wanted to cry to the knocking one to go away, that this moment of self-revelation was hers and she would not be denied, but when again the heavy hand fell she knew the moment had passed, was dead.

Slade stood in the doorway when she opened the door.

"Well, Inspector?"

Her eyes were hostile.

"I believe Mr. Swensen is with you, Lady Malverne. I am very sorry, but I must ask him to come with me at once. There has been an important development."

Her fury died, and new-risen fear gripped her with cold fingers. At its touch she flinched, a woman afraid, desperately afraid of something she could not understand, but of something expressed in the detective's eyes.

Swensen was beside her, talking in a low voice.

"You wanted me, Inspector. Well, what is it?"

"Please come with me, Mr. Swensen."

Slade turned and the woman said quickly, catching her breath, "I'll come too, Inspector."

"I'd rather you didn't, Lady Malverne," said Slade, but

he looked meaningly at the Swede, who nodded.

Slade walked to the end of the corridor, and presently was joined by Swensen, who came alone.

"You said an important development, Inspector?"

"I did, Mr. Swensen."

They walked to the South Tower, and Slade led Swensen up stairs that were dark and eerie, even with the sunlight glinting through the old-time arrow-slits. Swensen trod with hardly any sound, and his step was springy.

Slade paused where the stairs turned. Sergeant Clinton was bent over something lying on a stone platform.

"Good God!" muttered the Swede, "not—not *another!*"

"Another murder—yes," nodded Slade.

Clinton stood back, and a bright beam leaped from the torch in his hand, to focus on the battered head of one of the maids.

Swensen winced.

"This is—horrible!" His voice sounded parched, about to crack.

"And do you recognize this, Mr. Swensen?"

Slade was stooping, pointing to an object lying alongside the body. Swensen saw that it was an Indian club. Slade picked it up carefully, holding it in his handkerchief.

"Do you?" he repeated.

Then Swensen's voice broke.

"It's mine!"

He was staring with wide eyes at the blood and hair adhering to the heavy teakwood bulb of the club.

XI.

Do you mind if I have a drink, Inspector? I feel I need one."

Slade nodded.

"All right. Let's go into the lounge. Clinton," he said, turning to his assistant, "you know what to do. Let me know when you're finished."

The Yard inspector and the Swede went down to the lounge, and Brooks, his normally impassive face enlivened with an excitement he could not subdue, brought whisky, glasses, and a siphon.

"I'll help myself," said Swensen.

He poured himself a liberal glass of whisky, drank it quickly, and mopped his mouth with his handkerchief. He lit a cigarette, and Slade waited for him to speak. He spoke when he had calmed himself sufficiently to take long, steady pulls at the cigarette.

"Well, Inspector, what do you want me to say?"

Slade had filled his pipe and lit it. From the direction of his gaze just then he was apparently absorbed in the tiny check design of the other's flannel trousers.

"I think you had better tell me something I can accept—on the evidence."

There was no mistaking the Yard man's meaning. The other flushed.

"Do you mean to say you think I—"

He gulped.

"I mean to say very little, Mr. Swensen. I'm going to ask the questions."

"All right." The cigarette end glowed very redly. "I didn't do it."

"You know nothing about it?"

"Not a thing."

"Good, now we can start."

Swensen's eyes widened.

"Start? What on earth—"

"That is your club, Mr. Swensen?"

"Yes, certainly. I've told you it is. As a matter of fact, I have three pairs with me. Indian club exercises keep me in perfect trim for athletics. Swinging them expands the chest, and allows the lungs—"

"I have no doubt you're right, Mr. Swensen. But just at the moment one thing only interests me, your ownership of that club."

"I can see that. But obviously some one got into my room and took it. The fingerprints on the haft will prove the real culprit."

"That's what I'm afraid of."

"What are you getting at?"

"The only fingerprints on the haft, Mr. Swensen, are yours, and they're very plain, absolutely unmistakable."

The muscles in the Swede's high forehead contracted, a pulse began beating visibly in his throat.

"How did you come to have my fingerprints, Inspector?"

"They're on my cigarette-case. Remember I gave you a couple of cigarettes earlier this morning?"

Swensen nodded.

"That's right. I forgot." He pushed a hand over his face, his lips munched in his effort to maintain a firm control. "Have you searched my room?"

"Not yet, we haven't the key."

"True, I have the key in my pocket." He produced it. "But I never lock the door." He met Slade's mildly inquiring gaze. "I've never had occasion to lock it."

"No?"

"What do you mean—no?"

"It's locked now."

"Locked? But I don't understand. I didn't lock it, I've never locked it. There must be some mistake."

"That we can soon prove. Let's go up there."

They went to Swensen's room, and the Swede

stretched forth his hand to open the door, but, as Slade had said, it was locked.

"Strange," muttered Swensen, placing the key in the lock and opening the door.

"I thought it was merely a precaution," said Slade. Swensen swung round and faced him, his fists knotted. The Yard man's face was calm, his gaze steady. He puffed his pipe and little blue streams of smoke issued from the corners of his mouth.

"Yes, Mr. Swensen?" he inquired.

The Swede's hands unfolded, the anger passed from his face, and he grinned wryly.

"Nothing. I guess you've got me on the end of a pin, and I can't exactly blame you if you make me wriggle."

Slade nodded slowly.

"I'm sorry. I only hope for your sake you wriggle cleverly, Mr. Swensen. Things look pretty conclusive."

Again that baffled, defeated look swept the Swede's face, but it did not linger. He grinned at Slade, chin up, and the detective admired him for his pluck. He might be a callous, scheming murderer, he might not. But he had most definitely qualities as a man that Slade could appreciate. There was nothing of the rodent about Kurt Swensen.

"Well, jab the pin, Inspector. I'm ready to wriggle, and —I'm in condition."

It was a mild flinging back of the gauge Slade had cast down.

"Very well," said the Yard man, "did you use your clubs this morning?"

"Yes, for about a quarter of an hour, before I went down to the lake."

"And they were all there, wherever you keep them?"

"Yes. They fit a small rack on one side of a travelling-trunk. I should have noticed had one been missing. I couldn't help noticing, as a matter of fact."

"I see. You just took out a pair, swung them, and put them back?"

"That's right."

"Lock the trunk?"

"No, no reason to."

"And you say you didn't lock this door?"

"No, for the same reason—or, rather, lack of one."

"And when did you last leave this room?"

"Shortly after breakfast. I came up for some cigarettes, sat down by the window, thinking about things, you know, and then went downstairs. I've hung about all morning until the others had gone, then I went to see Lady Malverne. You found me with her. That's all I've got to say."

"May I see the trunk with the other clubs?"

"Certainly, go ahead. That's the trunk. One over in the far corner."

Slade pulled the trunk down, opened it, and swung aside a portable shelf of clothes. Fitted against the side of the trunk, as the other had explained, was a rack with steel clips holding five Indian clubs. One place in the rack was empty. Slade was about to shut the trunk when he changed his mind. Taking out his handkerchief, he pulled a club from its clips, scrutinized it, and returned it to the rack. This operation was watched steadily by Swensen.

The third club Slade took from the rack drew a sharp exclamation from him.

"What's the matter now?" demanded Swensen, coming forward.

Slade stepped to the window, held up the club, and the other glanced at it over the detective's shoulder. Swensen took a deep breath.

"Good God!" he cried. "Am I going crazy? Not—not a second one!"

There was nothing Slade could say. The evidence of this other club he had extracted from the Swede's trunk spoke for itself. Like the club that had been used to kill the maid, this other club had blood and hair smeared on its bulb. But the blood was dried and the hair was darkish brown, whereas the hair on the other club was fair, like that of the murdered maid.

"What—what does it all add up to, Inspector? This is way beyond me."

Slade stared hard at him.

"This club, Mr. Swensen"—he tapped the club with the dried bloodstains—"was the weapon used to fell Bill Pegwell."

"But you must be mistaken, Inspector! I—I can't see that—"

Swensen faltered. Slade's gaze was accusatory, unyielding.

"I am not mistaken, Mr. Swensen. What have you to say regarding this?" He pointed again to the club. "Of course I must warn you against making any statement that will incriminate yourself."

Swensen licked his lips.

"But, Inspector, I swear I know nothing about this club, how those bloodstains got on it, or—or about knocking out this man Pegwell. Why, if I did, then the diamonds—"

He paused again.

"Exactly, Mr. Swensen. If you did know anything about it—if you were the person who used this club to fell Pegwell, then you would have that necklace . . . somewhere. You see where this leads us, Mr. Swensen?"

"But, Inspector, appearances are entirely against me. I know nothing, absolutely nothing."

"You will have a chance of repeating that later—"

"Then you're going to arrest me?"

"I'm afraid I have no alternative, especially if your fingerprints are on the haft of this second club. In that case I could not run the risk of not arresting you, Mr. Swensen."

Slade saw the other's face pucker with concentrated thought, and he guessed what was passing through the Swede's mind.

"I should not advise you, Mr. Swensen, to attack me and forcibly handle this club, so that your fingerprints will be found on it."

The other's mouth twitched.

"Damn you, Inspector, you think too fast!" He grinned sheepishly. "All right, the cards are stacked against me. But let me say one thing."

"Very well."

"Would you say—you're investigating this case, you know—that the person who knocked out Pegwell and stole the necklace is the same person who killed the girl—and the unknown man in the car?"

"I should say so, yes," returned Slade.

"Good." Swensen eased a finger round his collar. "I didn't shoot the man in the car, and I have never had a gun since I landed in this country."

"Maybe you will remember how easily you decided how the car came to be in the lake, Mr. Swensen."

The Swede's face flushed.

"Confound you, I told Lady Malverne that would be dragged up."

"Then you had anticipated . . . trouble?"

Slade's tone was suave. In time the other caught himself and stayed a flow of hot, passionate words. He lit a fresh cigarette and waited for his anger to cool. Anger, he could see, would get him nowhere with Slade.

"Trouble, of course I'd anticipated it! This whole business is a frame-up. That's as obvious as a rick in a cornfield. Some one is very anxious to see me in a jam."

"That is your explanation?"

"Isn't it explicit?"

"Perhaps."

"And to stick this thing on me won't you have to dig up some sort of motive?"

"Naturally. But wouldn't you consider a hundred and fifty thousand in jewels sufficient motive for three murders? It's a full fifty thousand a-piece."

Slade had not chosen the words with the special purpose of lashing the other to wild fury. He had not spoken in a mocking tone, but had kept his voice controlled and even. However, Swensen's reaction was violent. He swung back a fist and rushed at Slade.

"Damn you, you can't make—"

Slade dodged the fist driving at his face, and neatly turned on the ball of his foot, to bring his own left fist round in a crashing blow against the side of the other's head. Swensen sprawled his length.

He was not knocked out, but the blow had been dealt with sufficient force to make his head spin. He climbed dizzily to his feet.

"God, you pack a bruising left," he grunted. "But thanks all the same. I might have made a fool of myself if you hadn't done that. I mean"—his gaze measured Slade—"a worse fool than I have."

"I think we'd better go downstairs, Mr. Swensen. After you, please."

Slade's manner intimated that he, for one, had forgotten that occasion had ever demanded his knocking the other down. Swensen shrugged, turned about, and went through the door. Slade followed him downstairs to where Clinton was waiting. When the sergeant saw the second club his eyes lit.

"Shall I get through to the Yard?" he asked.

"Yes, and have this club tested for fingerprints. Frenton's man hasn't gone yet, I take it?"

"No, he's still here."

Half an hour later Lady Malverne returned to her room, weeping, Mrs. Clammer trying her best to console her. The result of the testing of the second Indian club for fingerprints and of Slade's talk to the Assistant Commissioner in charge of the C.I.D. had been the arrest of Kurt Swensen for the murder of one Maud Fading, maid at Steyning Towers.

Lucie Malverne was beside herself.

"Judith," she told Mrs. Clammer, "they shan't do this to me and not expect me to hit back."

"But, my dear, Inspector Slade had no alternative. The facts—"

"Facts!" cried the woman in love. "Facts are only things as we see them. They may be wrong—we may be wrong, short-sighted. The facts may not be facts. Do you mean to tell me, Judith, you think Kurt murdered Maud?"

"No, I don't. I like him, but—"

"There you are—but. Why must there be a but? Tell me that. Because the police have to arrest some one. Well, I won't bring any charge against that Bill Pegwell, and then they won't be able to hold him. He, at least, has not murdered anyone. They can only hold him if I wish to prosecute—"

"I don't know about that, Lucie, but don't be foolish, my dear. It won't help you. Perhaps this arrest of Kurt is a good thing in a way you don't see it. You said just now facts are only things as we see them. Perhaps we don't see this with the—the right focus."

The other woman stared at her.

"Judith, that is nonsense, and you know it. How can Kurt's arrest be for the best? In heaven's name how?"

"Well"—Judith Clammer's grey eyes lifted to the other's face—"he says he isn't guilty—"

"Of course he isn't!"

"And that therefore some one has framed him. I think he means some one has done their best to make it appear that he is guilty."

"That is obvious. Using his Indian clubs, locking the door. . . ."

Lucie Malverne sank into a chair, tired, staring with haggard eyes into the future, forgetting what lay around her.

"Very well, Lucie, my dear, if some one was so anxious to get rid of him that they went to all these lengths to have him arrested—he is better arrested."

The two women faced each other.

"What do you mean, Judith, what are you hinting at?" the younger whispered, tense, hands crushed to her throat.

"If Kurt hadn't been arrested, perhaps he would have been placed beyond such a possibility."

Lucie Malverne's face drained white.

"Murdered!"

The word was like a sigh through the room.

"Yes, murdered," declared Judith Clammer.

"But why, why?"

"You know why, Lucie. You know who hates him, who would have him out of the way, would prevent him from marrying you and taking your wealth."

The fingers lying on the white throat pressed until red marks appeared under their tips.

"No, Judith, that cannot be true."

She was contradicted, and the contradiction was offered in level, even tones, suggestive of a brain that thought clearly and saw things distinctly.

"It *could* be true, Lucie. It could be so true that, if you are honest with yourself, you will admit that was one reason why you have not already married Kurt Swensen. You were afraid of a storm ... a violent storm."

Lady Malverne's fair body sagged.

"Judith, it's not possible. No, you are wrong. You must be. Some one else is responsible. That person responsible was here, at Steyning Towers this morning, and now . . ." She shuddered, and her hands fell limply into her lap. "No, Judith, I tell you it is impossible," she said huskily.

But Judith Clammer was as undeviating as Fate, as remorseless.

"That's what you said when I told you Kurt had been arrested. 'Impossible!' you cried and rushed downstairs like a madwoman. But it wasn't impossible, Lucie. He was arrested. And you won't be able to help him by losing your nerve and going off at half-cock. You've got to pull yourself together, dear. If you love him at all, you've got to do that for him. You've got to show your face to the world and make the world see that you believe in him."

The grey eyes were misty, but very wise and tender.

"But, Judith, I do love him, I do believe in him. I'll

never think him capable of such a terrible thing. I couldn't bear to think that all the while he was in here, telling me that he loved me and that he hadn't taken the diamonds, he knew Maud lay on those dark stairs, her head crushed."

Judith Clammer nodded.

"That will make it easier for you. You will not have to pretend."

"Pretend! That's what I've done ever since I married Julius. My life has been one long pretence, Judith, and now, when I can really live, take happiness in both hands—this is what I get." She rose, colour returning to her cheeks. "I'm going to London, Judith. I'm going to be near him, if necessary to fight for him with every penny I have."

"Well, if those are the resources he can count on he ought to feel easy. You've got enough pennies to sink a liner."

But already Lucie Malverne's thoughts had turned half-circle again.

"You really think, Judith, Kurt is safer now he is under arrest?"

"I think now he is arrested you might hear of Barry coming back from Paris," said Judith Clammer with brutal directness.

XII.

The following morning the world's Press announced in large, bold headlines the arrest of Kurt Swensen, the successful Swedish-American Olympic champion, for the murder of a Sussex girl at Steyning Towers. In England the arrest created a furore of excitement. Editorials pondered how the arrest of Swensen for this particular crime would aid in the recovery of the missing Malverne diamonds. The Tears of Death, the more sensational writers noted, had once more justified their grim title.

But where were they?

Excitement reached fever-heat when the later afternoon editions carried news of a startling development. The body of the dead man found in the submerged car in the park of Steyning Towers had been identified as that of Butterick, the insurance company's staff detective!

Then who was the short, sandy-haired man who had posed as the real Butterick?

Find him, cried the now confident "crime correspondents" in the evening editions, and you will soon have the Malverne diamonds.

However, the public was not told all that transpired on that memorable Monday. It was not told the result of a debate at the Yard between departmental chiefs. It was not told of the sending of Kurt Swensen's dossier by the Baltimore, Maryland, police by cable. Swensen had once been arrested for nearly killing a nigger by hitting him on the head with a heavy block of wood. He had protested that the negro had been drunk and had attacked him first, and he had acted in self-defence; he had been acquitted by a court who held little sympathy for the black man's alcoholic exuberance.

Nor was the public told anything of the direct new

lead Slade obtained when he visited Reisenberg's office in Hatton Garden and interviewed Tessa Pegwell.

The public was told that the girl Maud's fingernails had been found to be stained with tiny particles of human blood and that, under their fashionable points, small fragments of torn human skin were discovered. A Home Office expert left no doubt as to what these discoveries meant. The girl had fought her assailant and lashed out with her hands, and her nails had scratched.

The public was also told that no scratch marks were found on Kurt Swensen's body.

But it was not told that when Slade walked into Max Reisenberg's office he was surprised to see a strip of plaster adorning the Jew's left hand.

Without making his interest too apparent, for the news of the Home Office expert's findings had not by then been circulated, Slade mentioned that the plaster had not been on Reisenberg's hand when the Jew had left Steyning Towers.

"No, it was a damned bush at the side of the road, Inspector. My wife's hat blew off, and I had to go and get it. Those thorns were sharp, as I've reason to know."

"I expect they were," agreed Slade, thinking that bruises on Maud Farling's throat had proved that her assailant had caught her by the left hand, while he swung the club with his right.

He got down to the business that had brought him to Hatton Garden.

"Did you mention anything about this deal in diamonds, Mr. Reisenberg, to Mrs. Pegwell? You understand, of course, what I am trying to arrive at. Whether she received any information from you that would have aided her husband."

"I understand perfectly, Inspector. No, you can be sure, perfectly sure, that she got nothing from me. I gave that girl a job because I pitied her, married to a crook. I said to myself it wasn't her fault, I'll give her a chance. Now see what I get for it. Trouble, loads of trouble. And but one compensation."

"And that is?"

"I can kick her out." The Jew smiled crookedly. "I have already told her that she goes at the end of the week."

Slade sat back. He knew Reisenberg's type, and wondered what sort of proposition he had put up to the girl, and if she had slapped his face. Perhaps her finger nails were responsible for the strip of plaster on the Jew's left hand.

"She is here now?"

"Yes, in that office."

Reisenberg pointed to a door behind his chair.

Slade rose. "I'd like to have a word with her."

"I'll ring for her to come in," said Reisenberg, stretching forth a hand to press a table button.

"Don't bother," said Slade. "I want to see her in private, and, anyway, I'm afraid your presence would spoil my chance of learning what I've come for."

The Yard man received a baleful look from the other.

"Cigar, Inspector?"

Apparently, from Reisenberg's manner, he and the Yard man had not finished their own interview.

"No, thanks, Mr. Reisenberg."

"Well, as you will." A fat hand waved airily as the lid of the cigar-box dropped. "But, Inspector, you're not going to believe all that girl tells you?"

"That depends what she tells me."

"Of course. But you must remember she will be vindictive about me. I've given her the sack, you know."

"As long as she tells me and not Mrs. Reisenberg, I don't think you need worry, Mr. Reisenberg."

The Jew coloured. He coughed to cover a momentary, but very real, confusion.

"Tessa—Mrs. Pegwell—is naturally inclined to resent my asking questions about her husband's being at Steyning Towers. I'm concerned now with only what she might tell you out of spite. Do you understand me,

Inspector?"

Slade felt like saying he understood precisely how much of a worm Max Reisenberg was; but his reply was, "I think I do, Mr. Reisenberg. And I think you should understand that I have come here solely to learn what I can about the whereabouts of that missing necklace."

Reisenberg patted his fat hands together.

"Good, then we understand each other perfectly, Inspector. A cigar now, perhaps? No. A pity, they are good cigars. But"—shrewdness crept into eyes and tone—"do you think she will be able to help you regarding the whereabouts of the diamonds?"

Slade smiled bleakly.

"I cannot say without seeing her first."

The reply was a snub, delivered directly. Reisenberg had enough sense not to continue his unfortunate fishing for news.

"Naturally," he said, rising from his chair, his manner as smooth as silk. "Now I will show you into her office, Inspector. This way."

He held open the door.

"Some one to see you, Tessa. Inspector Slade of Scotland Yard."

He said it with malice oozing from every pore. Slade felt like delivering a hearty kick in the seat of the man's well-stuffed trousers. Instead he jerked the door to after him with an abruptness that threatened to break the frosted-glass of the upper half.

He turned, to find regarding him a girl with wide eyes and fluffy brown hair. Her face was round and intelligent; she was neatly dressed in a brown woollen suit, and although make-up was carefully applied to her face, there was a well-scrubbed look about her. At first glance Tessa Pegwell created a favourable impression on Slade. She stood waiting for him to speak, a little frightened, but under perfect control, and in the raised line of her chin Slade discovered determination.

He knew that he would have to fight for what he

would win from her, and he would win something only if
he were fortunate.

"You are Tessa Pegwell?" he asked.

A slim shoulder rose and dropped again.

"Do you have to start at the very beginning?" she
inquired. "You've come to question me about my husband.
I've been waiting for you all morning. Well, before you
ask anything let me tell you something. I'll only speak if
you are willing to make a bargain with me. But what I'll
tell you, as my part of the bargain, will be plenty."

Slade might have smiled, and so enraged her. A slip of
a girl offering to barter with the law of the land. Actually
Slade rather admired her. She was driven back on her
last-line defence, fighting for her husband, and she
thoroughly intended not to be the loser in the bargain.

Annoyance pencilled little lines in her white forehead
as Slade did not answer.

"Well?" she repeated. "Are you going to take me . . .
seriously?'"

It seemed that second thoughts had given her some
doubt. Probably she realized the limitation of her
bargaining powers.

"Yes, of course I'll take what you have to say
seriously, Mrs. Pegwell," said the Yard man, "but you will
have to remember that your husband is in custody on a
charge of breaking into—"

"I know all that."

She was brusque. Her chin was lifted again in its
aggressive tilt.

"Yes, I believe you do. You drove with him to Steyning
Towers, didn't you, Mrs. Pegwell?"

She considered the question gravely.

"I don't think there's any need for me to answer that
question, Inspector Slade."

"Not here, Mrs. Pegwell. But it will be different when
you are in a court, on oath."

She did not flinch.

"I'm sorry, but you're not stampeding me. I've still got

my bargain to make. You want the necklace called the Tears of Death. Very well, I want Bill released. My bargain is the necklace for Bill—and no tricks."

With difficulty Slade kept surprise from his face. She knew where the diamonds were. It was even feasible that she had them in her possession, although he could not at the moment perceive how Bill Pegwell had managed the miracle. Or was she putting up a bluff, a wild, desperate bluff?

What he read in her eyes did not answer the question. He found himself surprised that such a girl should have married a man like Bill Pegwell. She was not the usual veneered drab of the lower classes who clung to men with a will to come by easy money. There was a subtle poise about her that, if not exactly suggesting breeding, did, most definitely, suggest personality.

"You have the necklace, Mrs. Pegwell?"

He did not expect her to admit possession, but he saw that the situation demanded direct tactics. Parrying and dissembling would get him nowhere with this young woman.

"I have not, but I know who has, if that interests you."

Just a tinge of mockery to the last words. An older woman would have omitted it—wisely. Mockery is born of emotional stimulus; and a woman whose emotions are in danger of being stimulated is placed at once at a distinct disadvantage. Still, she was doing very well, Slade allowed. She was sticking to her point.

"It interests me considerably. But I have no way of knowing if you're bluffing or not."

"Of course you haven't," she said, in clear tones, "and I think, Inspector, that gives me the advantage."

She was perceptive too, and clear thinking, and she had that mental courage born of far-sighted appreciation of just whither an argument would lead. Further, she was determined, by not allowing him to digress, to do the leading herself.

"A theoretical advantage, Mrs. Pegwell. Your husband

is arrested, and for all I know you may be an accessory—"
She interrupted.

"Our bargain doesn't call for advantage or disadvantage, theoretical or otherwise, Inspector Slade. I can lead you to the Malverne diamonds. In return for doing so I want my husband released, and any charge made against him dropped unconditionally."

Bright spots of colour flamed high in her cheeks. The emotional tide, Slade saw, had turned.

"Isn't this a little melodramatic, Mrs. Pegwell?" he asked, feeling melodramatic himself, but realizing that he had to humour her to some extent.

"If you had a husband arrested by the police, Inspector, perhaps you would call it melodramatic. I don't. And if he were released only to be arrested again I still shouldn't call it melodramatic. That is why I said—and repeat—unconditionally."

The term was ambiguous, and perhaps she did not realize that. But Slade was wise enough not to quibble. Her meaning was anything but ambiguous.

"I'll promise you, Mrs. Pegwell, that I'll see what can be done. A formal charge, naturally, is made by Lady Malverne. Only Lady Malverne can revoke the charge."

"That isn't good enough, Inspector. I want Bill released."

"If he isn't you won't tell what you know?"

"I certainly shan't. You can arrest me too. That won't alter my mind."

No more would be gained by staying and endeavouring to persuade her into another frame of mind.

"Very well, Mrs. Pegwell, I can't promise anything just now. Not even that you won't be arrested. But I'll call on you this evening, perhaps with news."

As he turned to go her reserve broke.

"Tell me, Inspector," she asked, slightly breathless; "Bill —he wasn't hurt bad, was he?"

There was a winsome look about the face that a few moments before had been set in lines of grim determination.

"No. It was a nasty crack, nothing more. Probably leave him with a sore head for a few days, but there's nothing to worry about."

"You're not—not—"

She hesitated. Tessa Pegwell the suppliant was vastly changed from Tessa Pegwell the bargainer.

"No, I'm telling you the truth, Mrs. Pegwell. You have no reason to be worried about your husband's health."

"Thank you."

Reisenberg, spoiling a good cigar, jumped to his patent-leather-shod feet as Slade came out of the girl's office.

"Was she . . . difficult?" he asked, shooting a sidelong glance at the Yard man.

"I haven't decided yet, Mr. Reisenberg. Good day."

Slade left a very thoughtful Max Reisenberg behind him as he passed through the doorway. He went back to the Yard and the conference that was in session, there to learn that Lady Malverne, annoyed at the arrest of Kurt Swensen on a murder charge, had come to London and through her solicitor very forcibly intimated that she would bring no charge against Bill Pegwell.

"She's going to be difficult, Slade," said the A.C. when the conference was concluded and the two were in the latter's office.

Slade was minded of Reisenberg's last question before he left the Jew's office in Hatton Garden.

"Shall we have to release Pegwell?"

"Not necessarily," said the A.C. "We can alter the charge, we can hold him on suspicion—but not for long. And where the shoe pinches is Swensen. He's under arrest. Well, we can't just go on merrily making charges and dropping them. Yet this fingernail evidence of the murdered girl leaves a loop-hole in the case against Swensen. He hasn't any scratches on his whole body, not recent ones."

"And Reisenberg has."

Slade explained the Jew's story of getting his wife's hat and scratching his hand on a thorn-bush.

"What do you make of it, Slade?"

"Frankly, I think the murders are connected directly with the stealing of the diamonds. They were different threads in the pattern of the same plot."

"Yes, I'll concede that. It makes sense. If it didn't I should be more perturbed than I am. What else?"

"Well, we've concentrated on the human side of the case, the suspects, their alibis, and the cases against them. But there is another side to the case."

"What's that?"

"The diamonds. They are somewhere. Some one has them. Perhaps if we concentrated now on that side of the case we should come back to the murder angle."

"Walk back round the circle you've made?"

"In a sense, yes."

"And that means Pegwell's wife."

"If her story is not a piece of bluff."

"Did it sound like bluff to you?"

"No, I think she knows something. Probably not as much as she makes out, because she would naturally try to impress us in order to secure her husband's release. But I'm pretty sure there is something useful to be learned from her. But she'll stand to the bargain."

"Two women, eh, determined to be cussed? Lady Malverne and Bill Pegwell's wife, and both about the same man. Think this is an instance where the same stone might bring down two—er—feathered creatures? I suppose I shouldn't say birds in this connexion."

Slade smiled dutifully at the mild joke.

"I think it may be worth trying. We could keep Pegwell close-watched. In fact, he might be more useful free than in custody now that Swensen is being held. If he is linked up with some one else we may get a lead when he's not so careful."

"True, although it's a risk, either way one looks at it, Slade. However, I'll arrange for Pegwell to be brought to

London for questioning, and then we'll have him formally released on the grounds that the charge has been retracted. Think you might do something with his wife when she hears that?"

"I think it's very likely. It would be important, of course, to get our information from her before she sees her husband."

"Still sticking to your theory that she was with him on that expedition, eh?"

"I'm certain of it. Any news of the bogus Butterick, sir?"

"No, Slade. That gentleman has disappeared into the blue. If he isn't the murderer he's an accessory, mixed up in it somewhere. And by the way Swensen has decided not to talk any more. Just shut up like a clam. Of course, we've got to be careful. After all, he's an American citizen, and a popular figure in the athletic world."

The A.C. rose, and Slade knew the interview was over.

"I'll report this evening, sir, after seeing Mrs. Pegwell. I suppose nothing's come of the hunt for some fingerprints of the bogus Butterick?"

"Not a thing. It was a last hope, anyway."

XIII.

When Slade stood before the front door of the small house in Clapham where the Pegwells lived he half expected to find that Tessa Pegwell had taken refuge in flight. He was aware of a sense of pleasurable surprise when in answer to his ring the door opened and the girl stood before him.

"Good evening, Inspector."

"Good evening, Mrs. Pegwell. You've seen the evening papers?"

He was taken into the tiny but comfortable sitting-room, and a worn armchair was pushed forward for him. The furniture was reminiscent of that to be found in suburban second-hand shops. Good of its kind, but its best days had long been passed.

"Yes, and I feel sure now that you can't hold Bill any longer."

There was a new note in her low voice. It might have been of hesitation or of last-minute doubt in her own ability to go through with this thing.

"We've considered the case very carefully, Mrs. Pegwell, and while I cannot say that the police can make a 'bargain' as you suggested, I think I can tell you that in return for important information you may be able to give us you will find the charges against your husband will not be pressed."

"That means—just what, Inspector?"

"That he will not be brought before a magistrate's court and the charge made officially. Of course, your husband might object at the sudden dropping of the case, and press for a hearing—if he is innocent. He might wish to counter us with a charge of wrongful arrest."

"I don't think you need contemplate that, Inspector."

"No, I don't think so, but I want to make the situation

very plain, Mrs. Pegwell, at this stage."

"I understand. What guarantee shall I have that— that Bill will be released?"

"No official guarantee, of course. Even my word is not official, but I can tell you that the charge will not be brought against your husband by Lady Malverne. Does that satisfy any doubts you have?"

Her glance was dubious.

"I suppose it will have to."

Slade pulled an argumentary rabbit from his hat.

"Perhaps there is one aspect of the case you have not considered." Round eyes watched him reflectively. "The sooner the diamonds are found and restored to their owner the better will be your husband's position regarding the police. You must realize that, in the circumstances, we cannot view his position in the case as anything but seriously compromising. And your husband has a record."

The wide eyes narrowed.

"You don't realize, Inspector, that Bill was framed that first time. He swears it. And, knowing Bill, I believe him. That's what made him feel he had to—to strike back, to do something to sort of make the balance even, and—"

She stopped, realizing too late how she had committed her husband.

Slade nodded.

"That's very unfortunate—"

She bridled.

"We don't want sympathy, Inspector. Just a chance to earn a living and enjoy our lives. Instead of that, what chance has Bill of getting a job, with detectives calling round to inquire where he is, what he is doing? This is the third place we've lived in since Bill came out, and still a man from the local police station calls round."

"Is your husband on remand?"

"Not now."

"Very well, Mrs. Pegwell, I'll bear all this in mind, and

if you can really help us I'll see if we—well, can't help in some way. But don't expect anything, then you won't be disappointed."

The expression on her face indicated how little she was ready to expect. Slade changed the subject abruptly, and got down to business.

"Now, the diamonds, Mrs. Pegwell. What do you know? Who has them, and just how did you come to find out? I need hardly warn that anything save the truth would be futile. We shall check your statement closely. By the way, I had better tell you that we shall expect a signed statement, stating that you offer the information voluntarily. You have no objection?"

"No."

Her lips barely opened to emit the word. She was staring at the opposite wall, trying desperately to think, to see whither she was leading herself. In a few moments her one chance of helping Bill would be gone, bartered for what?

She glanced at Slade. His face was grave.

"I shall have, first, to make an admission, which I do reluctantly," she said.

Slade remained silent.

"I went to Steyning Towers with my husband."

The detective nodded.

"I know. He gave that fact away himself."

She shook her head confidently. "Not Bill, Inspector. You can't make me believe that."

Slade said nothing. He had decided not to help her. Her story must be her own. Realizing that she could not draw him into explaining how he had learned she was with Bill, she continued, resignation in her tone and manner.

"We arranged for me to wait a certain time . . . while Bill was gone. I know you're not concerned with what happened before that, Inspector, but I had argued with Bill against trying his hand at that job. But, as I told you, he was still smarting about the police framing him. He swears he was framed, and this was to be his challenge. If you knew Bill you'd know that argument is wasted once he has set his mind on doing something."

"I think I know him sufficiently to realize that, Mrs. Pegwell," said Slade, remembering the process of his own interviews with Bill Pegwell.

"Well, we went. Bill hired a car, and I waited. I waited, actually, an hour longer than we had arranged, and he didn't turn up. I knew then that something had happened —to Bill; and I started up the car. I'd got on to the main road running by Steyning Towers—I'd been parked in a lane, you see—when I saw some one break from the high hedge running along the Towers side of the road. This person was a woman, and I gave her a lift to the station."

She paused, smoothed the skirt of her dress, and lifted her glance to the detective's face.

"I had a feeling that I must know where that woman went to, Inspector. I can only explain that feeling by saying that I knew something had gone wrong with Bill, something had happened to him, and that this woman had come from the grounds of Steyning Towers. To me it seemed she might know what had happened. I was a little frightened, and I suppose more than a little desperate. You see, my husband may be a bull-headed fool at times, but I happen to love him. I felt things were left up to me, and if I had a chance of helping him I should take it. This woman was my chance. She got into the back of the car when I held open the door of the seat beside mine, and she didn't talk. Just said she had missed the bus.

"I drove her to the station, as I said, and then I realized that she was going away without my knowing anything about her or even if she knew anything about what had happened to Bill. I made up my mind to follow her. I garaged the car in the next village, and went back to the station. It was late, and not many trains were running to London. I saw nothing of her until I was in the train and the train was moving out of the station. She then ran across the platform and jumped in, I suppose, an empty compartment. That made me more determined than ever to find out something about her. I was scared, I must admit, and I was tired, and behind all the excitement I felt that I was being a fool. Yet I was *happy*. You understand? It was a chance to learn something, and I was taking it.

"The woman left the train at East Croydon. I followed her on to a bus, and to a block of flats somewhere along the main road towards Purley, isn't it? I think it sounds all very like a thriller novel now, but at the time I felt I was doing the only thing possible, the only thing for me to do. I followed the woman into the flats—"

For the first time Slade interrupted.

"Did she act in any way that might suggest she knew she was being followed?"

"No, she went straight up the stairs to her flat."

"Didn't take a lift?"

"I don't think it was working. Anyway, if she wanted to be unobserved, wouldn't it be better to take the stairs? Other late-comers might have used a lift that was still operating?"

Slade nodded.

"Perhaps you're right. Go on, Mrs. Pegwell, please."

"When she had gone into her flat I opened a door that led on to a wide balcony. There were flower-borders near the coping, and the balcony seemed to run along the whole front of the building. Fortunately her window overlooked that side of the building, and I saw a light shining through curtains that had not been drawn together properly. I knelt under the window and watched. She must have put through a trunk call, because it was a long time before she got the number she asked the exchange for. Whoever she was talking to must have doubted what she said, I think, for after some moments she took something from the pocket of her overcoat, and held it up. The light, Inspector, shone on the Malverne necklace."

Slade started.

"You're sure?"

"There could be no mistaking that necklace. I had never seen it before, and I don't know much about precious stones. They've never made up part of my life, as you'll know, Inspector. But that was the Tears of Death necklace that Bill—"

She caught herself in time.

Slade was watching her with narrowed eyes; it was a wild, improbable-sounding story; such a story as a woman anxious to bluff the police might concoct. Yet there was something so essentially sane about Tessa Pegwell, perhaps a slight challenge in her manner, that Slade was assured her words had described an actual experience. It was as though she herself realized how bizarre this story of her amateur sleuthing sounded, and had told it in spite of the scepticism it might invoke.

In her own way Tessa Pegwell was a clever woman. Her instant response to Slade's query about the lift revealed that she could think clearly. She must know that a story of this kind could not be accepted unless she could offer more details, times, the name of the block of flats, the garage slip, etc.

The story must be true. Fantastic, a ridiculously simple sequel to two murders and the mountain of mystery Slade had faced at Steyning Towers—but a sequel, none the less, that contained the ultimate solution of this unusual case.

"What did you do then, Mrs. Pegwell?"

The calmly uttered question appeared to rouse her from a reverie. The fingers crumpled against her cheek slipped into her lap and again made that smoothing gesture across the skirt of her dress. They were long, white fingers, unadorned save for the slim gold band that was sign manual of Bill Pegwell's possession.

"I came home. It was very late. I walked a considerable distance before I was able to stop a late

Green Line bus that took me to Brixton. I walked home from Brixton."

Slade took out a notebook.

"Now, a few details, please. The name of the garage where you left your car?"

"I don't know the name, but I have a bill in my handbag. I'll get it."

She went out of the room, and returned a couple of minutes later with the garage slip.

"I'll keep this meantime, if you don't mind, Mrs. Pegwell. We shall have to get in touch with the garage people."

"If you think the car was stolen, Inspector, you can save yourself the trouble. Bill will tell you where he hired it. But I should like it returned as soon as possible. We haven't too much money, and cars by the day are expensive. Then, too, I shall have to look for another job at the end of the week."

There was plenty of pluck about her, Slade thought, as he slipped the garage receipt into his notebook. A man couldn't have faced a grim prospect with more fortitude. He realized that Tessa Pegwell was a person who commanded his respect.

"What was the name of the block of flats?" was his next question.

"Dunbar Court. A floodlit sign shows it up at night. I should say the building is very recent. It stands well back from the road, and the end flats have large sun-trap windows."

"What was the number of this unknown woman's flat?"

"Seventy-three. The door was green, I remember— anyway, it looked green in electric light."

"You didn't get her name?"

"No, she didn't speak at all in the car. When I dropped her at the station I tried to find out where she was going and she said Brighton. But I knew from the way she said it that she was telling a lie. I guessed she wanted me to know nothing of where she was going, and that fact suggested London. It made me want to follow her more certainly than before, and I suppose it was her telling me that obvious lie that caused me to make up my mind to leave the car and follow her on the train."

"And she left the train at East Croydon?"

"That's right."

"Know the number of the bus she took?"

"Not for certain. I was too anxious to be sure and catch the bus. I had to wait until she was on it, because if she had seen me she would have recognized me, and that would have ended any chance I had of discovering something about her and what she was doing. However, I've got an idea the bus was a Number 12. I can't be sure, though. It's just an idea I have. I may have seen the number as I got off it, but I can't be sure."

"Now, how about times, Mrs. Pegwell?"

She smiled faintly. She had practically no idea of how the time had passed that night. She knew when she left the rendezvous in the side-lane, and when the train left the country station, but was not sure what time it arrived at East Croydon, and after that time had ceased to have any meaning for her. She had been too tired to worry, at first, and after she had seen the diamonds in the woman's hand too excited.

Slade made some notes in his book before putting the next question: "Can you describe the woman at all, Mrs. Pegwell? Were there any distinguishing features about her—I mean, her appearance, her voice, for instance? She did speak, I understand."

"Oh, yes, she spoke, but only when I asked her a definite question. I got the impression that she was not English."

Slade glanced up quickly.

"Oh! Why?"

"Well, she spoke English well, but with a slight accent. Not much, but it was apparent. And I may be wrong, but I should say her accent is more apparent when she is excited. And she was certainly excited on Saturday night. She hid it well when she was in the car, but I saw her later, when she was 'phoning."

"And you've no idea how long that 'phone call took to get through?"

"No, not really, but I should say over half an hour."

"Half an hour is a long time to wait."

"I know. It seemed hours to me."

"And there is not much doing on the trunk lines at that time of night."

"I'm sorry, Inspector, I can't help that. I admit I can't give you any real idea how long it took for that call to come through, but if I stood in the witness-box I'd still say it was at least half an hour."

Slade dropped the point.

"Now, her appearance. Anything you can tell me? You saw her through the window of her flat."

"Yes, she has reddish hair. Not ginger, but dark—auburn, I suppose she calls it. Her face was very white. Startlingly white, I should say, with no make-up at all save her lips, which were brightly coloured with a dark-tinted rouge. And her eyes were dark, and, like her mouth, very bright."

"That's all you can tell me?"

"I'm afraid so."

"What about her hands? Were the fingernails coloured? Did she wear any rings; if so on which fingers? Would you say her teeth were false? What was her age—about? Didn't you hear anything she said over the 'phone, or make out some of the words as you watched her lips move? Did she have any particular gesture that would identify her among a number of similar-looking women? You see, Mrs. Pegwell, those are the details I want now, details that will help me."

She nodded mutely, feeling that, after all, she had been very unobservant. She couldn't even guess at the woman's age, with hope of being within five years. And how could she tell whether or not her teeth had been her own?

"I'm afraid you must find me very disappointing, Inspector," she said apologetically, while feeling that she had no reason to make an apology.

Slade smiled.

"On the contrary, Mrs. Pegwell, I think the average woman would not have done half so well. I cannot expect you to notice details with a trained eye. I just mentioned a few things in the hope that you would remember some detail you had forgotten."

She shook her head. "No, I can't help you any more. That's all I know. And"—she hesitated—"that's my part of the bargain, Inspector."

Slade got up.

"You won't have reason to regret giving me this information, Mrs. Pegwell," he promised. "But of course you realize that now you have other interest for the police."

Her eyes widened; she looked startled.

"Other interest?"

"Certainly. You'll be a valuable witness in the prosecution at the trial."

"Oh, I hadn't thought—"

"Perhaps the one witness on whom the whole case will depend. You see, you'll be of real value to the Crown's case, and"—his tone became grave—"nothing must happen to you, Mrs. Pegwell."

She stood very still.

"You think I shall be in danger?"

He shrugged.

"I can't say. I can only warn you, and point out that two murders have been committed already. Presumably because those diamonds are worth the taking of a very big risk, and there is some one involved who is prepared to take that risk. If you require police protection, naturally I will see that—"

"No, Inspector, no! Bill wouldn't I couldn't! You see, with things as they are . . ."

She stopped, breathless.

"Yes, I think I see," said Slade slowly. "But I shall warn your husband when he is brought to the Yard for questioning. You will have to be careful, and we may have to take steps without consulting you."

"I shouldn't want that, Inspector."

"We wouldn't want to have to force such attention on you, but you must realize that the circumstances are very unusual, Mrs. Pegwell. I am sure your husband would be relieved to know that his wife has ample protection."

That last was a skilful point. It effectively ended further protest at the moment, and while she was still contemplating this possible new development that Slade had envisioned the Yard man bade her good-night and left.

He went to the nearest telephone kiosk, put through a call to the Yard, and twenty-three minutes later a Flying Squad car picked him up and whirled him through Southwest London at a speed that flagrantly flouted the results of Mr. Hore-Belisha's campaign for road safety.

But a sharp disappointment awaited Anthony Slade. He arrived at 73 Dunbar Court to find it untenanted. In short, the bird had flown.

XIV:

The resident agent of the large block of modern suburban flats known as Dunbar Court was in no gentle mood at being roused from his paper and pipe to answer Slade's questions. He appeared to resent the intrusion upon his evening's peace as something personal. It wasn't till Slade said, "Very well, Milford, if you prefer to talk at the Yard, get your coat. I am investigating two murders and the theft of the Malverne diamonds . . ." that the agent's manner changed.

"Good God!" he cried. "Not the Malverne case!"

"Do we get any assistance from you?" said Slade.

"But I've got to think of the reputation of this property. There's been a lot of money spent, and we want good tenants—"

"Well you've started the wrong way. We have information that one of your tenants was in possession of the Malverne necklace. That tenant was occupying No. 73—"

"She's moved out."

"So we know—now. We went up to call on the lady, and got no reply. The occupant of 75 says she moved out this morning. Well, that's not many hours' start. But it's too much, Milford."

"What the devil can I do?"

"We want to see inside 73, and we want anything you've got filed about her."

"I can manage that, I suppose."

"We're in a hurry. We've got to question her neighbours, see if they know anything."

"But"—the agent made a feeble gesture with the hand holding his pipe—"this block of flats prides itself on its privacy, Inspector. I repeat, I've got to look to the property's reputation. That's partly my job."

"Very well. Give us what assistance you can, and I'll see our inquiry doesn't harm the reputation of Dunbar Court, Milford."

"Good. That's a deal."

A new eagerness crept into the agent's voice. He seemed reassured.

"Understand," he said, "I don't want to be difficult, but I've got a job, and it's a good one as jobs go to-day. I don't want to lose it, see?"

"Get a move on, man. We're not imperilling your job."

Slade was annoyed and irritated. At the back of his mind lay the thought that now he could not check completely Tessa Pegwell's story. Had she tried to trick him?

Milford's failure to respond to the obvious need for speed did nothing to allay the doubt.

Slade, Clinton, and a fingerprint man, accompanied by Milford, went back to Flat 73. The agent opened the door with his pass-key, and the Yard men entered a typical small modern flat, comprising two rooms with a small bathroom.

Slade glanced round at the furniture.

"She brought in none of her own stuff?" he asked the agent.

"No, it's only furnished flats this side, unfurnished the other. We don't encourage tenants adding to the furnished flats; they might make a mistake when they shift out."

"Then she took nothing out with her?"

"Only her bags, if that's what you mean."

Slade turned to the fingerprint man.

"Right, go ahead. Pick up all you can."

The man set to work immediately, much to the mystification and increasing interest of Milford, who, at first, was inclined to object to graphite powder being sprinkled on the proprietors' furniture.

"Now, Milford, what name did she give?"

"Mrs. Savarin."

Slade started. Savarin. He had heard that name mentioned recently, but could not at the moment recall where or by whom. But he was certain it was in connexion with the Malverne case.

Savarin ... it was unusual . . . foreign.

"Was she a foreigner?"

"She might have been. Can't say I took any interest in her. Too many here for me to worry about 'em separately, as it were." Milford scratched his head. "She took it for three months, that's our lowest period, you know. But she moved out before the first week was up. I admit that's a bit queer."

"What's that?" Slade cried. "Took the flat on a three-months' lease and left before the first week was up?"

"That's right."

"Well, she may be coming back. She may only have moved away for a few days."

Hope sprang anew, until Milford shook his head lugubriously and began picking a tooth with a grubby fingernail while watching the antics of the fingerprint man.

"No, it ain't like that. She's gone. She come to me and said, 'Mr. Milford, I'm leaving my flat. I find I've got to leave on urgent business for South America. It's a pity I took the flat, but I didn't know then just how things would turn out.' So she gives me the keys, collects her bags, and leaves Dunbar Court. And you say she's walked off with the Malverne diamonds?"

"I don't say she's done anything of the kind, Milford. Forget I mentioned the Malverne diamonds. Get me?"

The agent swallowed in a manner that, from his facial expression, was singularly uncomfortable. He spluttered as he recovered his breath.

"I get you all right. I know how to keep my mouth closed. Don't worry."

"What time did she leave?"

"About half-past eleven this morning. Might have been a bit nearer twelve. She had a cab from East

Croydon come and collect her bags."

"Clinton," said Slade, "take our friend for a walk on the balcony for a few minutes. I'm going to put through a 'phone call."

The indignant Milford was escorted outside by the smiling sergeant, and Slade, watching the fingerprint man's back, put through another call to the Yard. He was switched through to his own department and to Sergeant Farrar.

"Farrar," he said, "get the boats that sailed for South America to-day covered, see if it was possible for anyone leaving Croydon about noon to get aboard. If it isn't possible, have a notice put through to the docks and get the local men to go over the passenger lists for every day this week. Name might be Savarin, but I doubt it."

He hung up.

As he watched the fingerprint man rig his apparatus afresh he told himself that he doubted very much if she intended to go to South America at all. Perhaps she was in the habit of telling people she was going in the opposite direction. Brighton . . . London. South America . . . the U.S.A., Canada, the North Pole. . . .

He went out to where Clinton and Milford were staring at the lights of Croydon, stretching like a gleaming river at the base of a deep-welled canyon of darkness.

"Milford," said Slade, "had this Mrs. Savarin red hair?"

"Sort of. Dark red it was."

"Did she give any references?"

"No. We don't ask for them. A month's money in advance is all we take, and that's generally sound enough."

"Been no letters for her since she left?"

"No, nor postcards."

The humorous enlargement failed like a damp squib.

"Had she any initials on her bags and travelling-trunks?"

"No. If there were any I didn't see 'em."

"Now, what about 'phone calls? Have you a house exchange for this block of fiats?"

"No, every subscriber has a separate number, connected direct with the exchange."

"I see the number of Mrs. Savarin's 'phone is an Uplands number and the 'phone hasn't a dialling disk."

"That's right. We come under the Uplands exchange, just outside the London dialling area."

"So every outgoing call has to be asked of the exchange operator?"

"Yes, of course."

"Thanks, Milford, that'll be all, I think. No need to keep you any longer. One word, don't forget—don't talk."

The man slouched away, muttering to himself. Clinton and Slade returned to the flat, where the fingerprint man had finished his task.

"How many, Irvin?" asked Slade.

"Four different people all told, two sets, but some of the second set are a bit old."

"More than a week?"

"Yes, a month or so, I should say."

"And the other set?"

"Well, the first set is a man's and I should say, a woman's prints, and the woman's are all over the place, but I've an idea the man tried to wipe out most of his. There are roughly cleaned surfaces near most places where I picked up his prints. The second set, another man and woman's, I think, have some of the prints underlaying the first, but never overlaying."

Slade nodded.

"All right, Irvin. You can leave it now. Clinton, we'll return to our friends in 75."

The occupants of Flat 75 were a middle-aged couple named Bridgewater. When Slade and his sergeant disturbed them for the second time that evening they were engaged as they had been upon the first occasion, practising the solution of a contract problem. However,

the cards were put on one side as the detectives re-
entered, and Mr. Bridgewater, taking off his spectacles,
thought the occasion called for a drink. He produced
whisky and a siphon.

Over his drink he mused, and glanced at his wife.

"I don't think there's much we can tell Inspector
Slade, is there, Annie?"

"No, Ted. I only saw the woman once, as she was
coming in and I was going out. Let's see, that would be
last Thursday. She came in on the Wednesday. Yes, it
was Thursday. I remember distinctly because it was the
day before the quarrel."

"Quarrel?" queried Slade.

He saw Mr. Bridgewater frown at his wife.

"It was nothing, Inspector; I'd rather not talk about it,
you know."

"But, Mr. Bridgewater, if it concerns the woman who
recently occupied No. 73 it may be important, and I must,
I'm afraid, insist on being told."

"There you are, Ted," said Annie Bridgewater, "I told
you she was no good. And that man too. If you hadn't
pushed him down the stairs—hard . . ."

Slade turned to Mr. Bridgewater.

"I think you'd better tell me," he said mildly.

"Well, on Friday when I left our flat in the evening—I
was going to the cinema—I walked into the corridor as a
man left No. 73. He was definitely the worse for wear.
Liquid wear, if you get what I'm driving at, Inspector
Slade. Drunk, insolently drunk. He came at me and said,
'Are you another damned Swede?' Then he burst out
laughing, and tried to put an arm round my neck. I'm
afraid I wasn't too—er—impressed by his friendliness,
and told him to leave me alone. At that he became more
demonstrative, if you understand, and said he didn't
mind who I was as long as I wasn't a Swede. Well, I
hardly relished the idea of being seen by another of our
neighbours with that inebriate clutching me familiarly, so
I—I—well, I pushed him down the stairs."

Mr. Bridgewater ended his explanation with a violent rush of words, and he blushed furiously.

"Good for you, Ted," stoutly maintained his wife. "I hope you broke some bones."

"My dear!"

"So I do, Ted, so don't make me say I don't."

When Mr. Bridgewater's blush had faded Slade inquired,

"How tall was this man, Mr. Bridgewater?"

"Oh, a couple of inches shorter than I am. About five seven and a half or eight, I should say."

In Slade's mind was a picture of the bogus Butterick. That had been about the man's height.

"And his hair? You noticed the colour?"

"Yes, I couldn't help noticing. He had his hat in his hand. It was dark, rather thin on top, you know, but dark and very oily."

Slade's glance met Clinton's. The two Yard men had been thinking along the same line. Clinton shrugged.

"Had he a moustache, Mr. Bridgewater?"

"No, he was clean-shaven."

Several more minutes passed while Slade continued to ask questions that failed to produce any helpful response. At last he and Clinton took their departure and left the Bridgewaters to return to their study of contract.

"What do you make of it, Clinton?"

The sergeant was ready to throw in his hand.

"I'm stumped. It's the woman Tessa Pegwell told you about. That part of it's all right. But this dark-haired man doesn't fit in anywhere. He isn't the man we thought was Butterick, although his height is about right. Furthermore, he isn't Barry Birchall, Lady Malverne's step-brother. Birchall is fair. Not as fair as Swensen, but no one would call him dark. Besides, Birchall was in Paris when the diamonds were stolen. Even more certainly he was in Paris when the real Butterick was murdered, according to the medical report and the check that 'phone call from Paris gives us."

Slade nodded. Clinton was right. This new dark man fitted in nowhere that they knew. He might be the husband of the red-haired woman, Mrs. Savarin. But that told them nothing.

"We'll be getting back now, Clinton. I've given Farrar a job, and I want to get on to the Uplands exchange and have that mystery 'phone call that took half an hour to come through looked up. And I want the Croydon police to sort out the taxi-driver who called for Mrs. Savarin this morning."

"You hoping for anything from that angle?"

"Not much, Clinton, I must confess. She probably took a train at East Croydon for London—Victoria or London Bridge—and got herself conveniently lost."

They returned to the Yard, and Slade flung off his coat and got down to work again. He rang through to the Uplands exchange, and made an official request for information. While the records were being searched he got on to the Croydon Police, and set the wheels in motion for the local men to pick up the taxi-driver who had called at Dunbar Court for Mrs. Savarin.

By the time he had finished explaining to the Croydon police the Uplands exchange was ringing through again, with information.

Uplands 86190, Mrs. Savarin's number, Slade was informed, had put through a call to Paris at twelve fifty-seven on the night in question. Connexion had been made finally about one forty.

Slade asked for the Paris number, and was told it. Abelard 7810.

At once something clicked in the detective's brain. The association of two ideas had produced a single illuminating ray of light.

Savarin, the elusive name, and Abelard 7810.

Barry Birchall's Paris address was—Slade checked from his notebook—34 bis Rue de Savarin; and the number he had checked up from Steyning Towers as the incoming cable call was Birchall's number, Abelard 7810.

"Now what do you make of it, Clinton?" Slade asked his assistant.

Clinton considered.

"There's a connexion somewhere, yet it isn't possible from what we know that Birchall can be directly involved. A man can't be in two places at the same time—not two places as far apart as Steyning Towers and the Rue de Savarin in Paris."

"Seemingly that is so."

"Why seemingly? His sister spoke to him. She would know his voice. She wouldn't make an alibi for him, would she?"

"No, she wouldn't do that, Clinton, with feeling between Birchall and Swensen running pretty nearly to high tide."

"And you did check that number."

"True, I did. But voices can be faked. We mustn't forget that."

"Then check with Paris. Get the Surete to send a plain-clothes man to make a few quiet inquiries. That should settle the point."

"And if it does?"

Clinton raised his arms and dropped them.

"It's too much for me," he confessed. "There's a connexion between the woman and Birchall. She might have heard him say something about the diamonds and used him."

"How?"

"I don't know, I'm guessing."

"What makes me suspicious, Clinton, is her using as a pseudonym the name of Birchall's street in Paris. Looks as though she wanted to be careful to remember the right name, and not trip up. So she chose a name she couldn't forget."

"Or else," suggested Clinton, "she chose a name that would be hard for Birchall to explain if explaining became necessary on his part."

"You think that, eh?"

"I think it's a possibility we shouldn't overlook while we're considering everything else. Birchall might have been used pretty shabbily."

"Yet the chances of his being connected with the woman and the flat at Croydon are mighty small, Clinton."

The sergeant had a bewildering reply.

"So was the chance of the car being found in the lake, and the real Butterick, ever being produced for identification. There's some very real brains at work on this case, and a cool head. Whoever was duplicating Butterick, now I look back on it, did a fine job. He acted just so that we'd be glad to have him out from under our feet."

"Then you see a connexion, Clinton, between the car in the lake episode and this adopting of the name Savarin?"

"I don't say I see a connexion, but it looks to me as though the same brain might have thought out both moves."

"Yes, I see your point, and I agree. The *Surete* will be the only means of putting our doubts at rest. I'll have a call put through right away."

That call was given Post Office priority, and fifteen minutes later an official request was made of the French police regarding the occupany of 34 bis Rue de Savarin. Scotland Yard was promised a speedy report.

"You'd better drop it now, Clinton, and get some sleep. I'll wait to hear if Farrar has dug up anything and if the Croydon people find the taxi-driver. Then I'm leaving myself. We may yet have some late hours on this case before we've got the diamonds."

XV.

The next morning Slade was at his desk early. The Malverne diamonds case was growing in extent, the number of leads the police had now to cover meant close and hard routine work, with the chance of finding little of real value; but routine work that had to be done. Farrar's efforts with the companies with shipping lines to South America had produced no result save a fair assumption that the red-haired woman could not have travelled on the day she left Dunbar Court. The Croydon police had traced the driver of the taxi that had been called to Dunbar Court, one William Meggie. As Slade had supposed, Meggie's fare had told him to drive to East Croydon station. The local police had found a booking-clerk at the first-class counter who remembered the woman. She had taken a first-class single to Victoria.

And there that particular trail ended. A couple of Yard plain-clothes men were sent to Victoria, but Slade knew that the chance of finding her trail at the big London terminus was about as hopeful as his chance of buying a winning ticket in the Irish Sweep.

The question seemed to resolve itself into one of: had she gone aground in London or sailed abroad?

Close watch was to be kept at all ports for a woman answering her description.

About ten o'clock news came from Paris. A *Surete* detective reported that M. Barry Birchall was still residing at 34 *bis* Rue de Savarin, that M. Birchall, so far from being able to journey to England to take part in stealing a fortune in jewels and murdering two persons, had been confined to his bed from Saturday morning until Monday night. It appeared that M. Birchall was suffering from some disorder of the liver.

"That's scotched our chance of a Paris lead," said Slade to Clinton when the news came through. "Now we know it is impossible to include Birchall. His alibi's as sound as a rock."

Half an hour later another lead failed them. The photographed and developed fingerprints of both sets taken in Flat 73 at Dunbar Court were unknown in the files of the Yard's Records Department.

Slade, in short, was left high and dry.

Swensen remained under arrest, and Bill Pegwell was being brought up from Sussex. He arrived about quarter-past eleven. In the office of Department X2 a fresh fire of questions was levelled at him. He kept his head and his temper, and replied civilly, and, so far as it was possible for him to make a favourable impression, he made it. A few definite facts were precipitated in the course of this new experiment. Firstly, Bill knew nothing of the red-haired woman and didn't want to know anything. Secondly, when it was pointed out that, owing to the information with which she had parted, his wife might soon be in danger Bill's attitude towards the police changed considerably. He showed himself ready to co-operate in any way he could—"as long as you don't ask me to be pleasant to that dirty swine Reisenberg."

It was Bill's one flare-up.

It became apparent, too, that Bill had been definitely the victim of circumstances. He had been playing a lone hand in his effort to obtain the diamonds (once more he explained his reason why, this time to various grave official nods that were not in the least approving of his filibuster attitude), and had run counter to interests that obviously involved the employ of several persons.

His opinion sought, Bill doggedly adhered to his original statement of his belief that Reisenberg had cracked him on the head and stolen the necklace.

Bill was allowed to walk out of Scotland Yard, as he thought, a free man. Actually, two plain-clothes men were detailed to watch him and the divisional plain-clothes men throughout London were told to be on the look-out for him. His every movement would be reported. As the A.C. said to Slade after Bill had been 'released,' "We're running a certain risk, Slade, but we've got to have a 'draw' for our game, and Bill Pegwell and his wife will suit excellently. I might have some twinge of conscience, Slade, if Pegwell were a good citizen, but he isn't. He's got to prove himself. He's only beginning to realize what citizenship entails on the part of the citizen." So that morning passed, much covered but little achieved, and no advance made over the previous day's record in the case.

Slade called to see Lady Malverne after lunch. He found Mrs. Clammer still with her, and Lady Malverne herself somewhat changed. She was taking Swensen's arrest harder and more to heart than Slade had thought she would. He could see that even Mrs. Clammer's salutary influence was beginning to lose its initial potency, and he felt sorry for both women.

Lucie Malverne was surprised when she learned the reason for the detective's call. He wanted to know if her half-brother had ever complained of liver trouble. She told him no, not to her knowledge, and gave him the name of the doctor who had attended her half-brother and herself in London. As he left Lady Malverne's town house Slade saw Sir Vincent Brugman stepping out of his new Rolls Royce Phantom III. Plainly Lady Malverne was prepared to spend plenty of money in Swensen's defence. Brugman was the ablest defence counsel in the country.

Being essentially thorough, Slade called upon the doctor who had attended the Birchalls before Lucie's marriage to Sir Julius Malverne. Dr. Murray was a Scotsman with laughing blue eyes and scarcely no trace of a burr in his voice.

"Liver?" he queried. "Lord no, man! Barry Birchall was as strong as an ox. Not a robust-looking ox, I'll agree. But his strength was sound, and his body was sound. And if anybody asked me I'd say the same about his brain. A keen fellow, but with a lazy-bone in his carcase—or maybe several."

Slade returned to the Yard, thoughtful. Barry Birchall's liver was assuming, in the detective's mind, more significant proportions, and it was not long before the detective was asking himself if a clever young Englishman had managed to fool a Paris detective. The answer he sought might only be secured after a trip to Paris and a personal investigation. But that would mean holding up the case at the opposite end, which Slade didn't wish to do.

An ironical comment on this was a report from the man set to watch Captain Furniss, now in his little bachelor flat in St. John's Wood. The Captain had gone to a local public-house and consumed various quantities of weak whisky-and-soda, he had called in at a library, he had bought some tobacco in Hampstead, he had taken a bus back to his flat. . . .

Slade pushed the report aside. The trivial details, important in a consecutive chain, with every link apparent, were tantalizing when one sought an indiscrepancy, one little unreconciled fact upon which one would be able to pounce and then exclaim, "This doesn't fit? What is the real explanation?" Everything in the Captain's humdrum London day fitted, was self-explanatory.

Slade had reached this point when he had a fresh idea. The Paris police might be able to make something of the untraced fingerprints.

A photographic copy was dispatched by air mail.

That concluded another day's work on the case. Still the Press maintained its pristine enthusiasm for the case. Photographs, double-column articles, general articles on the blood-red histories of famous jewels, continued to be printed. Editors still managed to squeeze a few words into the leader column about police activity. Gossip-writers made literary hay in the sunshine of Lady Malverne's past smiles and of pictures of Kurt Swensen.

Then an American news agency with an international *clientele* released the story of Swensen's killing the negro. On that Tuesday evening Slade read the stuff that was a day old to him dished up in new, sensational garb.

And underlying the whole of the Press activity, enthusiasm, and interest, lay a new question: Why was Pegwell released?

Not too much was said about Pegwell, for editors were still chary of the law of libel; but they were uneasy, and obviously chaffing because Scotland Yard had not allowed them on the inside of the wicket-gate.

Barry Birchall's name, significantly, was not mentioned. Fleet Street had as yet received no hint that the police hunt for the Malverne diamonds might not be confined to the British Isles.

Wednesday morning, however, the case received fresh impetus. No less than information from Paris. One of the fingerprints in the set sent by Slade to the Quai des Orfevres was identified as having been made by a gentleman known to the Paris police as the brother of the Red Doll.

Details were provided.

The brother of the Red Doll was a gentleman of no good repute who specialized in aiding presentable swindlers, the high-class card-sharpers. He had worked with the demi-mondaines, and was believed to have connexions with several of the leaders of the Paris dope-ring.

There was the Red Doll herself. She was known to have used two names, Aimee Deparis and Lucille Bourget, but she was best known by the name with which she had appeared in the Folies du Casino Rouge—La Poupee Rouge, the Red Doll.

A man had been shot at the Casino. Rumour had it he was a lover. The truth was never known. The gun was never found. The Red Doll disappeared. The management of the Casino saw to that.

Six months afterwards Robert Deparis had his fingerprints taken by the police, but he escaped imprisonment. Elections were pending, and votes were wanted. Robert Deparis, the brother of the Red Doll, was lucky.

He too disappeared.

The French police, in their report to Scotland Yard, included the information that both brother and sister were known to be excellent linguists. They were believed to be of Italian and Gascon extraction. Certainly both could speak English and German as fluently as French, and their French was as perfect as their Italian.

Slade saw that he was up against a clever couple of rogues. There could be no doubt. The French police descriptions of brother and sister made mistake impossible. Robert Deparis was the dark-haired man who had been thrown downstairs by Mr. Edward Bridgewater while on his way to the cinema. The Red Doll was the auburn-haired woman of mystery who had left Steyning Towers with the necklace.

How did it all square, knit together, and become of one piece?

Obviously whoever had secured the necklace after cracking Bill Pegwell over the skull had managed to pass the diamonds to Aimee Deparis. She had been ready to run with them to her flat in Dunbar Court, where she was to lie low until joined by her accomplice.

But the accomplice?

Not Reisenberg. He had not contacted Dunbar Court. He had been watched. Not Swensen. He was in a cell. Not Bill. He too had the same alibi as Swensen. Not Furniss. The little Captain had been watched. He hadn't stepped farther out of his home neighbourhood than Hampstead. Mrs. Clammer? Hardly. She would have been with Lady Malverne. Suspicion against the one would have to include the other. And Slade could make out no possible case against Lady Malverne. There was no interest in purloining her own necklace, so far as he could see. Had it been a joke (thought of the prone Bill placed it obviously beyond the amateur confines of a joke) she would not have kept it up sufficiently long to allow Swensen to be arrested.

This left the servants.

But they had been at Steyning Towers. Slade went over the statements he had taken down at the Towers when he interviewed the staff. They were all English. None could have been of Italian or Gascon extraction. And the Friday night ruled out that possibility. On the Friday night Edward Bridgewater had seen and shoved downstairs the red-haired woman's confederate, her brother. Therefore he could not be numbered among the staff at Steyning Towers.

But could he have been Butterick?

Slade went over every detail of the bogus detective as he remembered the man. Had his hair been false, a wig, still the man could not have assumed his utterly English *role* without being English. Slade found himself unconvinced that Robert Deparis, excellent linguist though he might be, could have taken the *role* of Butterick, the sandy-haired detective. The man had been perfect in his part. No foreigner, with only an acquired English background and knowledge of English ways, could have hoped to pass that acid test under the eyes of two detectives from Scotland Yard. To have attempted the feat would have been praiseworthy, to have succeeded impossible.

Yet some one had done it. Some one who, Slade believed, was English.

Did that mean a third member of the party?

The only person who could have answered that question satisfactorily was dead, the maid Maud Farling. She was probably killed because she accidentally discovered that the character of 'Butterick' was a disguise. The real Butterick doubtless never had a chance to discover who killed him.

Two persons or three?

Slade couldn't make up his mind, and the annoying part was that he had no additional means of determining this numerical answer.

The Red Doll might have a lover who had been brought into the plot.

Who?

She had rung up Barry Birchall's Paris number as soon as she had successfully gone to earth with the gems. Could Birchall be the mysterious third? But if so, how had he fitted into the scheme? He had been in bed over the week-end with a liver complaint.

He had an alibi. Even if he hadn't been in bed he was in Paris, because he had rung up his sister and spoken to her.

His alibi was unassailable.

Or so it seemed.

Slade got up and lit his pipe. He began walking up and down the central square of carpet in his office, like a jungle animal confined to a cage. He was restive. He knew that under the surface of all this that was floating in his mind was the truth, concealed because of the cleverness of some shrewd brain.

The trick had been pulled successfully. At least, so far. Two murders had been committed, with probably only one planned, Butterick's. The maid's had been forced upon the murderer as a protective measure. But the diamonds had been stolen, and got away. By luck largely, because Bill Pegwell had almost upset the apple-cart.

He could hope to find no clue in the murder of Butterick. That had been carefully planned. There was a gun, but it was probably in the mud at the bottom of the Thames or the Seine now. The murder of Maud Farling offered one clue. The evidence of her fingernails. She had fought for her life and her nails had marked her murderer.

Of the two men arrested, neither had been marked, and one had had no opportunity to murder the girl. Reisenberg *had* been scratched, and, significantly, on the back of the left hand.

But there was another clue—the use of the Indian

clubs.

That looked like a knowledge of Kurt Swensen's habits and effects, and spite.

Spite against Swensen brought the pointer back opposite Barry Birchall's name.

Slade couldn't be sure that this line of reasoning was getting him anywhere, but he felt that he had surveyed the prospect of the case more closely than he had hitherto, and he realized that only a visit to Paris would enable him to put his mind at rest.

He went to the A.C.'s office, and explained what was in his mind.

The A.C. was perturbed.

"But why waste time trying to prove the impossible is the impossible, Slade?"

"I'm not so sure it is, sir," replied the chief of Department X2. "This case is schemed to a pattern, and I think I can discern some of the pattern. The woman, her brother, that Paris 'phone call; they're all extra to the case we're engaged on here. They don't join anywhere except as regards Swensen."

"Those clubs?"

"Yes. I'm certain whoever murdered Maud Farling will regret trying to throw the blame on Swensen, and he—or she—will also be marked with scratch lines. I'm sure of that."

"Well, Reisenberg?"

"He's still in the running, and if he makes a false step we shall have him. But this Dunbar Court angle doesn't seem his line of country. Not his nature to deal that way."

"That only leaves you what you can discover in Paris."

"I'm afraid so, sir."

"Very well, Slade, I've enough confidence in you to know that it wouldn't be a wasted journey."

"Thank you, sir."

"But there remains Swensen. He's becoming a bit of a problem. Did you know Lady Malverne's briefed Sir Vincent Brugman?"

"I saw Sir Vincent as I left Lady Malverne's house. But personally I think Swensen's safer where he is at the moment."

"What d'you mean?"

The A.C. looked at the departmental chief sharply.

"Those clubs point to feeling against Swensen, bitter feeling. No one would have gone out of his—or her—way to use them unless Swensen was to be involved if they were found. And think of what it means, not only taking a club from his room, but putting back the one that crashed against Pegwell's head. Swensen might be in danger if released."

"And therefore point the way to the murderer if the latter made a move against him."

"But there's Mrs. Pegwell for that, sir. We don't want to lay too many spoors on the ground. It would look suspicious if suddenly Swensen were released—as well as Pegwell."

"Dammit, you're right, Slade. It's a devil of a case, however one looks at it."

"Could we hold Swensen safely until the end of the week, sir?"

"Yes, I think so, Slade. Why?"

"The case might begin to work out by then if anything comes of the Paris investigation."

"I see." The pale eyes of the A.C. smiled. "So you're going?"

"I think it would be advisable sir . . . before he recovers from this attack of liver and disappears."

The smile disappeared from the A.C.'s pale, water-coloured eyes.

"I agree, Slade," he said slowly. "Good hunting."

XVI.

Leaving Clinton in charge of Department X2's handling of the Malverne case, Slade flew to Paris by airliner, and was met at Le Bourget by Inspector Dulac of the *Surete Generale*. It was some years since Slade had last seen Durac, then a first-class sergeant. An extradition case involving the capture and transportation of a Scots swindler had brought the two detectives together. But Dulac had a long memory.

"It is good to see you again, my friend," he beamed at the man from Scotland Yard. "Allow me to welcome you to France. I hope your stay will not be too short."

"The present exchange rate wouldn't allow me to stay too long," Slade smiled.

"Ah, I see you have not changed! But what is this case you are engaged on? I learn that you are interested in the movements of a certain Englishman living in Paris, a M. Birchall."

"Movements or absence of movement," said Slade.

Dulac raised a puzzled face as he hailed a taxi.

"I do not understand, monsieur."

As the taxi raced them into Paris Slade explained in brief outline the case upon which he was engaged and why he had come to Paris. Dulac's dark eyes gleamed. His French imagination was roused by the peculiar problem Slade had set himself.

"But this is most interesting!" he exclaimed, and sank his voice. "You are attempting to prove the impossible is possible. That is excellent." More formally he added, "I am sure you will succeed."

"I hope so, Dulac. Barry Birchall is a stumbling-block that trips me every time I try to figure out the case from a fresh angle."

The French detective nodded his head lugubriously,

and a carefully manicured finger touched his short dark moustache. He presented a neat, rather dandy appearance, but Slade knew from past experience that Dulac was a policeman first and last. He was one of those men whom it is a mistake to judge only by their outward appearance.

"There have been reports in the Paris newspapers, of course," he told Slade. "This Kurt Swensen is too well known for his arrest not to be broadcast, as you say. And those Tears of Death, a fortune in cold carbon . . . yes, the case is most interesting. More, it is stimulating. But your personal theory, my friend? Who do you think is the murderer and thief?"

"As we say in England, Dulac, I'm sitting on the fence. Every theory I've contrived conflicts with another—ultimately, at any rate. That is why I had to come to Paris. I felt that there was an even chance of discovering something at this end that would perhaps point to—well, a fresh lead."

Dulac nodded again, and produced a cigarette-case and matches.

"True," he murmured. "Well, I can tell you this, my friend, the man we sent to the Rue de Savarin learned only one thing, this M. Birchall had been confined to his room and his bed. He learned that from the *concierge*, who stated most positively that liver trouble had kept M. Birchall from venturing outdoors. But, of course, that was only an inquiry."

The Frenchman's dark eyes gleamed at Slade.

"You mean, Dulac, what the *concierge* told your man might not be the truth?"

Dulac's shoulders lifted in an elegant motion.

"I mean anything may be the truth. If this Birchall is far-sighted, he could have bribed the *concierge*. We shall see. But first we must eat, and you, my friend, are my guest. Indeed, we must celebrate."

At a small, discreet restaurant situated somewhat along the Grands Boulevards the French detective regaled his English *confrere* with a *dejeuner* that was truly gastronomic. Dulac was like a small boy showing off his toys to a friend. He metaphorically discarded his policeman's cap for the chef's hat. Slade must realize just how such perfection of the culinary art was obtained, and Dulac took endless pains to assure himself that Slade understood the processes and kitchen tricks he explained. From food he turned to wine, and on that subject Dulac, who had been bred and born in the vineyard country of the Haute-Marne, rhapsodized until coffee and cognac were produced.

"And now, my friend, a cigarette that is like the charm of a beautiful woman under the stars. Jules!" He called the garcon. "Those Egyptian cigarettes."

Slade, who frankly would have preferred his pipe, accepted a second cigarette after the first, and held the tip in the flame of Dulac's match.

"I am not taking up too much of your time, I hope, Dulac," he ventured, by way of politely drawing the conversation back to the business that had brought him to Paris.

"Monsieur, I am at your service—entirely," said Dulac, smiling broadly, and flicking the end of his moustache with his left finger-tips. "Command, and we shall proceed."

"I should like to call on Birchall. But first I'd like to question the concierge and perhaps some neighbours in the next apartments."

Dulac smiled.

"Truly a wise plan. Shall we depart?"

"I think so. It was an excellent lunch, and I—"

"No, no!" Dulac waved an arm with determination. "It was a little something, not much. What you call a snack. Tonight ... ah, that is another matter! To-night, my friend, I shall set before you the finest *diner* in Paris, in all France. I, Jean-Jacques Dulac, promise you."

Slade was not altogether cheered at the prospect, but he smiled bravely.

"You are very thoughtful, Dulac."

"It takes no thought, my friend. Food and wine—they are in my blood."

Slade lowered his glance to the Frenchman's slim waist, and wondered how he performed the miracle. But he was too polite to inquire.

They drove to the Rue de Savarin, an uninteresting thoroughfare in a middle-class residential district south of the Rue Lafayette. The *concierge* at 34 *bis* was a small, short man with a developing paunch. He smoked a pipe of decidedly Teutonic appearance, and greeted his visitors with suspicion until Dulac announced himself. Then wariness crept into the man's manner, and he put his long pipe aside.

Slade and Dulac had agreed that it would be best for the Frenchman to tackle the *concierge* and Birchall's neighbours.

For some ten minutes the Englishman stood by listening to a crackling fusillade of French. When Dulac had fired what was apparently the last shot the French detective turned to the Yard man.

"The *concierge* says he was not bribed to say M. Birchall remained in his room. M. Birchall, he contends, is not given to parting freely with his money, even when he asks a service of some one, and he asked the *concierge* to fetch a doctor for him late Saturday evening. The *concierge* brought Doctor Legrand from the Rue de Jamappes. There can be no doubt, my friend. This Birchall has a clear alibi, I am afraid, and you have come on the wild-goose chase."

"Did he say if Birchall has been out of his room recently?"

"Yes, yesterday for the first time."

"Another point Dulac. I take it there is a telephone in the room, with the number Abelard, 7810."

"A moment, my friend, I will verify."

There was another crisp exchange of crackling words, and Dulac nodded.

"That is right, monsieur. There is a telephone in M. Birchall's room with that number."

"Then why did he have to send the concierge for the doctor? Why didn't he 'phone?"

Dulac's eyes narrowed.

"Ah, you are shrewd! Yes, that is a point." Again he questioned the *concierge*. "He says he does not understand either. Perhaps M. Birchall did not know of a doctor living in this neighbourhood."

"What is the number of his apartment?"

Dulac asked the *concierge*.

"Seventeen, my friend."

"All right, let's go up."

Apartment 17 was on the second floor. Apartment 16 was opposite.

"Let's inquire there first," said Slade, pointing to the door with 16 on it.

"Very well."

Dulac knocked, and the door was opened by a white-haired man with a very pink face. The French detective explained that he was from the police and would like to ask some questions. They were shown inside.

Again Dulac carried on the conversation, acting this time more as interpreter for Slade, whose French, though sound enough, was not equal to a high-pressured argument.

M. Paillon, the occupier of Apartment 16, was a school-master and a bachelor who apparently took little interest in his neighbours, their lives or their mistresses. He was content with his books and his leisure to read. He knew M. Birchall, was on a nodding acquaintance with him, but he had never been in the Englishman's apartment, and could not say if at any time within the past few months he had been visited by a red-haired woman. Anyway, the world was full of red-haired women.

Yes, he had known that M. Birchall had been confined to his bed. He had met Dr. Legrand on the stairs. The doctor attended the homes of several of M. Paillon's pupils, and they knew each other sufficiently well to stop and pass the time of day. The doctor had mentioned his patient in Apartment 17, and said that whatever was wrong with the man, it was only slight and temporary. He had been unable to place his finger on the exact place of the internal trouble, although from M. Birchall's complaining it was clear that the liver was affected. Yet samples and testings of M. Birchall's urine had not pointed to any radical infection. Dr. Legrand was inclined to think the man was making a lot of fuss over nothing at all. He had told his patient as much, but M. Birchall had insisted that the doctor visit him until the mysterious 'pain' had vanished.

"What do you make of that, Dulac?" Slade asked the French detective.

"It seems to me that this M. Birchall took very great pains to assure himself that several people should be able to testify to his being here over last week-end."

Slade nodded.

"Exactly what I think, Dulac. Very great pains. An absolutely perfect alibi. Ask M. Paillon if he knows when Dr. Legrand first visited Birchall. I should like to check what the *concierge* said."

"But certainly."

However, M. Paillon was able to substantiate what the *concierge* had told them. Dr. Legrand had informed him that he had first been called in to the patient's bedside on Saturday evening between a quarter to nine and a quarter-past.

"The perfect alibi, Dulac," said Slade when the French detective told him what the schoolmaster had said. "It was between those times that the diamonds were stolen. The perfect alibi," he repeated softly.

"So it would seem," murmured Dulac. "But take heart, my friend. Such perfection is rarely human. There may yet appear a flaw in what is seemingly flawless. It means we must watch them more closely."

They left the helpful and pink-faced schoolmaster and

crossed the landing to Apartment 17. Their knock brought a fair-haired young man to the door. This time Slade took the lead.

"Mr. Barry Birchall?" he inquired.

"That is my name, gentlemen," he replied in English. "What can I do for you?"

"I'd like to ask you a few questions," said Slade, producing his card of identification. "I am Inspector Slade from Scotland Yard. This is Inspector Dulac of the *Surete.* You have no objection, I hope?"

"Not at all. Come in, gentlemen. I must admit I fail to understand what reason there is for your visit, but perhaps you will explain."

They were shown into a room with the window-shades drawn, so that they were in a poor light.

Birchall nodded to the windows.

"I've had a bad liverish attack, and I find the sunlight doesn't help matters. You don't mind the blinds being drawn? I'm only just recovering, still under the doctor, as a matter of fact."

"Not at all," said Slade, glancing at Dulac. The Frenchman was staring with studied idleness round the room. "You know your sister, Lady Malverne, has had a very valuable necklace stolen?"

"Oh, so that's what you've come about! Well, Inspector, I must say you are certainly thorough, but you've come a long way for nothing if you think I know anything about it. Lucie herself can tell you—probably has"—he shot a quick glance at the English detective—"that I've warned her against being careless with her jewels."

"Yes, she has told me that. On Friday evening you 'phoned her at Steyning Towers—"

"Pardon me, Inspector, not Friday evening—Saturday." There was a half-smile on the speaker's face. "I remember distinctly, because it was only a few minutes afterwards that this internal trouble started, and I had to send Adolphe—the *concierge*, you know—for a doctor."

"Yes, Saturday evening," nodded Slade. "My mistake. Actually, Mr. Birchall, I was hoping that you would be able to tell me something about a clever Frenchwoman known as the Red Doll."

Slade cursed the poor light in the room. He could not be sure whether or not the man had started at mention of the woman's name.

"The Red Doll, Inspector? 'Fraid that means nothing to me. Who is she?"

Was he fencing? Slade could not be sure.

"A crook, I believe. Inspector Dulac knows more about her."

Dulac, appealed to, smiled charmingly.

"Very little about her, Monsieur Slade. But her brother, Robert Deparis, he was a different proposition— for the police of Paris."

Again Slade wished those window-shades had not been drawn. Dulac, speaking casually, had caused the other to start. Slade was almost certain of that. But in the poor light the other's recovery had been well cloaked.

"Well, I'm sorry to disappoint you, Inspector Slade," said Birchall, "but the Deparises, brother or sister, are no acquaintances of mine—to my knowledge." He shrugged in a gesture of mild disavowal. "One meets so many people in a city like Paris who are not to be considered even chance acquaintances. But why, may I ask, are you interested in this woman, this Red Doll as you call her?"

Slade made up his mind in a hurry, and played a bold card.

"I believe she has the Malverne diamonds, Mr. Birchall."

Out of the corner of his eye Slade saw Dulac nod covert approval.

Birchall sat very still.

"And you are anxious to find her, naturally, Inspector," he said.

"Naturally," repeated Slade.

"But why come to me?"

This time Slade played an ace.

"Because on the night of Saturday last she is known to have put through a call to Paris."

"Well?"

There was a sudden tension in the atmosphere of the room. In the thin yellow light men's glances travelled quickly, searching. Slade, turning his glance from Birchall to Dulac, saw the Frenchman playing with a button on his sleeve, but he was staring at Birchall's shoes. Slade looked in the same direction. There was nothing out of place about those shoes.

"She called Abelard 7810, Mr. Birchall."

"Abelard 78— Why, good heavens, that's my number!"

Either Birchall was a marvellous actor or he was being told something startling for the first time. He rose to his feet quickly, and sat down again with the same quick, abrupt movement of his body.

"Now you know why I rather expected you to know of this Aimee Deparis," said Slade.

"But, Inspector, this is incredible! You must have made a mistake—"

"The exchange may have, Mr. Birchall. I can assure you I have not."

"Yes, of course, that's what I mean. No call came through to me late on Saturday night."

Dulac spoke.

"Are you quite sure, monsieur?" he asked softly. "M. Paillon seems to remember hearing your 'phone ring about one o'clock Sunday morning."

Slade wasn't sure whether Dulac was bluffing or whether he had actually asked that question of the schoolmaster. But it was a clever move on the French detective's part, and showed that he was following every statement Birchall made.

"Sunday morning early," murmured Birchall, as though thinking aloud. "Let me see now Oh, yes, I think that was when Dr. Legrand rang me back to inquire if I was feeling any better."

True or not, for the moment Birchall had saved himself—until Legrand could be interviewed. But the tension in the room could still be felt.

"Of course," murmured Dulac, "that would explain it, M. Birchall. Yes, Dr. Legrand."

There was a faintly mocking note in the Frenchman's tone. Slade saw the man seated opposite him squirm, and he wondered what Dulac was doing. He knew the French detective had all his countryman's intuition and imagination, but he doubted very much if those qualities would help Dulac in dealing with an Englishman.

He had reason for such a doubt, he thought, when Birchall took the bull by the horns.

"But I say, I must protest, Inspector Slade," he said. "Going to Paillon, I mean. It looks as though you came here expecting to find I'd got a tale ready concocted."

Again it was Dulac who replied.

"When one is dealing with a Deparis," he said, in the same soft tone, "one has to take many precautions. Perhaps Aimee and her brother Robert have put their heads together, M. Birchall, and conspired to make things awkward for you to explain. Had you thought of that?"

"But I don't know the Deparises!" Birchall protested. "I keep telling you that. How could they conspire against me if I don't know them and they don't know me?"

"Ah, a riddle, monsieur! And the answer?" Dulac shrugged. "Perhaps they do know you, although you don't know them."

"What do you mean?"

Slade was certain that this time there was a note of strain in the other's voice.

"I mean that I must really raise the blind of this window, monsieur," said the French detective, rising.

"But I object. My liver—"

Dulac took no notice. He was at the window, fumbling with a knotted cord.

"I never did like this sort of window-shade," he said. "One always has to fumble."

"Will you leave that cord alone?" cried Birchall. Dulac continued fumbling, taking no notice of the other. Slade sat rigid, wondering what on earth the French detective was trying to prove. If he wanted to see Birchall's face more clearly, then surely—

Slade's thought was suddenly diverted. Birchall had grabbed the cord out of Dulac's hands. Slade, watching, saw that the Frenchman made no effort to hold the cord. But the next instant Dulac's left hand swung round, palm flat and smote the other's face with a resounding smack.

"*Nam d'une pipe!*"

The other sprang back, snarling, his hand raised to where the French detective's blow had fallen.

Dulac stood back. As by magic a snub-snouted automatic had appeared in his hand. He spoke in rapid-fire French, giving the other no chance to interrupt. Finally Slade saw the man cower back under the threatening muzzle of Dulac's automatic, and drop into a chair.

"For God's sake, Dulac, what's happened? What's it all about?" cried Slade.

"My friend," returned Dulac, "raise the blinds. I was too clumsy."

Quickly Slade adjusted the cords and pulled. The shades rolled up, and sunlight invaded the room. The Yard man turned, to see Birchall, sweat beading his face, shrink back before the advance of the French detective.

"Now we shall see."

Dulac's left hand sped out in the direction of the seated man's head. There was a short cry, and then Slade saw Dulac's hand come away from the other's head, in his fingers clutched a wig of fair hair.

The seated man's hair was dark, and thin on top. . . .

"Good God!" cried the English detective. "Robert Deparis!"

Dulac smiled.

"The brother of the Red Doll, yes. He was clever, Monsieur Slade, clever enough to convince you he was an

Englishman. But he could not fully convince me he was not a Frenchman, so I took occasion to make sure. At the psychological moment he was the Frenchman."

XVII.

That night Slade flew back to Croydon airport. As the large Imperial Airways 'plane droned high over the Channel and a moon stole out of the east he sat back in his seat with a sense of well-being not due entirely to the excellent *diner* the generous Dulac had provided. Slade's mind was at ease.

He knew he had turned a corner in the Malverne case. He had broken the perfect alibi. He had connected the Red Doll with Barry Birchall, who in turn connected in the case with his hatred of Kurt Swensen.

The diamonds, the bloodstained clubs, the murders of Butterick and the maid at Steyning Towers; they made a clear sequence now. They would lead him, Slade felt assured, to the solution, the arrest that would return the diamonds to their owner and send a cold-blooded, scheming murderer to the gallows.

Of course, he had no idea where to look for Aimee Deparis. Her brother had been taken to the French police headquarters without opening his mouth. He had found the game up so far as he was concerned, and he became silent, presumably on the not altogether wrong assumption that silence could not endanger him any further.

Arrangements had been made for the Parisian police to hold Robert Deparis on a technical charge, pending a demand from the London police for his being handed over as an accessory in a capital crime.

Sufficient for Slade that, at the moment, Robert Deparis might be left out of his calculations. Meantime, however, Dulac and the Parisian police were making every effort to uncover some further connexion of the Deparis brother and sister. A plain-clothes man was left in the apartment at 34 *bis* Rue de Savarin. Search of the apartment had produced nothing in the nature of a helpful clue. Apparently whoever had been the brains behind the plot had wisely insisted that no tangible clues that could aid the police in the event of things slipping up should be kept.

There was no book with telephone numbers or addresses in the apartment, and Dulac's search had been very thorough.

Dulac had stormed and raved at the impassive Deparis, but the man had remained unmoved. He had refused to say to what apartment or cupboard that key belonged, and he refused to make any statement involving himself or anyone else.

Forced, in his own defence, to explain why he was living in disguise in the Rue de Savarin in an apartment known to be rented in the name of an Englishman, Barry Birchall, he stated baldly that he was helping a friend, and would neither enlarge that statement nor retract from it.

Slade reviewed these new facts as the 'plane sped towards the white cliffs of Albion. They fitted, he saw, into the new case he would have to construct. At the moment the most discernible thread in the new pattern was Robert Deparis himself.

Edward Bridgewater's testimony proved that Deparis was in London on the evening of the Friday. On the Saturday evening he was in Paris, disguised as Barry Birchall. . . . Or was he? Had he gone to Paris *after* the diamonds had been stolen, and, disguised as Birchall, allowed the Englishman to go to England to contact his sister?

That was a fresh snag, early in the building of the new case. In some way or other Slade would have to settle the time of Deparis's leaving London and arriving in Paris. On that depended everything. Conversely he would have to prove the times of Birchall's leaving Paris and arriving in England.

He had cleared a lot of ground, but there remained

much to be done.

Beginning with the hypothesis that Deparis had left England late Friday night (that would not have been difficult, he was seen in Croydon by Bridgewater), he and Birchall must have exchanged positions, one gone to Paris when the other came to London. Then Birchall and Aimee Deparis had been in England to act together. Birchall had got from his sister (prior to the previous Tuesday, when he was believed to have returned to Paris, according to Mrs. Clammer) the facts about her forthcoming deal with Reisenberg, and had planned accordingly. He had realized that the insurance company would be bound to send a detective to Steyning Towers— perhaps he had inquired—and had resolved upon a bold entry into the field. Kill the insurance company's detective, take his part, and make a safe walk-out on Sunday. He would have several hours' start before the insurance company discovered that their man had disappeared, and the chances were that the body in the car in the lake would not be found for weeks or months.

It was sheer bad luck for him that his half-sister had dived into the lake that morning.

It was a bold plan, as Slade perceived it, yet sound enough at bottom. Aimee Deparis would be in the grounds to receive the necklace, and would be well away with it before the police even realized that it was stolen.

There point number two ran counter to the plan. Bill Pegwell had happened on the scene. Birchall had made the most of his opportunity. There was the opened safe, the necklace in a cracksman's hand. A quick blow and—.

Slade paused.

There was another snag.

The Indian club! How did that work? It suggested that whoever slugged Bill had been armed with the club— prepared, in short—when he followed him into the room where the safe was. Yet Birchall would not have known that Bill would be there. Going to rob the safe himself, he would not have taken a club, unless he had had some thought in mind to involve Swensen. . . .

Slade paused again.

There might be something to that, he saw. There was bad blood between the two men, Swensen and Birchall. The latter wanted to put some grit in the slipway of the Swede's progress towards the altar with his half-sister and her late husband's fortune. Murder would be a very effective grit to use.

Perhaps at first Birchall had only considered involving the Swede in the robbery, but the idea had grown into something else, more ugly, when he saw Bill Pegwell kneeling by the open safe. Perhaps he had tried to murder Bill then, had stolen the necklace, and had returned the club to the Swede's trunk, knowing it would be searched. That would not have been difficult. He knew Swensen, and his habits, presumably, and it would not have been difficult for him to have procured keys to the rooms at Steyning Towers. Quite the reverse, it would have been childishly easy.

The case he was building up, constructing out of freshly made theories, was becoming very, very possible, and it was, furthermore, knitting together with a solidness and smoothness of edge that won the experienced detective's appreciation and whetted his interest.

Of course, there was the third unforeseen development, so far as Birchall himself was concerned. (For the moment Slade was passing over Tessa Pegwell's appearance on the scene, and its highly important development.) The third unforeseen development was the maid's entering 'Butterick's' room while he was his true self, without disguise.

What had happened then?

Birchall had seized her throat, to prevent her from shrieking his true name. She had clawed and fought and finally fallen unconscious. By then, of course, he knew that Bill Pegwell would not die, and suspicion had not fallen as he had intended it to fall—on Swensen. So what did he do?

Looking at the body of the unconscious maid gave him a terrible idea. *She* should fix the direction in which suspicion should turn. In a matter of seconds he was inside Swensen's room, had taken another club, returned to his room, pulled the unconscious figure of the maid into a dark corner of the stairway, and had brutally bludgeoned the life out of it.

A callous act, brutish and deliberate, an act for which no pity could loosen one's feeling of nausea and loathing; but an act, as Slade realized, that might have been readily dictated by the opportunity of a moment. Once given the mental impetus, Birchall had acted automatically.

And up to a point the horrible, unnecessary murder of the maid had achieved the object the murderer had in mind at the time of its commission—Swensen had been arrested. Those two clubs had clinched the case against him. Something more than mere unsubstantiated protestations was needed to convince the critical mind that Swensen was not guilty.

And only one point remained in Swensen's favour.

He had not been scratched by the girl's fingernails. If Birchall bore the marks of her nails the case against him was complete.

There was an outside chance that she had scratched some one else, a member of the servant staff who would not own up to the fact because of what such an action on the part of the maid suggested.

Brooks . . . for instance . . .

Slade smiled. He saw that this new case was exacting. Mathematical accuracy of fact was demanded if it was to hold together. Find Aimee Deparis, he was sure, and it would not be long before the rest of the facts and details fitted into their proper niches, and the edifice would be complete, with Birchall under arrest, awaiting trial.

And would that trial cause a sensation!

There was enough material in the case to make a

whole book. The human interests at play were unusual and equally powerful. The plot was deep, sound, and would create a stir throughout the civilized world when it was pieced together in a law-court.

The 'plane flew across the wide acres of Sussex farmland, passed over Surrey, and dropped over the airfield at Croydon. A Flying Squad car was waiting to rush Slade to the Yard, where the Assistant-Commissioner was staying, refusing, with a fine sense of public duty, to forsake a desk the sight of which filled him with tired longing for a bed.

Small wonder, the A.C. had put in a fifteen-hour solid day.

"Sit down, Slade," he said when the chief of Department X2 entered his office, still with his overcoat on. "You've lost no time getting in, I see. Well, I hear you've uncovered something. Will it take long?"

"I can let you have an outline in a quarter of an hour, sir."

"Good. Shoot, then. I'm listening."

Slade told the A.C. of the investigation in the house in the Rue de Savarin, and of its outcome. He finished with an account of the last activities of the Paris police before he left Le Bourget for Croydon.

The A.C. was impressed. As Slade's story unfolded his lassitude appeared to leave him. He leaned forward across his desk and followed the detective's words closely.

"Excellent, Slade," he nodded when the chief of Department X2 had completed his narrative. "So the hunch was successful?"

"It was scarcely a hunch, sir. I felt that Paris might give us another lead."

"I know, I know." The A.C. waved a hand. "But now this woman, this Red Doll. How're you going to get on to her? She'll take a bit of unearthing. You've nothing that points to her whereabouts in this country—always supposing, of course, that she is in this country," he added.

He looked to Slade for an answer, and the latter could not keep to himself the anxiety he felt on this very point.

"I'm afraid it's going to be a bit of a puzzle," he admitted. "Her brother won't talk. The Paris police are working hard to uncover something that will give us a lead, but I'm not pinning much expectation to the outcome. This affair has been handled pretty slickly. The only course I've got open to me is to hammer again at Lady Malverne and Mrs. Clammer. They might be able to tell me enough about Birchall to give me a lead to where he is. Where he is the woman will be."

"Yes, that follows, of course. But it's a bit thin, isn't it, Slade? What reason have you to suppose that they will be able to give you any extra information of this kind?"

"None," said Slade, with honesty.

The A.C. rose and paced his office.

"If they fail you?"

"There's still Captain Furniss."

"And he's worth—what?"

"Very little, I'm afraid, sir."

"And you've no other line?"

"Only Birchall's acquaintances—he must have had some. Perhaps he was a member of a club. The man can't very well disappear without leaving any trace."

"If he's as clever as what you've told me seems to prove, Slade, I'm not so sure. Good at disguise, a quality that is generally complementary to that of a good actor. He'll be elusive—he has been, dammit!—and he'll give you a long run. It'll be a question of who tires first unless he slips up. And we've no reason for supposing that such an intelligent criminal should slip up—obviously."

All of which was perfectly true, but to Slade, just returned from an air-trip, following a tiring day's investigation, very disheartening.

"You're thinking of Swensen, sir?" he asked, trying to follow the trend of his superior's thoughts.

"I am, Slade. We're in the deuce of a position there. I agreed to the arrest of this man, and now he's a liability.

The case against him is breaking down more and more with each day passing. You thought it might be as well to keep him until the end of the week. I agreed again. But I ask you, Slade, does this case look like settling itself in that short time? You've done a lot of valuable work. You've gone far enough to show that this is one of those complicated affairs with a clever brain controlling everything, almost, that happens. Good enough. We can re-orientate our minds, as it were, get to grips with a new sort of problem. But confound it, we can't solve it in that time, not with two principals unfound! And they might be anywhere in these islands—anywhere."

Definitely, Slade thought, the A.C. was tired. He was not usually so perturbed as he appeared now, or, rather, he usually did not allow himself to appear so perturbed. A different matter.

"I know Clinton has kept things covered this end," he offered mildly.

The A.C. swung round, a slip of a smile on his thin mouth.

"I know I'm barking, Slade. Take no notice of it. I'm nearly asleep on my feet, man. Your department's only to be congratulated, I realize that, and I'm not complaining, or even expecting you to do more than is human. But you must realize our position. If Swensen is released without something to cover his release, some other arrest or stimulating development in this case—we're sunk. There'll be another outcry in the Press. They'll want another purge, and all that tripe; as though stirring us up with a politician's ladle is going to help in solving a case like this Malverne affair. No, Slade, what's beginning to get under my skin is the urgency for an alternative to Swensen. We did the right thing there. We had to arrest the man. Confound it, the man would swing, even now, in an open court, on the case we could build against him. You know that very well. Yet that alternative has to be found. It's like asking you to perform a miracle, I know. But keep hard at it, Slade. Don't let up for an instant.

Lady Malverne's stirring up trouble with all her millions, and the trouble's going to land in one solid mass in this office if you're not a miracle-worker. And now good night, man. I've kept you long enough, and myself too long. You've done a good job, but remember what I said. We want a miracle now, Slade."

XVIII.

Slade repaired to his own office in no easy frame of mind. The glow of pleasurable anticipation occasioned by his contemplation of the build-up of a new case during his 'plane trip had died, killed by the A.C's words of urgency and gloom.

He found Clinton seated at his desk, slowly sorting a pile of papers. The sergeant was half asleep.

"Well, Clinton, how's the fort been holding out?" he asked, taking off his coat and dropping into his own chair. The sergeant swung round.

"The A.C.'s getting het up," he confided.

Slade nodded.

"I know. I've just seen him. He looks half dead, and sounds as though he won't last the night."

"Bad as that, eh?"

"Worse, but keep it to yourself. Farrar dug up anything?"

"No. It may be good news, it may be bad. There's no news from any of the ports, and they're all on the lookout for her. Don't think, myself, she can slip through without getting caught."

"She can if she's like some others in this case, Clinton."

The sergeant's eyes narrowed with interest.

"Which others?"

Slade told him what he had told the Assistant-Commissioner, and when for the second time he completed the recital he saw that the sergeant's square face had drawn as long as was physiologically possible.

"So, Clinton," he concluded. "Birchall and Aimee. They're a prize pair and in this together. We've got to find 'em, that's the miracle the A.C. expects us to work. Do you feel like performing a miracle?"

"I feel more like going into a trance," the sergeant confessed mournfully.

"Wouldn't help at all." Slade knew he was being facetious, and he gave way to the feeling, wisely. Facetiousness can be a balm to tired nerves. "Birchall's the new fox, and he's left us no trail. We're just running anyways across country, and we may be miles out in our running, while the fox just licks his paws and scampers back to his hide-out without sweating from one pore. It's hardly decent, but it's the sort of thing that friend Frenton down in Sussex says makes our life interesting."

Clinton made no explosive remark as Slade had known him to make on similar occasions in the past. Instead, he sat with his square face resting in one brown hand, his eyes dolefully regarding the ink-stained desk immediately below his nose.

"I wonder," he said slowly, "if Birchall has a private 'plane?"

"You wonder what?"

Slade's interest was captured.

"A private 'plane," said Clinton, looking up. "I was thinking about Barry Birchall to-day, while you were in France, as a matter of fact—"

"Why, especially?"

"I got thinking about those rumours concerning Sir Julius Malverne's air-crash."

"Go on," said Slade. "I can tell the bee's buzzing very annoyingly in your bonnet, Clinton."

The sergeant smiled—at least, his face creased in an expression that passed for a smile with him.

"And now, listening to what you had to say about this development in the Rue de Savarin, it's suddenly struck me—what if Birchall is an out-and-outer? I mean, he wanted this necklace. All right. Suppose there was something fishy about that 'plane crash. As I said, I've been thinking about it to-day, and I rang up the air-club to which Sir Julius belonged, and I learned that Birchall belonged to the same club, but that he left shortly after the . . . accident."

Slade took out his pipe and filled it.

"That's interesting, Clinton—very. And you think it ties up with what we know now?"

"It might. This is how it strikes me. He wanted that necklace—Birchall. He plans to get it. He wanted Malverne out of the way. He got him out. Did something to his 'plane. I looked up the case. The police were never called in. The air-ground people settled it as an accident among themselves, but probably that was some hush-hush stuff. You know."

Clinton's prose style was losing anything it had ever had of elegance, but the man, like Slade himself, was tired. That was obvious. He had remained at the office in case something should turn up, and he had probably thought himself well-nigh silly with the various facets of the case. Mentally, he had gone roaming far afield to discover something new.

"Yes, I know, Clinton," Slade nodded. He felt a world of sympathy for his sergeant. Clinton was a stout fellow, and could be depended upon to think along sound lines. Nothing flamboyant or bizarre about Clinton's mental flights; they always obeyed the geographical and geometrical axiom that the shortest distance between two points is a straight line. "But you wouldn't suggest that the murder of Sir Julius Malverne was necessary as a preliminary move to the stealing of the Tears of Death?"

"Not ordinarily, I wouldn't," said Clinton, "but we've got to remember one thing."

"What's that?"

"Sir Julius always kept the necklace in his London bank. An amateur cracksman like Birchall, say—if he is one—with finesse and brains, couldn't get at it. The only bird who could fly off with that necklace would be a professional with blow-lamp and gelignite, and it would be a big job at that. Normally we could say the necklace and the other Malverne jewels were safe. But with Sir

Julius dead, what happens? His widow commences to sell the stuff. Unloads it pretty quickly, as I've found out. Then she decides to get rid of the hoodoo necklace. But to put the deal over, womanlike, she's got to cart it down to her place in Sussex. Then the bright boy who made this possible by removing the husband gets his chance—and takes it."

Slade sat still, smoking.

"Clinton," he agreed, "there's something in that—definitely something in it. It may go farther than you suppose. Julius Malverne out of the way, Birchall might suppose, would give him a chance to lift quite a bit of his half-sister's fortune. Then appears Swensen, who upsets the prospects, gives rise to a jealous quarrel, and Birchall is bitterly resentful. Follows the present case, with its attendant murders and the probable reason for them."

Having made his contribution, Clinton proceeded, like most cautious individuals who are prone to be too cautious in a moment of doubt, to retract from the effectiveness of his statement by throwing doubt on its plausibility.

"Of course," he said, "it sounds all right. I saw that. But it would be a devil of a lot of work for one man."

"Where do you get the one-man part of it?" asked Slade. "We know Birchall's in with the Deparis couple. There may be others. It's an organized affair. We've plain evidence of that. As for his own part in the scheme, how much work would be necessary to rig a 'plane so as to set it on fire when it reaches a couple of thousand feet? Very little, with tanks full of petrol," he added, answering his own question. "Then what? Then the waiting while the widow recovers from the shock—if recovery is necessary. After that the lifting of the loot. No, Clinton, it was your suggestion. Don't pull it to bits for no reason at all except that you made it yourself. It stands up on its own feet."

"But if the crash wasn't an accident arranged beforehand?" said Clinton, stabbing at a sheet of paper with a pencil.

"Don't keep firing torpedoes, Clinton. One might strike something. Heavens, we can't prove it one way or the other at this stage. In fact, I'm not worrying about that. What does concern me is the possibility of a new lead from the air-club. You see?"

"You mean from that angle we may get a new lead about Birchall?"

"Yes, of course. He's a flier. We weren't told that before. It opens up new possibilities. It might explain the apparent spiriting away of our unfound Red Doll. It means, in effect, we've got to warn the Continent about a lone 'plane with two passengers, a man and a woman."

"Which probably landed days ago," said the forthright sergeant.

"There's one thing about you that warms my heart, Clinton. You're never afraid to look on the gloomy side of anything." Slade stirred the dottle in his pipe and struck another match. "What if it did? Can one hide a 'plane by putting it in one's pocket? A 'plane is a far more interest-awakening vehicle than a car. There aren't so many in the world, but what the flight of a stranger in the home brood is noticed by some one. Not like a car in a car-park. That 'plane is somewhere, to be traced. If it isn't, then it was set on fire, and a combustion of that sort will be remembered for quite a while, especially when the tangled wreckage reveals that a 'plane has crashed. By the way, has there been any notice in the papers during the past few days of a 'plane crash anywhere?"

Clinton picked up the house-'phone and put the request to another department.

"Yes," he said, dropping the receiver, "one, yesterday, on a hill outside Paris."

"Paris—a hill?" Slade sat up. "Are there any hills outside Paris?"

"Sorry," said Clinton, with a straight face, "Paris in Maine, U.S.A."

Slade slumped down again in his chair.

"Well, I don't think even as resourceful a person as

Birchall appears to be would fly the Atlantic, with the Continent so conveniently near. Not unless he wanted a lot of publicity. So we may presume that if he has a 'plane it is still intact, and is either in this country or on the Continent, Clinton—"

"Or in the sea."

The sergeant offered the third alternative with no hope in his voice.

"In which case the Malverne diamonds are probably already adorning Neptune's trident. But somehow, Clinton, I have a feeling that they aren't. A man who has done so much to get them—and what they're worth— would take precautions to disappoint Neptune, I think. What was the air-club Sir Julius and Birchall both belonged to?"

"Tri-Wings. Their ground's out in Surrey, near Caterham."

"We'll call there to-morrow, Clinton, for what the visit's worth. I think we can consider this session closed. Nothing at all turned up?"

"Nothing, except a continuous string of growls from the A.C's office."

Clinton returned for a few short hours to the bosom of his family, while Slade sought his bachelor's bed. The next morning both were back at the Yard by half-past eight. Slade had arrived first.

"I've already 'phoned the Tri-Wing ground," he greeted Clinton. "They're expecting us. There's a club-house, with a resident secretary. It's a pretty exclusive sort of place, I understand."

They drove into Surrey in a fast police car. The secretary, a tall, thin man with a decidedly weather-beaten look and hairy hands, and a voice that for some reason made one think he was about to burst into song, greeted them and took them into the deserted lounge.

"Nothing wrong, I hope?" he asked anxiously. "The club's always had a good name, and I don't want to think we're due for some bad publicity."

"No," said Slade. "We want some information."

The secretary's face lightened. "Good!" he exclaimed. "For the moment I thought we'd got a dope-runner in our midst, or something equally ghastly." His mouth pursed. "What sort of information?" he asked quickly. "Naturally, we want to help the police, if we can. But you must realize that in a club of this nature there are certain privileges expected by the members, one of which is privacy, and—"

"We're not here to ask for divorce information," grinned Slade, who had shrewdly guessed the nature of the secretary's fresh doubt.

The man, whose name was Myers, looked relieved.

"In that case, just ask me, Inspector, and I'll answer to the best of my ability. How about a drink? Purely a private offer, you know," he added, grinning.

Slade, who did not usually accept a drink while on such a mission as the present, agreed, and nodded to Clinton, who also complied. Slade realized that Myers would prove more likely to be talkative with a drink in his hand, and he would not drink without the others joining him.

"It's early in the day to start," smiled the secretary, "but we don't often have the police here—thank God!"

He was a likeable sort of man, thirty-fiveish, and apparently keen on his job. Mentally he was on his toes the whole time Slade was with him.

"I want to go back to a rather tragic episode you will remember, Mr. Myers," began Slade, when the secretary set down his glass, and again looked uneasy.

"Don't tell me," he muttered. "I know—Sir Julius Malverne's crash."

Slade nodded.

"What's turned up?" asked Myers.

"Nothing, so far as I know. I thought you people were certain here that it was a straightforward accident?"

Slade gave the other a keen look, and Myers realized that he had prepared the trap for his own feet.

"Of course," he said quickly. "But when a man of Sir Julius's public prominence meets such a death there are always rumours ready to circulate, you know. We've had to be very careful. I thought for the moment some one had been starting another tale about the crash, and you had come down about it."

From the secretary's manner it was plain to Slade that the crash had been anything but a straightforward accident, as he would have them believe, and that the affair had been to some extent glossed over. Earlier that morning he had read through a filed newspaper report of the inquest, at which ground mechanics had testified that the machine that was wrecked had been prone to trouble with its petrol feed. The charred remnants of the 'plane and its occupant had made a detailed examination of the possible cause for the crash impossible.

"Of course, I appreciate what you say, Mr. Myers," said Slade tactfully, "but I can assure you that I am not here to investigate the truth of a new rumour regarding the accident to Sir Julius."

The secretary breathed more freely.

"But I believe," continued Slade, leaning forward, "that Sir Julius's brother-in-law, Mr. Barry Birchall, was a member of this club at one time."

"That's right," nodded Myers. Plainly mention of Birchall's name gave him no qualm. "Matter of fact, when those two were on the ground I was like a cat on hot bricks. They didn't exactly love each other's looks, you know."

"So I've understood. Know any reason for the dislike?"

"No. Mutual antipathy, I should say."

"And Mr. Birchall left the club shortly after the accident occurred?"

"Well, about a month after, I should say."

"Did he give any excuse for leaving—or was he asked to leave?"

"Oh, nothing like that, Inspector. I rather liked Birchall, and was sorry to see him go. But he told me his girl-friend didn't like his flying about in the ether. Of course, I didn't soak that up, but I admit she was a pretty girl, and a fellow would want to keep his feet on the ground when she was about."

"This girl and Birchall. Likely to be anything serious in it, should you say?"

The secretary flashed the detective another appraisive glance.

"So it's really Birchall, and not the accident that interests you, Inspector?" he countered.

Slade smiled.

"You're perceptive, Mr. Myers. But the girl and Birchall?"

Myers rubbed a hand along his jaw.

"No, I shouldn't say Birchall would have been the sort to saddle himself with her—permanently, you understand. She was a damned good looker, blonde, with good figure and what they call come-hither eyes on the films. Expensive, I should say, and if my opinion was asked I should say Birchall hadn't too much of the ready; anyway, barely enough to satisfy that girl. Looked like ex-front line of the chorus to me."

All this was informative.

"Gold-digger type?"

"Absolutely. But the sort, I should say, who could do her digging in a very entertaining way."

"Know her name and address by any chance?"

"No, Inspector. 'Fraid I can't help you there." Slade wasn't sure whether Myers was being cautious or telling the truth. "Susie was what Birchall called her. I remember that."

"And you last saw Birchall and the girl about five months ago. That right?"

"Yes. Birchall hasn't been back since he left. The accident to Sir Julius's 'plane was about six months ago, and Birchall left a month or so after that. Yes, it would be about five months ago that I last saw him, and he had the girl with him then."

"Did he have a London address while he was a member?"

"Only an hotel, and it wasn't always the same. He had a place in Paris, if I remember rightly."

"Yes, I think he had," said Slade, in a tone suggesting that the other had reminded him of something important. "What did he do with his 'plane when he left?"

"Sold it."

"To another member?"

"No, the club bought it for the school."

A blank expression filled Slade's eyes.

"So he sold his 'plane?"

"You find that surprising?" asked Myers, trying to conceal his eagerness.

"Perhaps. Left nothing in it, I suppose? Or in his locker on the grounds?"

"Only an old pocket-wallet. I didn't bother to send it after him because it was obviously a throw-out. Nothing in it ... at least, nothing except a cutting from a newspaper, a small advert."

"You still have it?"

"Somewhere." Myers smiled. "We never throw anything away here."

"Could I see it?"

"Yes, of course. I'll see if it's still in the 'Found' cupboard."

He was gone about six or seven minutes, and when he returned he held in his hand a shabby morocco wallet.

"Here it is," he said, passing it to Slade.

The detective turned it over. There were no initials on the outside. He opened it, and extracted a small cutting from a newspaper. The cutting read:

OPPORTUNITY of earning £50. Services of first-class air pilot
    required. Must be unmarried and unemployed. Apply, giving de-
tails age, experience, etc., to Box T512, *Daily Signal*.

"Mind if I keep this cutting and wallet, Mr. Myers?" asked Slade. "I'll give you a formal receipt, of course."

"Why, no, there's no objection that I can see," said the secretary, his facial expression revealing that he had tried hard without success to find one.

"And you've heard nothing since of Birchall?" asked Slade, as he passed a hastily written receipt to the club secretary.

"Not a thing. Am I going to?" he queried shrewdly.

"Perhaps," Slade smiled.

A few minutes later the two Yard men were driving back to London.

XIX.

When, some hours later, Slade called at Lady Malverne's Town flat, he found Mrs. Clammer's unsmiling reception rather more bleak than he expected.

"I called to see Lady Malverne," he explained.

The other woman nodded.

"I can understand that you wouldn't call to see me, Inspector," she said frostily. "However, if it's about Sir Vincent Brugman—"

"It isn't," Slade assured her. "I wanted to talk about her half-brother."

"Barry!" The bleak eyes stared straight at the detective, as though they would discover what lay in his mind. "How can Barry interest you, Inspector?"

"I want to get in touch with him."

"Then why not try his Paris address? I gave it to you."

"He isn't in Paris."

"Well, what can Lucie do about that? Barry is a bird of passage. He's here, there, and anywhere else, according to where his fancy takes him."

Slade had the impression that she was still trying to gauge him secretly.

He tried a fresh tack.

"You told me at Steyning Towers, Mrs. Clammer, that Lady Malverne asked Mr. Swensen to throw her half-brother out of this flat. Am I right?"

"You are. I did tell you that."

The bleak eyes were wary.

"How long ago was that?"

She appeared to consider for some moments.

"Oh, about two months."

"Two months."

"Yes, couldn't be less."

"You are sure?"

His insistency annoyed her.

"Look here," she said frostily, "just what are you getting at, Inspector? I don't like the sound of this questioning. If you've got anything against Barry tell me. What's the object of this dancing round the mulberry-bush?"

Slade had thought his method rather direct. Her description rather disappointed him.

"I want to know when Barry Birchall was last in this country," he said.

"I thought I told you that too. Last Tuesday—or, rather, Tuesday of last week," she was careful to explain.

"Yes, that's what you told me—"

"Well, don't you believe me?" she snapped.

"Certainly," said Slade soothingly. "What I am trying to find out is when you last saw him in the flesh. You see—"

"I don't," she snapped again. "You didn't say anything about seeing him in the flesh—which I shouldn't want to do, anyway. I'm no sexual peeping Tom," she declared, with fine lack of restraint, which brought a smile to Slade's mouth. "I didn't say I'd seen him. Is it likely Barry would show his face after being thrown out on his neck? The boy's a bit of a ne'er-do-well, as I've never denied. But he's no fool. He's no match for that big blond Swede when it comes to brawn, and he's kept out of his way. But Barry's got a snap and bark like a terrier. Every time he's been in the country for the past two months he's taken a delight in ringing up his sister and being abusive. You saw what he was like that night at Steyning Towers."

Slade played a high card, but played it with caution.

"Suppose I told you that Barry Birchall was not in Paris that night, Mrs. Clammer?"

The woman's face went stiff. He saw the change. The facial muscles at the side of her mouth drew taut.

"I shouldn't believe you," she returned, with spirit.

"But that wouldn't alter the fact that he wasn't there, Mrs. Clammer." Slade spoke softly; he saw that his words were a shock. "A man has been arrested by the Paris police for—well, let's say impersonating Mr. Birchall."

"Impersonating—"

She gasped. "Nonsense!" Colour stained her pale face, then receded rapidly, leaving it paler than before. "Why have you come here?" she challenged.

"I came to see Lady Malverne. But since I've been speaking to you, Mrs. Clammer, I've realized that you may be able to help me."

"Help you to do what?" Suspicion thickened her voice. "Hang Kurt Swensen?"

There was sarcasm too in the last question.

"Let's forget Mr. Swensen for a moment."

"I'm willing to forget him for ever, but you've locked him up in gaol, and that alters things," she said, a bite in the words.

Slade felt that he was opposed to an antagonist worthy of his blade.

"Mrs. Clammer"—he tried a new line—"my job is to get the truth. When I tell you that what you've just told me—that you haven't actually seen your nephew for two months—alters the case considerably, will you believe me? It *is* the truth," he emphasized.

She sniffed.

"Well, I don't pretend to see where we're getting with all this, but I'll accept what you say. I can't do otherwise. You'd gain nothing by telling a lie, anyway," she added shrewdly. "But what's the mystery about my seeing him—"

"No mystery. But you must realize that if some one in Paris could imitate his voice sufficiently well to trick his half-sister, that could also be done here, in London. In short, you've heard from time to time in the past two months of some one purporting to be Barry Birchall—"

"Purporting! Why, this is absurd! Of course, it was Barry."

"Did Lady Malverne *see* him?"

"No," she agreed, with less certainty.

"And you say you didn't?"

"No. But surely—"

"Just a minute, Mrs. Clammer, please. I suggest that you have no actual proof that Barry Birchall has been 'phoning his half-sister during these two months. If you allow—I'm only suggesting it as a condition; proof will be offered later, I assure you—if you allow that his voice could be imitated, then you haven't any proof, have you?"

She saw the contention, and had to admit the point Slade had made.

"That's true enough," she agreed, "but what's the meaning of all this supposing and demand for proof? What are you trying to do—"

And then the answer, the only possible answer, flashed with all the disturbing effect of fork lightning into her troubled mind.

"Good heavens! You think Barry—did it!" she gasped.

Slade said nothing, and she continued staring at him, emotional stress changing the expression in her eyes as the colour of water under a cloudy sky is changed.

"You've broken down an—alibi," she muttered, pausing before the word. "You've been hunting him. That's why you questioned me at Steyning Towers. I see now. The arrest of Kurt Swensen was a trick, a very subtle trick," she sneered, "in order to allay—"

Slade stopped her.

"Mrs. Clammer," he said, "I said a few moments ago I made up my mind to speak to you more freely because I thought you could help me. I didn't consider antagonizing you would help me. Grant me credit for that, at least."

It was a direct appeal to her intelligence, and the woman's brain was shrewd, her wits sharp.

"Well," she retorted, "what have you come to *prove?*"

The emphasis given to the last word revealed clearly that she still stood in the opposite camp.

"I think there's one person who can clear up this

matter definitely, once and for all," said Slade slowly. "I want to clear it up."

She stared at him for a moment, long and hard.

"His sister?"

"No. I don't think a man of your nephew's type, Mrs. Clammer, feeling as he does, would have confided much to his sister. Do you, frankly?"

"I don't. But if you think he made a confidante of his dear Aunt Judith you're vastly mistaken. Barry hadn't any more use for me than I have for my grandmother's bustle. His friends?" She moved her shoulders in a slight wriggle. "Has he any? Does Barry's type ever get real *friends?* You should be able to answer that yourself, Inspector."

"No, I don't think a mere friend would be able to help me."

The detective's tone conveyed the impression that he knew definitely who would.

She took him up.

"A woman, eh?"

"I think so," nodded Slade. "Can you help me?"

"Would he tell me about his women friends?"

"Possibly not, but you would know."

She looked startled.

"What makes you so sure?"

"I think Sir Julius would have talked, perhaps very pointedly, about any woman his brother-in-law was rather friendly with. And there was one. I've found out that much."

"You've found out a very great deal, Inspector. You mean Susie?"

"Yes, Susie. I confess, though, I don't know her surname. But I'm rather anxious to find her. I want her full name and address."

"You sound like a Post Office official. Full name and address! Susie Knight's her name, if you must know. Though I couldn't have told you it a month ago."

"How was that?"

This simple question appeared to exasperate her.

"Must I explain every little why and wherefore?"

"I'm afraid so, Mrs. Clammer. This, I feel, is very important."

"And how I came to know Susie Knight's surname is really necessary for your peace of mind?"

"Not only necessary," said Slade, keeping his temper, "but so important that I shouldn't leave without being told."

"Good God!" After she had recovered from what she thought was a deliberate affront the shrewd look came back to her face. "You've doubtless found out this girl's real worth. That's why you're pestering me. I can tell. Well, I'll give you your opportunity to cut short the interview, Inspector. I found out her name when she called to see me here, about four weeks ago."

"She came here!"

"Well, I'm glad something's surprised you."

"To ask about Barry?"

"Ask about Barry!" Mrs. Clammer laughed harshly. Her thin hands knotted, and she beat them on her knees. "No, to demand money. That's what she came here for!" she announced with startling distinctness. "Now you know. Make of it what you like. You can guess how much she got out of me! I told her I'd send for the police if she tried any of that kind of hanky-panky. I don't think she liked me."

Here was something fresh. A suggestion of blackmail. It fitted in with the case as Slade had outlined it. Obviously the girl had learned something about Barry Birchall's activities, realized that he had little money, and went to where she thought her knowledge would be well paid for. It was her misfortune to see the aunt instead of the sister.

But that was a month ago.

Did that mean that the affair at Steyning Towers had been planned then?

Whatever it meant, it was clear to Slade that this girl

would have some real information to give. He turned to Mrs. Clammer again.

"Did she say why she thought you should give her the money?"

"Naturally. She said she could send Barry to prison. He had left her, after using up her money, had promised to marry her and walked out on her. I soon showed her what her tale was worth. It was transparent. She thought to panic me into giving her money. She had nothing at all with which to *frighten* me. Just a bright girl with an idea that was not so very bright after all. She was smart, and took the chance. It just didn't come off."

What did this mean? Had the girl decided not to tell what she knew in face of her reception? Had Mrs. Clammer's attitude suddenly scared her?

There were a number of possible explanations to account for the girl's retreat in face of Mrs. Clammer's opposition. Mrs. Clammer was watching him closely.

"Did you get her address?" he asked.

She opened her hands and let them fall against her thin thighs.

"Dear me, you'd be a champion at parlour games, Inspector. You've always got a fresh question ready. Doesn't anything ever stump you?"

"Sometimes. Ladies who have wayward nephews—"

Slade stopped. Her glance was very direct, but the corners of her mouth twitched.

"Yes, that's a score off me, Inspector." She sounded slightly more friendly, and Slade had hopes of winning her confidence. "As a matter of fact, I didn't get her address, but she did let slip that she was living in Islington."

"Do you happen to know if Islington was her address six months ago?"

"No, I don't. Barry, before the quarrel, never spoke about her. He's deep and can be as silent as deep waters. But the type of girl he picked didn't altogether surprise me, Inspector. Hard, metallic, you know the kind."

"Gold-digger," suggested Slade, remembering what the secretary of the Tri-Wing Aero Club had told him.

"Yes, that's the word they use to-day. Gold-digger. Good word too. Vulgar, but descriptive. And, anyway, everything is vulgar to-day."

Slade was side-tracked.

"She went without any threat?"

"Of course she did. She had nothing to threaten. It was just a try-on. That much was plain, Inspector."

"Did she suggest that she had lived on intimate terms with him?"

"Well, she's a woman talking to another woman. Would she suggest their friendship was platonic, and expect the other woman to pay out of joy—or relief? No, she gave me pretty well to understand the type of friendship theirs had been. If I may be vulgar in turn, I should say it was all-embracing." She grinned. "To make things crystal clear she cleverly brought in a reference to my nephew's most distinguishing feature."

"What is that?" asked Slade.

"A birthmark. In shape, just like a fish, just over— well, where he sits down."

A hint of colour stained her cheeks.

"And you haven't heard from her since?" asked Slade.

"Of course I haven't. I should have been surprised— very much surprised—had she returned to have the police put on to her. I made my mind pretty plain to her. When she left we both knew where we stood—or, at any rate, she did. You can take my word for that."

"She didn't try to approach Lady Malverne?"

"I thought of that, and took precautions. True, I was not with Lucie all the time she was—well, running round the country with Kurt Swensen, but I should have known if the Knight girl had made overtures. You can take my word again, Inspector . . . the girl left well alone."

Mention of Swensen's name had put another thought into Slade's head.

"Mrs. Clammer," he said, "how long has Lady

Malverne known Mr. Swensen?"

The woman shot him a swift glance, as though he had asked something that took her by surprise.

"Why do you ask?"

"I should like to know."

"Very well, about seven months."

"Seven months. Since, then, before the Olympic Games? Did she meet him in England?"

"Yes, to your first question, Inspector. No, to your second. Lucie met Mr. Swensen in Switzerland before the Games were held. He was holidaying in Europe after an extensive training course, I believe. He joined the remainder of the Americans in Berlin, I believe. I'm not sure about that. But I know he first met Lady Malverne about a month before . . . before the air crash in which Julius lost his life."

She seemed to feel the possible implication of this statement, for she said, quickly, "You don't imagine, surely, Inspector, that Kurt could—"

Slade shook his head.

"I've been to Caterham this morning, and I'm certain there's no need to reopen that affair now."

"Thank God!" she murmured devoutly. "There've been enough rumours about that accident. And if the fools— the malicious fools," she added vindictively, "would only stop to find the facts they would realize that Kurt Swensen does not fly."

"Does one have to be able to fly to tamper with a machine that's on the ground?" asked Slade mildly.

She made a clucking sound.

"You're impossible, you really are," she said irritably. "You annoy me, Inspector."

"I'm sorry."

"You're nothing of the sort. But that's neither here nor there. The point is what you've said has disturbed me. You're right; you know you are and I know you are; and that only makes the matter worse."

"Why, did Sir Julius dislike Mr. Swensen during the

short time he knew him?"

"Julius was not the man to show his likes or dislikes," she countered, then added, after a thoughtful pause, "except to Lucie."

"I'd like to ask a more personal question, Mrs. Clammer," said the Yard man.

"Well, Inspector, I don't think I should be able to stop you. I'm certain you're used to riding roughshod over people's feelings."

"I must apologize if I have given you that impression. I didn't want to—"

"Nonsense! You know a policeman can get the answer he wants ultimately, although he may come up against an old duck like myself who's ready to quack it out with him. But you're comforted by the knowledge you're the representative of the law, for what that's worth to you. But I mustn't continue this drivel. You're too polite to ride roughshod over anything, and when I give an exhibition of bad manners you just sit there and smile as though some one had suggested a drink. By the way, will you have a drink, Inspector? This call has grown more social than I should have dreamed possible."

"No, thanks," smiled Slade. Mrs. Clammer was an amazing person. "I'd much prefer to have the chance of putting that personal question."

She sniffed.

"I might have known I couldn't drag a fresh scent across the trail," she sighed. "Very well, I'll tell you if it isn't something concerning my personal habits, though I don't think you'd be interested in them."

"I'd like to know your own summation of Sir Julius Malverne's character?"

The question apparently surprised her.

"Didn't I tell you at Steyning?"

"A little. You had no opportunity for enlarging."

"I don't know that I particularly want such an opportunity. But if you want it, here's my opinion of him. He was successful, overbearing, clever, fond of animals, and liked getting the better of people in argument or business. It didn't matter which, seemingly. He'd go a long way to gain his point, even if the point wasn't worth gaining, and he was jealous—if you can understand this—of his personal opinion of himself. In fact, he was a jealous man altogether."

"As a husband?"

She shook a finger.

"Now, Inspector, play fair. That's bringing Kurt Swensen into the picture, and I'm not going to do that. No, I won't do that," she added, with force.

Slade saw that he had obtained as much of her confidence as he could expect, in the circumstances, and, having been more successful than he had hoped with his questioning, he did not feel that it would be wise to continue his visit past its period of usefulness.

He rose.

"You've been very helpful, Mrs. Clammer."

"I'm not altogether glad to hear it, Inspector," she said bluntly, and walked with him into the hall. As he paused, waiting for the lift, she said, "Do you expect any sudden development . . . soon?"

Slade looked at her, his mouth compressed.

"Yes, Mrs. Clammer," he said, "a very sudden development, and very soon."

As the lift whirred him downwards he caught a last glimpse of her standing above him, staring into space.

XX.

Slade and Clinton turned their united energies to locating the whereabouts of Susie Knight. The aid of the local Islington police-stations and the Post Office sorting-offices in that district was sought, and by late afternoon it was apparent that there were no less than five Susie Knights resident in that part of London.

A divisional plain-clothes man paid a rapid call to each in turn, and Slade and Clinton, waiting impatiently, learned finally that the Susie Knight answering to their description lived at 44 Pompadour Terrace.

A fast police car took them to West Hill Road, out of which Pompadour Terrace turned. No. 44 was a four-storey house let into flats. Inquiry on the ground floor assured them that Susie Knight occupied a flat on the third floor. They mounted the wide staircase to the third floor. On a dark brown door was a card with the small printed notice, "Miss S. Knight."

Slade rang the bell.

The door was opened by a young woman dressed in smartly tailored suit, sheer silk stockings, and suede shoes that looked as though they had cost an even number of guineas.

"Well?" she asked, her tone deliberately forbidding friendliness.

"We're from Scotland Yard," Slade explained.

Her carefully painted and powdered jaw dropped.

"You've got the wrong address," she said, recovering quickly.

"I don't think so," said Slade. "You're Miss Susie Knight?"

"I am. But I don't have any copyright in the name. I imagine there are other girls who would answer to it as well as me."

"But you knew Mr. Barry Birchall fairly well, didn't you?"

There was no need for an affirmative reply. The expression on her face supplied it. Suddenly a mild storm broke out.

"Has that old tabby been telling tales about me?" she raged.

Slade took it quietly.

"Perhaps we'd better discuss things inside, Miss Knight," he suggested.

She drew back, and they entered the small flat.

"Well," she began, when they were seated, "what about it? You haven't come to inquire after my morals, have you?"

"I've come to learn when you last saw Barry Birchall," said Slade.

"Oh, about six weeks—no, a couple of months ago."

She said it in offhand fashion, but Slade felt that her manner was studied, to give just that impression, that it meant little to her. He watched her closely, and saw that her eyes were furtively watching both himself and Clinton, and every now and again their gaze strayed to a door at the far side of the room. Doubtless a door opening into the bedroom of the small flat.

"Not since?"

"No, we had a row. He left me flat."

"And is that why you went round to see his aunt?"

Her fury boiled again.

"So that old—"

But she didn't get far. The Yard man stopped her with a gesture, she realized she would do well to obey. There was something definitely perturbing about these two men from Scotland Yard, something that upset her mind and rocked her careful and studied poise.

"All right, you saw her," she muttered. "What of it? You've nothing on me."

Slade was irritated by that feeling that she was on

her guard, prepared not to reveal . . . something. He decided upon a bold bluff. He felt it would be the only measure likely to succeed with such a woman, who obviously knew her way about.

"Miss Knight, perhaps you don't understand one thing. I'm investigating the case of the missing Malverne diamonds. There are two murders in that case, and a lot of explanations are due. I think you could help us a lot."

"You—you think . . ." She broke off, panic in her wide, mercenary eyes. "I don't know anything about the—the diamonds."

The hidden suggestion in Slade's words had evidently shaken her more than she cared for them to see.

"I'm not suggesting you do, Miss Knight. But I'll tell you that what you could tell us, in turn, about a certain individual connected with this case may be very important. We want that explanation."

"You mean Barry?"

"Yes, Barry Birchall."

She sat still for some moments, then lit a cigarette. She got up, paced the room, stared for several seconds at the other door, then came back and sat down again.

"What do you want to know?" she asked. "You must realize that this won't be anything but . . . painful for me."

She cleverly inserted a slight sob, to give the words pathos. The effort was wasted.

Clinton grinned openly.

"You say you saw him two months ago, and haven't seen him since?"

"That's right."

"You quarrelled?"

"Yes."

"About what?"

"Well, he was getting tired of me, if you must know," she said savagely, but she overdid it.

"He just walked out of your life, as they say in the magazines?"

"Yes."

"In spite of the fact that he gave up flying for you, sold his 'plane, only two months—at most three months—before that?"

Slade's knowledge was disturbing.

"He said that?"

"That was the excuse he gave at the air-club."

"Then it was a lie!" she said heatedly, caution, for the moment, forgotten in a fresh blaze of anger. "I remember the day he told the secretary—what was his name, Myers—filleted sort of fish; never did take to him—told him he was resigning from the club. I remember distinctly. It was the day he was chuckling about a fellow called Meredith."

"Who was Meredith?"

"Some fellow who had a joke put over him, I think. Barry kept laughing and saying Meredith was going to make his fortune. Barry's fortune, I mean, not Meredith's."

"How?"

"I don't know. All I could get out of him was that this Meredith was some one who had answered an advertisement in a newspaper."

Slade and Clinton exchanged glances. Both experienced a feeling of rising excitement at the woman's words.

"And that," said Slade, "is how you remember the day Mr. Birchall resigned from his club?"

"Yes. Anything funny about it?"

"No. It's perfectly straightforward." Slade looked at her meaningly. "You lived with Mr. Birchall, didn't you?"

Her chin went up.

"What of it? Barry wasn't so bad when the going was easy. But he wasn't much fun when the weather changed. That was Barry. I haven't broken my heart over him deserting me."

"You would be able to recognize him if you saw him again, wouldn't you?"

She hesitated, said slowly:

"Of course."

"Even if you didn't see him, but read a description of him, you'd still be able to recognize him?"

She had paled.

"What are you driving at?"

"This."

Slade took from his pocket a police circular in which several sentences were ringed in blue pencil. He handed it to her, and she read:

Late yesterday evening the body of a man was washed up on

   the beach between Pevensey Bay and Eastbourne. Body was found

   by resident of one of the Martello towers on the Crumbles. Features

   were unrecognizable, due to period body had been immersed in the

   sea; but above the left buttock was a birthmark of peculiar shape,

   resembling a fish. . . .

She didn't read beyond that point. The paper fluttered to the floor.

"I did not know of that birthmark until to-day," said Slade, recovering the circular. "But I thought you would recognize the description. Birchall's birthmark was on the left side, wasn't it?"

"Yes," she muttered.

Slade rose and walked to the other door. She followed him with her eyes, but said nothing. He pushed open the door and looked into the room. Beside the bed were a number of strapped cases. On their sides were labels with "Via P. and O." in large letters, and others with "Cabin Class" on them.

Slade came back.

"Thinking of taking a long trip, Miss Knight?" he asked.

"My health," she said weakly.

"You may be right."

There was a touch of grimness about the detective's tone and manner.

"No," she murmured, fright hushing her voice, "you can't know. You can't!"

"Miss Knight," said Slade, "don't you think you'd better tell me the whole story?"

She stared at him miserably, all archness, all self-sufficiency gone.

"I daren't," she said. "It would mean . . ."

She choked.

"You've been threatened?"

She nodded in short jerks.

"Your life?"

"Yes," she managed to get out.

"Miss Knight," said Slade, "I think you are in an unfortunate position. You've got to make a choice. I should advise you to confide in the police. You must realize that, knowing what I do now, I couldn't let you leave on that journey to—Cape Town, was it?"

She stared at him, finding it difficult to make up her mind.

"Very well," she said at last. "It means my losing a nice packet of five hundred pounds, but in a way I'll be glad to get it off my chest."

"I think you'd be wise. Take your time. Afterwards I shall want you to make a statement, of course."

She appeared to consider this; then began:

"I didn't quarrel with Barry. He disappeared. He said what he knew about that man Meredith, who answered an advertisement in a newspaper, would make his fortune, and the idea seemed to amuse him. I don't mean getting the money amused him. I mean the idea of getting it just that way. Anyway, as I told you, he disappeared. I didn't hear anything for some weeks. Then one day I received a visit from a red-haired woman, who spoke with a slight foreign accent."

Slade glanced at Clinton; the sergeant was sitting forward in his chair, trying to visualize every possibility this startling new information offered for survey.

"She had a copy of a Sussex paper with her. I don't remember the date or the name of the paper, even. But it gave in a few words what you showed me just now, the fact that the body of a man had been washed up on the South Coast, and it mentioned the birthmark. As soon as I saw about the birthmark I began to cry. She stood over me and said, 'So you could identify him?' I said, "That's Barry Birchall. We've been living together for nearly a year. I can't be mistaken.' Then she laughed, and said I could—very easily. I could be so mistaken that my life wouldn't be worth a pair of cheap stockings. I got afraid, and asked what she wanted. She said she'd come to warn me to keep my mouth shut. The episode hadn't got into the London papers, and the chances are the body would be buried and forgotten—if I kept quiet. That seemed to be what she wanted. She said, further, that if I would agree to what she had to say I'd have nothing to worry about."

She paused.

"What did she say?" asked Slade.

"She said I would have to agree to leave the country if they told me to."

"They?"

"Yes, she kept saying they."

"Meantime they would leave you alone, unless you went to the police. That the idea?"

"Yes, and she told me not to move or try to get away, because I should be found, and I'd regret the trouble I had caused. I was mighty scared, I can tell you. But if they told me to leave the country, I was to go where they had arranged, and I should be given five hundred pounds."

"Was this decision sudden?"

"Yes. Early this morning the red-haired woman came

again. She had tickets and labels for the journey to South Africa, and I was to pack without delay. The boat is leaving Southampton to-morrow. I am to go to Waterloo to-night, where she will meet me and give me the five hundred pounds."

"Got any idea what made them want to get you out of the country so suddenly?"

"None at all."

Slade glanced at Clinton.

"Deparis's arrest has done this, Clinton. It's leaked, and the cat's jumped. Pretty smart movement."

"Yes, pretty smart," agreed the sergeant, who then turned to the woman.

"I suppose it was this red-haired woman's calling round here and intimidating you that gave you the idea of trying something on Birchall's aunt, wasn't it?"

She flushed.

"Yes," she admitted. "Funds had been getting low. Barry took me from a show I was in, and that upset the producer, who'd been nice to me up till then. Well, I couldn't go back, and jobs are scarce. It seemed I might get some sympathy money."

"You tried the right way to get it," grunted the sergeant scornfully.

"Listen," said Slade, "as I understand the arrangement, you are to meet this red-haired woman at Waterloo Station this evening. Right?"

"Yes."

"What time?"

"Quarter to eight."

"Where?"

"By the old coach."

"Any other instructions?"

"No, except that I'm to go to Regent Hotel in Southampton."

"Now, Miss Knight," said Slade, "I want to ask you something very serious. You've no wish to find yourself arrested as an accessory to murder, have you?"

She was cowed. This sober question completed her defeat.

"You—you think that?" she muttered.

"I think by agreeing to run away in this fashion, and saying nothing to the police of what you know about the body washed up near Eastbourne, you've placed yourself in a difficult position."

"But five hundred pounds—"

Slade lost what little sympathy he had for her. She was hard to the core. Money and her own security counted first in her mind.

"Five hundred pounds as against five years in gaol," he told her crisply.

She flinched, looked at her manicured hands, and whispered, "No—not that."

Clinton made a sound of disgust at this display. She did not appear to have heard.

"There's one way you can get yourself out of a mess, Miss Knight."

"How?"

"Go to Waterloo to-night, meet this woman, as arranged, and take the money, but do it so that we can make an arrest. The rest is up to us."

"Could I go on to Southampton then?" she asked.

Slade shook his head.

"No, definitely not. You'll be an important witness for the Crown, Miss Knight. There will be a lot of witnesses in this case, but few more important than you."

"What of the threat to kill me?"

"You'll get plenty of protection, I can promise you that."

She considered the prospect.

"If I don't agree?"

Slade smiled.

"Then we arrest you now."

"Arrest me now—" She stared at him. A broken laugh spilled from her very red mouth. "You don't leave me any option."

"I do. Voluntary co-operation or arrest. You've got the choice."

"You call *that* a choice?"

"You're lucky to have it."

"All right," she said irritably, "I kick in. I'll do this job, but what about the five hundred I get from the red-head?"

"We'll decide about that later. Anyway, it's not my business, and the money will be wanted as evidence later on. Perhaps the notes can be traced."

"You think of everything," she sneered.

Slade got up. "You've a 'phone here, Miss Knight?" he asked, ignoring the gibe.

"Yes, by the bed."

Slade went into the bedroom, and closed the door, so that his conversation could not be overheard. He rang the Yard and asked to have a plain-clothes policewoman sent to the flat in Islington. He picked up the travel tickets on the dressing-table, read the name of the booking-agents and the number, and passed the information over the 'phone to his own department. An independent effort would be made to check up on the person who had bought the ticket.

He went back to the outer room.

"You've thought of nothing else to tell me, Miss Knight?" he asked.

The woman's savage mood had returned.

"Yes—get out and leave me alone."

"I shall, in about twenty minutes. I'm having a plainclothes woman stop with you ... in case," he added significantly.

"What about that statement you want?"

"We'll let that wait till the red-haired woman has been arrested. You can add all that voluntary assistance to the statement. It'll help you."

"Help me! I like that! I've done nothing wrong. You can't start that bluster with me, Inspector, and expect to get away with it."

Slade didn't argue. The woman annoyed him, and the

strain of fencing with her was tiring. She was the bludgeoning type of witness who always returned to the same series of indignant questions.

Both men were thankful when the policewoman in plain clothes arrived and took over. Before he left Slade gave her implicit instructions out of hearing of the now moody Susie, and when he left with Clinton he was assured that those instructions would be carried out.

"Clinton, we're closing up fast, and some one's going to get a big surprise," he said as the two Yard men left Pompadour Terrace.

"Big surprise!" grunted the sergeant. "I'm past being surprised in this case. You arrive back hot-foot from Paris with a new case all lined up. Birchall's our man. You've broken his alibi, you've got a copper-bottomed motive, the whole case is watertight against him, even to the clubs found in the Swede's trunk, both murders, and the stealing of the diamonds. Then Birchall has to turn up as a six-weeks'-old corpse. Probably older. Depends how long he'd been in the water. It may be good detective work, but I'm hanged if it's satisfactory. It's made a monkey out of one of the finest built-up cases I've seen. It would have been dollars to doughnuts that Birchall would have swung when that case was brought into court. Swensen was in it up to his neck, as we made out *his* case. But Birchall was already gallows cold." The sergeant stopped, stared straight at Slade, and demanded, "Who the devil is the murderer now? That red-head?"

"I don't think so," smiled Slade. "She's been useful, but that's all."

"Don't tell me we're going to swing back to Maxie Reisenberg or Pegwell?"

"You'll see," said Slade, with the same knowing smile.

"Well," snorted Clinton, "there's only Captain Furniss left among the men in the case. I swear a woman couldn't have done it all."

"Aren't you forgetting the bogus Butterick?" said Slade.

"No, because there's this Robert Deparis."

"Who was in Paris at the time, Clinton."

"Oh, hell!" cried Clinton. "This is just lunacy. There's nobody left. The way this adds up there could not have been a bogus Butterick, yet I saw him with my own eyes. Where am I wrong?"

"Nowhere. You've just not taken something into consideration, Clinton."

"Something or some one?" queried the sergeant astutely.

"Something."

"Well, what's that?"

"This case is gaining momentum. Now, a scientist would tell you, Clinton, that momentum is the rate of change of velocity. There you are."

"Where am I?"

"Changing your velocity, gaining momentum."

"What is this, a conundrum?"

"No, a simple factor—the velocity of this case changed when Robert Deparis was stripped of his disguise as Butterick."

"But that's my whole contention," cried Clinton. "Why did he have to keep that disguise up?"

"For the same reason that the Butterick we knew was a disguise. It was all a lot of cleverly carded wool."

"Wool?"

"Yes, Clinton. But, thank heaven, we've now got it out of our eyes."

"You may have," grunted the sergeant. "But I'm still left with a bogus Butterick who, according to my present reckoning, couldn't have been there." He swore under his breath. "Yet I gave him a cigarette and poured him out a drink."

XXI.

At half-past seven that evening Department X2 of New Scotland Yard had converged on Waterloo Station. Slade's men were in position a full quarter of an hour before the red-haired woman was expected to meet Susie Knight by the old coach. One man covered the main entrance, another remained not far from the coach, yet another hovered between these two, as a sort of liaison officer; one man covered the entrance into the Underground, and another covered the southern approach.

Slade had planned with care. There was little chance of the woman, after she had made contact with the 'decoy,' escaping through the net he had prepared to catch her.

Susie Knight, with baggage, arrived about seven-forty, and waited by the coach. Suburban home-goers hurrying by, intent upon catching their trains, little dreamed of the drama unfolding about them. The plain-clothes police-woman sat near by on a seat, her face lowered over an open magazine. Had panic seized the 'decoy' she had only to glance in the direction of the woman detective to take fresh heart. In the Islington flat the woman had already demonstrated her preparedness. In the pocket of her severely cut overcoat was a serviceable automatic. The rest of Slade's contingent was armed. The chief of Department X2 was taking no chances.

Slade and Clinton mingled with the crowds surging backward and forward across the platform, that never-dammed stream of humanity that flows from early dawn till midnight across the platform of a large railway terminus.

Slowly the hands of the large clock reached towards seven-forty-five. At a minute past the quarter-hour a taxi drew to a halt by the kerb, and a red-haired woman wearing dark glasses alighted, paid off the driver, and walked into the station. Before the taxi could take its place at the rear of the cab-rank a detective had sprung on to the running-board and was asking the driver questions.

After answering, the driver obediently returned his cab to the kerb and waited, the detective seated in the darkened interior.

The curtain had been rung up on the drama.

The red-haired woman with dark glasses walked towards the women's cloak-room, hesitated, then crossed towards the coach. Again she diverted her direction, only to turn once more, and finally to approach the waiting Susie Knight.

"So you kept your word? Good. Here is the money," she said, "and remember—not a word if you value your life."

Behind the dark glasses keen eyes peered into Susie Knight's face.

"You understand?"

"Yes," murmured Susie, in a voice scarcely above a whisper.

She opened her handbag and pushed the roll of paper money inside.

Slade, unobserved by the red-haired woman, had seen the money change hands. Good enough. He pulled a handkerchief from his breast-pocket, and the policewoman and two plain-clothes men converged on the red-haired woman.

It was all done with dispatch, neatly, without fuss. She was hustled off the platform while the man from the southern entrance came up and superintended the packing of Susie Knight's bags into another taxi. Then he accompanied her to Scotland Yard, to await Slade's reappearance.

Meantime Slade and the others reached the taxi waiting by the kerb.

"Please get in, Mademoiselle Deparis," said Slade.

The woman flung him a savage glance.

"This is a terrible mistake," she said. "You will regret it."

Slade took no notice. To the man who had alighted from the taxi he said, "What's the address?"

"Seventeen Malbrook Mews, Bayswater."

"Right. Take her to the Yard and hold her."

The taxi sped away, bearing the policewoman, Aimee Deparis, and the plain-clothes man. The rest of Slade's men piled into two police cars, and the driver of the first, given the address by Slade, headed for Westminister Bridge and a westward drive to Bayswater.

Malbrook Mews was an unpretentious thoroughfare in a quiet backwater neighbourhood. The police cars parked one at each end, and the men took up their stations, one by each waiting car, one in front of No. 17, while another made his way round to the next street, to cover a possible rear entrance.

Slade and Clinton rang the bell of No. 17, and a dour-faced manservant answered the door.

"Your master in?" asked Slade.

The man would have closed the door quickly, but Clinton's right foot was already acting as door-stop. Slade pushed the man forward into the hall, whispered a few words that reduced him to startled impotency, and moved forward to the staircase with Clinton.

They mounted to a wide landing. A door was ajar, and through the opening a light was reflected.

A man's voice called in French, "That you, Aimee? Everything all right?"

"Come on," whispered Slade.

The two Yard men pushed themselves into the room, and Clinton shut the door and placed his back to it.

At a desk sat a man with pale face, a pair of spectacles bridging his nose, his thinning hair brushed straight back from his high forehead.

Clinton frowned. There was something familiar about the man, but he could not say what it was. The man rose, as Slade advanced, his fingers brushing the top of the desk.

"Ah!" he said, and looked long and piercingly at the chief of Department X2. "Then something has miscarried?"

"Aimee Deparis has been taken to the Yard," Slade informed the man. "I have come to—"

"Take me?" interrupted the other gently.

There was a slight smile on his mobile lips. He did not seem in the least perturbed at this invasion, unexpected as it must have been.

"Exactly," nodded the detective.

"'And you'll arrest me for the purloining of the necklace known as the Tears of Death?"

There was mockery, leaping mockery, in the measured tones.

"No," said Slade.

Clinton stared. He was lost in this polite parley of words. What was Slade's game? He could see that his chief was wary, eyes and body alert. What was Slade waiting for?

"Of course, I forgot," smiled the man. "You can hardly arrest a man for stealing what is rightfully his, can you?"

A pause; then:

"You mind if I smoke? This is rather a surprise, you know, and I feel I must ask time to recover my—um—poise."

His right hand had travelled to the pocket of his jacket. Slade's own hand had slipped into the pocket of his overcoat.

"I should be sure you found your cigarette-case," he advised.

The hand hesitated, dipped into the jacket pocket, hesitated again, while the smile on the other's face grew wider.

"Naturally."

The hand came out, holding a gold cigarette-case. He lit a cigarette, dropped the case on to the desk, and inquired:

"You've interested me greatly, Inspector Slade— Oh, pardon me, it is Inspector Slade, isn't it? You see, I do make a habit of reading the daily papers."

Slade nodded curtly.

The other resumed, while Clinton fidgeted.

"As I said, you've interested me greatly, Inspector, and I should like to know before we become melodramatic just how you figured it all out."

"I'm afraid this isn't the place," said Slade. "I arrest you—"

"My dear Inspector! A moment, please, I beg! Don't let us be hasty a second time." The gibe went home; Slade knew he was referring to the arrest of Kurt Swensen. "And you have Aimee. Such a personable woman, Aimee. I'm sure you'll agree. And you have brother Robert too. Quite a bag. You've found Barry, naturally?"

Behind the man's smooth facade was interest, quick and alive.

"We know what happened to Birchall," said Slade evenly, "and to Meredith. There can be no advantage in delaying me from making this arrest. You'll have to—"

"Yes, yes, of course I shall. What a one-track mind you have, Inspector. Most depressing. No imagination—or have you? I wonder? It took considerable perception to find me. Finding Robert was a help of course. But that doesn't explain everything. Ah, I have it! The Knight woman, yes, that must be the answer. Is she at the Yard too?"

"She is."

"H'm. Looks like the mesh of your net is pretty fine, Inspector. I shall have great difficulty in wriggling through. But I shall, you know that, don't you?"

The question was a direct challenge. Clinton, his hands in his pockets, felt perspiration forming on his face, and an uncomfortable sensation made itself apparent beneath his waistcoat buttons. There was something cold-blooded and coolly unscrupulous about this man smoking the cigarette that worried the sergeant. The hand grasping the gun in his pocket felt moist and sticky.

"The game is up," began Slade, when the other interrupted him again.

"*Please*, Inspector, let's avoid the melodrama. I hate that term, anyway. It is untrue. I never *play*. You understand? Apart from that, a game is never *up*. It is ended, but only for one player. For the other there is always the 'next time.' I know what I am talking about."

The cigarette was half burned through. He lifted his hand to his mouth, slowly removed it, and with amazing speed threw it into Slade's face. Clinton pulled his gun from his pocket, but the man was between the wall and Slade. To have fired would have risked hitting Slade.

The next moment the room was plunged into darkness, as the man's foot caught in a coil of electric flex and jerked the plug of the lamp from a wall-socket. Clinton bounded forward, collided with Slade, and threw him off balance. Before the sergeant could reach the window the man had hurled himself through it, on to a stone balcony.

Clinton clambered on to the balcony in time to see a pair of white hands release their grasp of the stone rail, as the body of the man merged with the darkness of a creeper spreading its arms against the wall of the house.

"Quick!" shouted Slade, a step behind his assistant. "Shoot!"

Clinton's gun bellowed, but they heard the bullet smack against stone.

Slade fired, an instant too late, for as the bullet tore through the night a laugh of triumph floated up to them. The two Yard men turned and raced down the stairs to the ground floor, burst along the corridor, and threw themselves across a tiny kitchen and out into a small garden full of shadows.

"He can't be far, and the back's covered," said Slade. "Keep under that wall, Clinton. I'll take the other. He's desperate, man, so take no chances."

Scarcely had they separated, however, than a shot rang out from the end of the garden, followed by another. Windows in neighbouring houses were thrown up, and an excited babble of voices rose.

Slade was aware of a figure jumping down upon him from a wall. He tried to throw himself aside, but his manoeuvre was only partially successful. A fist caught him behind the left ear, and he fell prone upon a flower-bed. Feet kicked his body, and desperately he tried to rouse himself. He twisted his head, saw Clinton sprinting across a patch of thin moonlight, and from somewhere farther along the street rose a woman's shrilling scream.

Then shots were firing again, and the shadows of the garden were pierced with bright flashes of flame. A light went on in the house, and Slade, rising to his feet, saw a group of figures gathered in the doorway of the kitchen. Another shot reverberated, and the light went out, followed by the tinkling of shattered glass.

A man swore, and Slade recognized the voice of one of his own men.

The chief of Department X2 was on his feet and dashing for the house. He realized what had happened. The man he had come to arrest, finding his retreat cut off, had doubled back, hoping to get through the house and that the noise of conflict would have drawn off any detectives stationed in the street. He had shot out the light, and taken a diving run through the knot of detectives.

The surprising swiftness with which he had turned about had all but brought his bold movement success. He had passed Clinton and the man who had entered from the front—the man who had cried out—but Slade knew both ends of the street were closed ... if he got through.

The Yard men reached the hall together. The figure of the manservant lay sprawled across the floor, and down his face flowed a stream of blood.

"Hit him with the butt," said Clinton.

They left the unconscious man and ran out into the street. As they passed down the steps a shot from the opposite pavement cautioned them against proceeding too rashly.

"He's got a sting," said Slade, "and he's desperate. Don't take chances."

In the shadows thrown by the trees lining the other side of the street the fugitive was, for a moment, safe. Slade took a whistle from his pocket and blew three short blasts. An answering blast came from each end of the street. A minute later the two police cars, headlights blazing, commenced to crawl towards each other. The twin ribbons of light illuminated the entire street, swept away the shadows from the opposite side, and revealed a figure lying on its stomach under one of the trees.

Clinton threw a shot high.

The other was not wasting his fire. He did not reply.

But when the cars were about twenty yards away he suddenly sprang upright, and jumped. With a lithe bound his hands reached a low branch; a twist of the whirling legs, and he was drawing himself up into shadow once more.

The Yard men tried a couple of exploring shots. They flew wide. Then Slade realized what the other's move meant. He would jump for the wall that bounded the backs of the houses in the next street; for the mews had only one row of houses facing directly into it.

"Snipe the wall!" he called, and ran into the roadway as the cars drew level.

A shot from the man in the tree put out a headlamp of one car. A plain-clothes man in the car replied, but the reply only drew a low laugh, followed by a mocking call.

"Not yet, Inspector. You're going to have a long run for your money. I hope you're in condition."

A dark shape curved through the space between the tree and the wall. As it dropped Slade's automatic barked. That mocking voice had directed his attention to the man's position in time for him to raise the weapon. The shot was effective. The dropping figure seemed to droop in mid-air, and a cry broke from the man's lips.

"He's hit!" roared Clinton.

But the groping hands reached the top of the wall, and with a great heave the man pulled himself level with the top as a fusillade of bullets spattered powdered brick-dust over the pavement.

Slade and his men were hurling themselves against a wooden door. Once, twice, they bunched themselves and leaped forward. At the third attempt the door splintered at the bolt and sagged open. They poured through, heedless of what their reception might be. But their elusive adversary was silent. He was not under the wall, but the ground where he had fallen was covered with bright fresh blood.

"He's hit bad," said Clinton. "Losing a lot of blood. He can't last."

"He's got to last," grunted Slade, determination in his voice. "We've gone a long way to get him, Clinton, and we've got to get him and have him patched up."

"You'll be disappointed, Inspector," said a slow, pain-laden voice, a few yards to their right.

Three torch-rays split the night, and focused upon the crumpled body of the man who had made a desperate bid for freedom.

Slade bent over him. His gun lay at the man's side, but he was too weak to reach for it. That drop from the wall had been too much. The man was sinking fast.

"Clinton," said Slade. "Send for an ambulance."

The sergeant turned to go, but he was within earshot as Slade said, "Sir Julius Malverne, I arrest you for the murders of Henry Meredith, John Butterick, and Maud Farling, and I warn you—"

"What's the good of warning a dying man, Inspector?" murmured the other.

XXII

At a later hour that night Slade sat in the Assistant-Commissioner's office. The tired look that had been so apparent on the face of the latter when last Slade had seen him, barely twenty-four hours before, was gone, replaced by an expression of eager anticipation.

"Well, I'll say one thing, Slade, you've upset a lot of apple-carts, but you finished the case within the week. In short, you've done the miracle. But how still defeats me. I follow the general lines, of course, but you must have hit on the solution all at once, I should say."

The words were equivalent to a question.

"Scarcely," admitted Slade. "When I got that information from Mrs. Clammer about the birthmark I checked up the files, and found the circular about the body washed up on the South Coast. Actually, I had to shake the truth out of the Knight woman before I could be sure. I faced her with the circular. It was a long shot, but it hit the mark —well, perhaps not in the centre, but certainly a glancing hit."

"I should call it a bull's-eye if I were responsible," smiled the A.C., nodding approval. "Good bit of work that. Shows what routine can do."

The A.C. was strong on routine.

"Then I suppose you found you had to substitute some one for Birchall?"

"Yes. It was a bit of a problem, but there was one piece over."

"I can guess that. The advert you found in the wallet."

"That's right, sir. The Knight woman's mention of a certain Meredith gave me a wider scope there. I was certain the secretary of the Tri-Wing Aero Club had been in trouble when talking about Sir Julius's crash. I saw then the pattern beginning to clear itself. Sir Julius had

hired an unknown unemployed airman, sent him up in a
rigged machine, and that was the supposed end of Sir
Julius Malverne."

"And, incidentally, the beginning of it all?"

"Well, not exactly. You know of the egotistic streak in
him. It was responsible for that confession he made
before he died. I think it had another outlet. He married a
pretty woman, and found her unresponsive. Actually I
believe she married him when the man she really loved
went off somewhere—in Africa, I think it was—and was
killed. He caught her on the rebound, as it were; and the
marriage wasn't a success."

"Do you think he was a sadist?"

"Not as the term is understood to-day. But he was a
very successful business man. He had a strong, positive
character, and I should say he was considerably piqued
when he found he had married an intelligent woman who
would not look up to him as the household god. For the
first time in his life he was made to realize that, in some
measure, he fell short. That was dangerous to his pride. I
should say he became furtive, watchful, and when Kurt
Swensen appeared on the scene in Switzerland, and
engaged the attention of Lady Malverne, he was
embittered. I think, to understand Sir Julius fully, one
must appreciate the other peculiar streak in his nature,
complementary to his egotism —I mean, his self-
sufficiency. It was responsible for his interest in precious
gems. He didn't want them for themselves. They were
locked in a bank. He wanted them for the sense of
possession they gave him, a feeling that he had more
than other men—yes, I should say he was assuredly
acquisitive, in that way. They gave him a strange
sensation of deep possession. With his millions, his gems,
his big business, he was complete, sufficient to himself.
Only his wife didn't quite fit in with this mental picture
of himself. He knew she did not love him, and lack of love
meant to him lack of possession. That another man
should step in and take what he considered rightfully his

upset his mental balance. He saw that, if he were off the scene, more than friendship might ripen between his wife and Swensen. So he began to plan a scheme that must have given him a great deal of perverted pleasure. He saw himself officially mourned and buried, Swensen married to his wife, and then himself reappearing and claiming what by law was his."

"You've dug deep, Slade. Go on."

"But there was a snag. Barry Birchall found out about Meredith, and had to be put out of the way."

"Just a minute, Slade. How did you get Meredith's Christian name?"

"From the *Daily Signal*. He had been advertising on his own for a job, and when he got the one Malverne offered he wrote to the paper explaining why he wanted to cancel the future adverts he'd paid for."

"And do you mean to say those dunderheads didn't put two and two together when the crash occurred."

"Oh, he didn't say who had employed him. He just said he had got the job advertised. They had no track of who put that particular advert in the paper. It was paid for in cash, and only appeared once."

"Then how the devil do you suppose Birchall found out the truth?"

"That I can only guess. Probably he saw Meredith on the ground with Sir Julius. Or he may have seen Sir Julius after the crash. There might be any one of half a dozen explanations of that."

"Yes, I suppose you're right. It's a moot point, anyway. Go on with your own account, Slade."

"Well, Birchall did find out, and thought to levy quite a sum from his brother-in-law. He was promptly put out of the way. Sir Julius had got in touch with the Deparis pair—as he says in the confession, he'd know them a long while, and had used them several times when putting over a big business bluff—and he knew they would do what he wanted if the price was sufficiently high. Perhaps he had something on them. I don't know.

However, with their help Birchall was got rid of, and Robert Deparis, a quite clever character actor, took on the role of the murdered man. The fact that Barry Birchall had quarrelled with Swensen helped this smart piece of duplicity; but there was another fly in the ointment."

"Susie Knight, of course."

"Yes. Sir Julius knew of her. Must have seen her at the air-club lots of times. When Birchall's body was washed ashore he sent Aimee round to make sure there was not going to be a leak. How effective she was you know. Then, in the middle of this situation, which had developed on its own, as it were, and had not been originally planned by Sir Julius, came the announcement of Lady Malverne's decision to sell the Tears of Death.

"That made the man who had bought them frantic. What could he do? Appear, and spoil his original plot for which he had already done so much, gone so far? Or lie low and let them be sold? Lady Malverne's decision to have the necklace brought to Steyning Towers gave him his greatest idea.

"Wouldn't a better plan be to have Swensen charged with theft of the necklace and murder? There would be the trial, the agony of cross-examination. That, surely, would be a marvellous personal triumph. And perhaps he could step into the picture then, and add the last ounce to his wife's humiliation."

"Good Lord, Slade, this sounds like the concoction of a madman's brain!"

The A.C. was sitting upright in his chair, his pale eyes narrowed.

Slade shrugged.

"I'm only attempting to give some sort of explanation for the confession he made. The case needs a lot of filling in, and the filling in can be done only when one understands fully what activated Malverne. He had waited and waited, was tired of waiting, and seized a fresh chance to attain the object he sought."

"M'yes, that's reasonable enough. Go on, man."

"He had to keep Barry Birchall out of the affair as a suspect. Swensen, you see, had to stand out clearly in the minds of the police. So the dead Birchall was given what he thought was a perfect alibi."

"The 'phone call from Paris?"

"Yes. Deparis was here in England, ostensibly as Birchall, until the Tuesday. Actually he was here on the Friday night. Probably he was out of funds. But he went through with the deception, and did it remarkably well. He and his sister are both excellent linguists. That made the bold scheme possible."

"Not so bold, Slade, when you come to consider. A check with the exchange should have satisfied us regarding that call. It was Mrs. Pegwell who was directly responsible for the Paris lead, wasn't it?"

"Yes. There Malverne was out of luck. Reisenberg was hated by Bill Pegwell, and Malverne, in Steyning Towers as the insurance company's detective, must have had a shock when he went to 'steal' his own diamonds to find a cracksman fumbling at the door of the room. But his facile brain, always quick to adapt a situation to his own advantage, saw how to transform this serious obstacle to good use. He crept to Swensen's room, got the club, and came back while Pegwell was at the safe. The rest we know."

There was a pause, broken by the A.C., who said, "That killing of Butterick was ruthless."

"True, but necessary to his plan," Slade pointed out. "Obviously he knew of the arrangements made with the insurance company, and he did not find it difficult to intercept Butterick. He knew the grounds of Steyning Towers, just where to run the car through the hedge, into the lake. I'll give him credit for a clever plan. The fact that he had had to kill Birchall made the killing of Butterick easier. He had a kind of unmoral justification, if you understand me."

"I think I do. But what of the murder of the maid?"

"She must have stepped into his room when his

disguise was off. There was no alternative, if he wished to save his neck. He killed her, choked her into unconsciousness, then went for another club. You see, that constant vein of hatred against Swensen makes a uniform pattern throughout the entire case. The maid's murder was the second that was forced upon him, the other being Birchall's, of course. He killed Butterick not because he had to, but because the murder of the insurance detective would provide himself with a *role* to play. It was a means to an end."

"I still can't help thinking, Slade, that it was terribly risky, going into his own household in that disguise. I can't imagine how the man could hope to get away with it. Some mannerism would betray him to the servants or his wife. The whole time he was there he was open to self-betrayal."

"Yes, sir, I know that's how it would appear to an onlooker, as it were." Slade hesitated, choosing his words with care. "But speaking from my own experience of the bogus Butterick, I should say there was actually very little danger. He was clever enough to foresee that."

"How do you mean, very little danger?"

"Well, he had changed his colouring and facial appearance. He appeared as a paid servant of a company, and was accepted as such, so that no one gave him much attention. He had only to keep his mouth shut—which he did effectively—and keep out of people's way for just over twelve hours, and the whole thing could be written off the slate."

"I begin to see what you mean. His role of detective was protection in itself."

"Yes. I took him as a sort of business necessity, and gave him little if any attention. The rest of the household ignored him. He was wise enough to cut a pathetic figure when the necklace was stolen, mumble about losing his job. That went down." Slade laughed harshly. "Yes, he took me in completely. Everything went off as planned. The 'phone call came through. That put Birchall out of our minds. Aimee got away with the necklace he managed to pass to her. Two unaccountable things happened to wreck the scheme, however. Tessa Pegwell was waiting for her husband, and pugnaciously followed Aimee. That, for us, was pure luck."

"You deserved a bit, Slade," smiled the A.C., "and in the ordinary course of things could reasonably expect a certain amount in such a case, one where the interests were very involved and overlapped at times."

This sounded like a masked compliment. Slade did not try to take off the mask.

"The other unaccountable happening," he went on, "was Lady Malverne's finding the submerged car, with the body. That was real bad luck for Sir Julius. Had that body not been found we might have been still searching for the real Butterick, a man who had found temptation too much for him."

"Just a moment, Slade." The A.C.'s eyes were twinkling. "Haven't you bowled your own argument out middle stump?"

"How do you mean, sir?" asked Slade, puzzled.

"Well, if Malverne had gone to all the trouble of having Robert Deparis act the part of the dead Birchall, with a faked alibi, so as to keep our attention centred on Swensen, not let it wander to the mercurial Barry, why should he arrange a plan that would have sent us seeking for Butterick? That would have taken our attention from Swensen."

Slade nodded.

"Yes, I agree. So far as the stealing of the diamonds was concerned. Although he may have had a plan that would have allowed of the finding of Butterick's body. But either way, Swensen had to explain his fingerprints on the blood-stained clubs. You admitted yourself, last night, sir, we could have made out a case from those that would hang him."

"True," nodded the A.C., frowning. "But Swensen wasn't scratched by the murdered maid. Malverne was.

You say the marks of fingernails run down in front of his left ear?"

"Yes, that's right. They've almost healed, but are still traceable."

"Well, now, what about this, Slade? It would make your own case more watertight, if you will permit me to say so. Suppose Sir Julius knew his wife's habit of swimming in the early morning, realized that, diving from the diving-platform, she must find the submerged car, and allowed for that."

"You mean, sir, he wanted the car found?"

"Yes, with the body, of course. Wouldn't that have strengthened the case against Swensen as a jewel thief and a murderer?"

Slade considered this.

"I think you may be right, sir," he admitted. "The only point is the gun that killed Butterick. Wouldn't he have planted that among Swensen's bags? He appears to have thought of everything."

"I don't think so, Slade. Wouldn't he argue this way? Swensen committed the murder of Butterick—I mean, this is how he would have thought we would have reasoned —in a coldly reasoning frame of mind. He got rid of the gun afterwards. Anywhere. In the middle of the lake, in a field. That doesn't matter. Pegwell was attacked in the same mental tempo, as it were. Hence no weapon was found. But the girl got him unawares, and he lost his head, clubbed her, and forgot the club. That seems to me to be pretty tight at the seams, Slade, and if he was as clever as you think, and as he certainly appears to have been, he could have argued along those lines. Don't you think so?"

"Well, to be perfectly frank, sir, I'm not sure he could. Pegwell and the murder of the maid were not factors when he planned Butterick's murder."

"True, I see that. But the murder of Butterick would be viewed by the police, Slade, as I said. That doesn't alter, whatever else happens. All he had to do was to arrange Pegwell's slugging and the maid's murder— afterwards, mind—to be consistent with my outline. See that? You said he was quick to adapt a situation to his own advantage. Well, then, couldn't that be the explanation?"

Slade had to agree that it could. He looked with barely concealed admiration at the Assistant-Commissioner. The man had to keep track of a score of major problems for the Yard's investigating machinery, yet in the space of a brief hour's talk he had grasped the Malverne case so thoroughly that he could explain a point that had all but defeated Slade himself. Small wonder, Slade reflected, that the brain behind those pale, watery-looking eyes was feared by the criminal fraternity throughout the land.

Slade rose.

"That's the case for the records, sir," he said simply.

"It does you credit, Slade," the A.C. acknowledged warmly. "That'll be all for to-night, man. You must be wanting your bed. The man Malverne wounded. Not bad?"

"Just a flesh wound, sir."

"Good. Well, good night, Slade. To-morrow we'll take up the questions of Pegwell and the Deparises. I don't want to move too hastily in either direction."

The A.C. picked up his 'phone.

"Good night, sir," nodded Slade.

Twenty minutes later he was smoking his pipe in the cool darkness of a taxi, glad to relax after a strenuous day.

THE END

Resurrected Press Books in A. E. Fielding's *The Chief Inspector Pointer Mystery* Series

MORE MYSTERIES BY LEONARD GRIBBLE

Available now, or coming Soon!
Like us on Facebook to see our latest books!
http://www.facebook.com/ResurrectedPress

Is this Revenge (1931) aka The Serpentine Murder
The Stolen Home Secretary (1932) aka The Stolen
Statesman
The Yellow Bungalow (1933)
The Death Chime (1934)
The Riddle of the Ravens (1934)
Mystery at Tudor Arches (1935)
The Case of the Malverne Diamonds (1936)
Riley of the Special Branch (1936)
Who Killed Oliver Cromwell? (1937)
The Case Book of Anthony Slade (1937)
Tragedy in E Flat (1938)
The Arsenal Stadium Mystery (1939)
Atomic Murder (1947)
Hangman's Moon (1950)
They Kidnapped Stanley Matthews (1950)
The Frightened Chameleon (1950)
Mystery Manor (1951)
The Glass Alibi (1952)
The Velvet Mask (1952)
Murder Out of Season (1952)
She Died Laughing (1953)
Murder Mistaken (1953) with Janet Green
The Inverted Crime (1954)
Sally of Scotland Yard (1954) with Geraldine Laws
Death Pays the Piper (1956)
Superintendent Slade Investigates (1956)
Stand In for Murder (1957)
Don't Argue with Death (1959)
Wantons Die Hard (1961)

AVAILABLE FROM RESURRECTED PRESS!

THE EDWARDIAN DETECTIVES
LITERARY SLEUTHS OF THE EDWARDIAN ERA

The exploits of the great Victorian Detectives, Poe's C. Auguste Dupin, Gaboriau's Lecoq, and most famously, Arthur Conan Doyle's Sherlock Holmes, are well known. But what of those fictional detectives that came after, those of the Edwardian Age? The period between the death of Queen Victoria and the First World War had been called the Golden Age of the detective short story, but how familiar is the modern reader with the sleuths of this era? And such an extraordinary group they were, including in their numbers an unassuming English priest, a blind man, a master of disguises, a lecturer in medical jurisprudence, a noble woman working for Scotland Yard, and a savant so brilliant he was known as "The Thinking Machine."

To introduce readers to these detectives, Resurrected Press has assembled a collection of stories featuring these and other remarkable sleuths in The Edwardian Detectives.

- The Case of Laker, Absconded by Arthur Morrison
- The Fenchurch Street Mystery by Baroness Orczy
- The Crime of the French Café by Nick Carter
- The Man with Nailed Shoes by R Austin Freeman
- The Blue Cross by G. K. Chesterton
- The Case of the Pocket Diary Found in the Snow by Augusta Groner
- The Ninescore Mystery by Baroness Orczy
- The Riddle of the Ninth Finger by Thomas W. Hanshew
- The Knight's Cross Signal Problem by Ernest Bramah

- The Problem of Cell 13 by Jacques Futrelle
- The Conundrum of the Golf Links by Percy James Brebner
- The Silkworms of Florence by Clifford Ashdown
- The Gateway of the Monster by William Hope Hodgson
- The Affair at the Semiramis Hotel by A. E. W. Mason
- The Affair of the Avalanche Bicycle & Tyre Co., LTD by Arthur Morrison

The Middle of Things
Ravensdene Court
Scarhaven Keep
The Orange-Yellow Diamond
The Middle Temple Murder
The Tallyrand Maxim
The Borough Treasurer
In the Mayor's Parlour
The Saftey Pin

R. Austin Freeman
*The Mystery of 31 New Inn from the Dr. Thorndyke
Series*
*John Thorndyke's Cases from the Dr. Thorndyke
Series*
The Red Thumb Mark from The Dr. Thorndyke Series
The Eye of Osiris from The Dr. Thorndyke Series
A Silent Witness from the Dr. John Thorndyke Series
The Cat's Eye from the Dr. John Thorndyke Series
*Helen Vardon's Confession: A Dr. John Thorndyke
Story*
As a Thief in the Night: A Dr. John Thorndyke Story
*Mr. Pottermack's Oversight: A Dr. John Thorndyke
Story*
*Dr. Thorndyke Intervenes: A Dr. John Thorndyke
Story*
The Singing Bone: The Adventures of Dr. Thorndyke
The Stoneware Monkey: A Dr. John Thorndyke Story
*The Great Portrait Mystery, and Other Stories: A
Collection of Dr. John Thorndyke and Other Stories*
The Penrose Mystery: A Dr. John Thorndyke Story
The Uttermost Farthing: A Savant's Vendetta

Arthur Griffiths
The Passenger From Calais
The Rome Express

Fergus Hume
The Mystery of a Hansom Cab
The Green Mummy
The Silent House
The Secret Passage

Edgar Jepson
The Loudwater Mystery

A. E. W. Mason
At the Villa Rose

A. A. Milne
The Red House Mystery
Baroness Emma Orczy
The Old Man in the Corner

Edgar Allan Poe
The Detective Stories of Edgar Allan Poe

Arthur J. Rees
The Hampstead Mystery
The Shrieking Pit
The Hand In The Dark
The Moon Rock
The Mystery of the Downs

Mary Roberts Rinehart
Sight Unseen and The Confession

Dorothy L. Sayers
Whose Body?

Sir William Magnay
The Hunt Ball Mystery

Mabel and Paul Thorne
The Sheridan Road Mystery

Louis Tracy
The Strange Case of Mortimer Fenley
The Albert Gate Mystery
The Bartlett Mystery
The Postmaster's Daughter
The House of Peril
The Sandling Case: What Would You Have Done?
Charles Edmonds Walk
The Paternoster Ruby

John R. Watson
The Mystery of the Downs
The Hampstead Mystery

Edgar Wallace
The Daffodil Mystery
The Crimson Circle

Carolyn Wells
Vicky Van
The Man Who Fell Through the Earth
In the Onyx Lobby
Raspberry Jam
The Clue
The Room with the Tassels
The Vanishing of Betty Varian
The Mystery Girl
The White Alley
The Curved Blades
Anybody but Anne
The Bride of a Moment
Faulkner's Folly
The Diamond Pin
The Gold Bag
The Mystery of the Sycamore
The Come Backy

Raoul Whitfield
Death in a Bowl

And much more!
Visit ResurrectedPress.com
for our complete catalogue

About Resurrected Press

A division of Intrepid Ink, LLC, Resurrected Press is dedicated to bringing high quality, vintage books back into publication. See our entire catalogue and find out more at www.ResurrectedPress.com.

About Intrepid Ink, LLC

Intrepid Ink, LLC provides full publishing services to authors of fiction and non-fiction books, eBooks and websites. From editing to formatting, from publishing to marketing, Intrepid Ink gets your creative works into the hands of the people who want to read them. Find out more at www.IntrepidInk.com.

www.ingramcontent.com/pod-product-compliance
Lightning Source LLC
Chambersburg PA
CBHW071300250626
47159CB00004B/1248